ELDORADO

1794, five years since the storming of the Bastille,
but the atrocities still continue, with the Scarlet
Pimpernel and his brave band of men robbing the
guillotine of many of its victims. In this adventure
Armand St Just falls in love with the lovely Jeanne
Lange, and in his desire to protect her betrays his
leader's trust, leading him into his greatest danger yet,
imprisonment at the mercy of Chauvelin and Héron.

———————

Also available in Knight Books are
The Scarlet Pimpernel and *The triumph of the Scarlet
Pimpernel*

BARONESS ORCZY

Eldorado

KNIGHT BOOKS

the paperback division of Brockhampton Press

ISBN 0 340 10424 4

This abridged edition first published 1971 by Knight Books,
the paperback division of Brockhampton Press Ltd, Leicester

Printed and bound in Great Britain by
Richard Clay (The Chaucer Press), Ltd,
Bungay, Suffolk

First published by Hodder & Stoughton Ltd 1913

CONTENTS

Part One

Part Two

Part Three

PART I

CHAPTER I

In the Théâtre National

AND yet people found the opportunity to amuse themselves, to dance and to go to the theatre, to enjoy music and open-air cafés and promenades in the Palais Royal.

New fashions in dress made their appearance, milliners produced fresh 'creations', and jewellers were not idle. Paris – despite the horrors that had stained her walls – had remained a city of pleasure, and the knife of the guillotine did scarce descend more often than did the drop-scenes on the stage.

On this bitterly cold evening of the 27th Nivôse, in the second year of the Republic – or, as we of the old style still persist in calling it, the 16th of January 1794 – the auditorium of the Théâtre National was filled with a very brilliant company.

The appearance of a favourite actress in the part of one of Molière's volatile heroines had brought pleasure-loving Paris to witness this revival of Le Misanthrope, with new scenery, dresses, and the aforesaid charming actress to add piquancy to the master's mordant wit.

The Moniteur, which so impartially chronicles the events of those times, tells us under that date that the Assembly of the Convention voted on that same day a new law giving fuller power to its spies, enabling them to effect domiciliary searches at their discretion without previous reference to the Committee of General Security, authorizing them to proceed against all enemies of public happiness, to send them to prison at their own discretion, and assuring them the sum of thirty-five livres 'for every piece of game thus beaten up for the guillotine'. Under that same date the Moniteur also puts it on record that the Théâtre National was filled to its utmost capacity for the revival of the late citoyen Molière's comedy.

The Assembly of the Convention having voted the law which placed the lives of thousands at the mercy of a few human bloodhounds, adjourned its sitting and proceeded to the Rue de Richelieu.

Already the house was full when the fathers of the people

made their way to the seats which had been reserved for them. An awed hush descended on the throng as one by one the men whose very names inspired horror and dread filed in through the narrow gangways of the stalls or took their places in the tiny boxes around.

Citizen Robespierre's neatly bewigged head soon appeared in one of these; his bosom friend St Just was with him, and also his sister Charlotte; Danton, like a big, shaggy-coated lion, elbowed his way into the stalls, while Santerre, the handsome butcher and idol of the people of Paris, was loudly acclaimed as his huge frame, gorgeously clad in the uniform of the National Guard, was sighted on one of the tiers above.

The public in the parterre and in the galleries whispered excitedly; the awe-inspiring names flew about hither and thither on the wings of the overheated air. Women craned their necks to catch sight of heads which mayhap on the morrow would roll into the gruesome basket at the foot of the guillotine.

In one of the tiny *avant-scene* boxes two men had taken their seats long before the bulk of the audience had begun to assemble in the house. The inside of the box was in complete darkness, and the narrow opening which allowed but a sorry view of one side of the stage helped to conceal rather than display the occupants.

The younger one of these two men appeared to be something of a stranger in Paris, for as the public men and the well-known members of the Government began to arrive he often turned to his companion for information regarding these notorious personalities.

'Tell me, de Batz,' he said, calling the other's attention to a group of men who had just entered the house, 'that creature there in the green coat – with his hand up to his face now – who is he?'

'Where? Which do you mean?'

'There! He looks this way now, and he has a playbill in his hand. The man with the protruding chin and the convex forehead, a face like a marmoset, and eyes like a jackal. What?'

The other leaned over the edge of the box, and his small restless eyes wandered over the now closely packed auditorium.

'Oh!' he said as soon as he recognized the face which his friend had pointed out to him, 'that is citizen Foucquier-Tinville.'

'The Public Prosecutor?'

'Himself. And Héron is the man next to him.'

'Héron?' said the younger man interrogatively.

'Yes. He is chief agent to the Committee of General Security now.'

'What does that mean?'

Both leaned back in their chairs, and their sombrely clad figures were once more merged in the gloom of the narrow box. Instinctively, since the name of the Public Prosecutor had been mentioned between them, they had allowed their voices to sink to a whisper.

'It means, my good St Just, that these two men whom you see down there, calmly conning the programme of this evening's entertainment, and preparing to enjoy themselves tonight in the company of the late M. de Molière, are two hell-hounds as powerful as they are cunning.'

'Yes, yes,' said St Just, and much against his will a slight shudder ran through his slim figure as he spoke. 'Foucquier-Tinville I know; I know his cunning, and I know his power – but the other?'

'The other?' retorted de Batz lightly. 'Héron? Let me tell you, my friend, that even the might and lust of that damned Public Prosecutor pale before the power of Héron!'

'But how? I do not understand.'

'Ah! you have been in England so long, you lucky dog, and though no doubt the main plot of our hideous tragedy has reached your ken, you have no cognizance of the actors who play the principal parts on this arena flooded with blood and carpeted with hate. They come and go, these actors, my good St Just – they come and go. Marat is already the man of yesterday. Robespierre is the man of tomorrow. Today we still have Danton and Foucquier-Tinville; we still have Père Duchesne, and your own good cousin Antoine St Just, but Héron and his like are with us always.'

'Spies, of course?'

'Spies,' assented the other. 'And what spies! Were you present at the sitting of the Assembly today?'

'No.'

'I was. I heard the new decree which already has passed into law. Ah! I tell you, friend, that we do not let the grass grow under our feet these days. Robespierre wakes up one morning with a whim; by the afternoon that whim has become law, passed by a servile body of men too terrified to run counter to his will, fearful lest they be accused of moderation or of humanity – the greatest crimes that can be committed nowadays.'

'But Danton?'

'Ah! Danton? He would wish to stem the tide that his own passions have let loose; to muzzle the raging beasts whose fangs he himself has sharpened. I told you that Danton is still the man of today; tomorrow he will be accused of moderation. Danton and moderation! – ye gods! Eh? Danton, who thought the guillotine too slow in its work, and armed thirty soldiers with swords, so that thirty heads might fall at one and the same time. Danton, friend, will perish tomorrow accused of treachery against the Revolution, of moderation towards her enemies; and curs like Héron will feast on the blood of lions like Danton and his crowd.'

He paused a moment, for he dared not raise his voice, and his whispers were being drowned by the noise in the auditorium. The curtain, timed to be raised at eight o'clock, was still down, though it was close on half past, and the public was growing impatient. There was loud stamping of feet, and a few shrill whistles of disapproval proceeded from the gallery.

'If Héron gets impatient,' said de Batz lightly, when the noise had momentarily subsided, 'the manager of this theatre and mayhap his leading actor and actress will spend an unpleasant day tomorrow.'

'Always Héron!' said St Just, with a contemptuous smile.

'Yes, my friend,' rejoined the other imperturbably, 'always Héron. And he has even obtained a longer lease of existence this afternoon.'

'By the new decree?'

'Yes. The new decree. The agents of the Committee of General Security, of whom Héron is the chief, have from today powers of domiciliary search; they have full powers to proceed against all enemies of public welfare. Isn't that beautifully vague? And they have absolute discretion; the agents of the Committee of General Security shall alone decide what constitutes emnity against public welfare. All prisons are to be opened at their bidding to receive those whom they choose to denounce; they have henceforth the right to examine prisoners privately and without witnesses, and to send them to trial without further warrants; their duty is clear – they must "beat up game for the guillotine". Thus is the decree worded; they must furnish the Public Prosecutor with work to do, the tribunals with victims to condemn, the Place de la Révolution with death-scenes to amuse the people, and for their work they will be rewarded thirty-five livres for every head that falls under the guillotine. Ah! if Héron and his like and his myrmidons work hard and well they can make a comfortable income of four or five thousand livres a week. We are getting on, friend St Just – we are getting on.'

'Then from this hell let loose upon earth,' exclaimed St Just hotly, 'must we rescue those who refuse to ride upon this tide of blood.'

His cheeks were glowing, his eyes sparkling with enthusiasm. He looked very young and very eager. Armand St Just, the brother of Lady Blakeney, had something of the refined beauty of his lovely sister, but the features – though manly – had not the latent strength expressed in them which characterized every line of Marguerite's exquisite face. The forehead suggested a dreamer rather than a thinker, the blue-grey eyes were those of an idealist rather than of a man of action.

De Batz's keen piercing eyes had no doubt noted this, even while he gazed at his young friend with that same look of good-humoured indulgence which seemed habitual to him.

'We have to think of the future, my good St Just,' he said after a slight pause, and speaking slowly and decisively, like a father rebuking a hot-headed child, 'not of the present. What are a few lives worth beside the great principles which we have at stake?'

'The restoration of the monarchy – I know,' retorted St Just, still unsobered, 'but, in the meanwhile —'

'In the meanwhile,' rejoined de Batz earnestly, 'every victim to the lust of these men is a step towards the restoration of law and order – that is to say, of the monarchy. It is only through these violent excesses perpetrated in its name that the nation will realize how it is being fooled by a set of men who have only their own power and their own advancement in view, and who imagine that the only way to that power is over the dead bodies of those who stand in their way. Once the nation is sickened of these orgies of ambition and of hate, it will turn against these savage brutes, and gladly acclaim the restoration of all that they are striving to destroy. This is our only hope for the future, and, believe me, friend, that every head snatched from the guillotine by your romantic hero, the Scarlet Pimpernel, is a stone laid for the consolidation of this infamous Republic.'

'I'll not believe it,' protested St Just emphatically.

De Batz, with a gesture of contempt indicative also of complete self-satisfaction and unalterable self-belief, shrugged his broad shoulders. His short fat fingers, covered with rings, beat a tattoo upon the ledge of the box.

Obviously, he was ready with a retort. His young friend's

attitude irritated even more than it amused him. But he said nothing for the moment, waiting while the traditional three knocks on the floor of the stage proclaimed the rise of the curtain. The growing impatience of the audience subsided as if by magic at the welcome call; everybody settled down again comfortably in their seats, they gave up the contemplation of the fathers of the people, and turned their full attention to the actors on the boards.

CHAPTER II

Widely divergent aims

THIS was Armand St Just's first visit to Paris since that memorable day when first he decided to sever his connexion with the Republican party, of which he and his beautiful sister Marguerite had at one time been among the most noble, most enthusiastic followers. Already a year and a half ago the excesses of the party had horrified him, and that was long before they had degenerated into the sickening orgies which were culminating today in wholesale massacres and bloody hecatombs of innocent victims.

His sister Marguerite, happily married in England, was the final temptation which caused him to quit the country the destinies of which he no longer could help to control. The spark of enthusiasm which he and the followers of Mirabeau had tried to kindle in the hearts of an oppressed people had turned to raging tongues of unquenchable flames. The taking of the Bastille had been the prelude to the massacres of September, and even the horror of these had since paled beside the holocausts of today.

Armand, saved from the swift vengeance of the revolutionaries by the devotion of the Scarlet Pimpernel, crossed over to England and enrolled himself under the banner of the heroic chief. But he had been unable hitherto to be an active member of the League. The chief was loath to allow him to run foolhardy risks. The St Justs – both Marguerite and Armand – were still very well known in Paris. Marguerite was not a woman easily forgotten, and her marriage with an English 'aristo' did not please those republican circles who had looked upon her as their queen. Armand's secession from his party into the ranks of the émigrés had singled him out for special reprisals, if and whenever he could be got hold of, and both brother and sister had an unusually bitter enemy in their cousin Antoine St Just – once an aspirant to Marguerite's hand, and now a servile adherent and imitator of Robespierre, whose ferocious cruelty he tried to emulate with a view to ingratiating himself with the most powerful man of the day.

Thus it was that more than a year had gone by before Armand St Just – an enthusiastic member of the League of the Scarlet Pimpernel – was able to do aught for its service. He had chafed under the enforced restraint placed upon him by the prudence of his chief, when, indeed, he was longing to risk his life with the comrades whom he loved and beside the leader whom he revered.

At last, in the beginning of '94, he persuaded Blakeney to allow him to join the next expedition to France. He had only been away a little over fifteen months, and yet he found Paris a different city from the one he had left immediately after the terrible massacres of September. An air of grim loneliness seemed to hang over her despite the crowds that thronged her streets; the men whom he was wont to meet in public places fifteen months ago – friends and political allies – were no longer to be seen, strange faces surrounded him on every side – sullen, glowering faces, all wearing a certain air of horrified surprise and of vague terrified wonder, as if life had become one awful puzzle, the answer to which must be found in the brief interval between the swift passages of death.

Armand St Just, having settled his few simple belongings in the squalid lodgings which had been assigned to him, had started out after dark to wander somewhat aimlessly through the streets. Instinctively he seemed to be searching for a familiar face, someone who would come to him out of that merry past which he had spent with Marguerite in their pretty apartment in the Rue St Honoré.

It was no wonder, therefore, when anon he was wending his way slowly back to his lodging he was accosted by a pleasant, cheerful voice, that he responded to it with alacrity. The voice, of a smooth, oily *timbre*, was like an echo of the past, when jolly, irresponsible Baron de Batz, erstwhile officer of the Guard in the service of the late King, and since then known to be the most inveterate conspirator for the restoration of the monarchy, used to amuse Marguerite by his vapid, senseless plans for the overthrow of the newly risen power of the people.

Armand was quite glad to meet him, and when de Batz suggested that a good talk over old times would be vastly agreeable, the younger man gladly acceded. De Batz at once proposed the *avant-scène* box of one of the theatres as being the safest place where old friends could talk without fear of spying eyes or ears.

'There is no place so safe or so private nowadays, believe me, my young friend,' he said. 'I have tried every sort of nook and cranny in this accursed town, now riddled with spies, and I have come to the conclusion that a small *avant-scène* box is the most perfect den of privacy there is in the entire city.'

But somehow, after the first ten minutes spent in de Batz' company within the gloomy shelter of the small *avant-scène* box, Armand already repented of the impulse which had prompted him to come to the theatre tonight, and to renew acquaintanceship with the ex-officer of the late King's Guard. Though he knew de Batz to be an ardent Royalist, and even an active adherent of the monarchy, he was soon conscious of a vague sense of mistrust of this pompous, self-complacent individual, whose every utterance breathed selfish aims rather than devotion to a forlorn cause.

Therefore, when the curtain rose at last on the first act of Molière's witty comedy, St Just turned deliberately towards the stage and tried to interest himself in the wordy quarrel between Philinte and Alceste.

The presence of St Just in Paris had as a matter of fact astonished de Batz not a little, and had set his intriguing brain busy on conjectures. It was in order to turn these conjectures into certainties that he had desired private talk with the young man.

He waited silently now for a moment or two, his keen, small eyes resting with evident anxiety on Armand's averted head, his fingers still beating the impatient tattoo upon the velvet-covered cushion of the box. Then at the first movement of St Just towards him he was ready in an instant to reopen the subject under discussion.

With a quick nod of his head he called his young friend's attention back to the men in the auditorium.

'Your good cousin Antoine St Just is hand in glove with Robespierre now,' he said. 'When you left Paris more than a year ago you could afford to despise him as an empty-headed windbag; now, if you desire to remain in France, you will have to fear him as a power and a menace.'

'Yes, I knew that he had taken to herding with the wolves,' rejoined Armand lightly. 'At one time he was in love with my sister. I thank God that she never cared for him.'

'They say that he herds with the wolves because of this disappointment,' said de Batz. 'The whole pack is made up of men who have been disappointed, and who have nothing to lose. When all these wolves will have devoured one another, then, and then only, can we hope for the restoration of the monarchy in France. And they will not turn on one another while prey for their greed lies ready to their jaws. Your friend the Scarlet Pimpernel should feed this bloody revolution of ours rather than starve it, if indeed he hates it as he seems to do.'

In a moment St Just's loyalty was up in arms.

'The Scarlet Pimpernel,' he said, 'cares naught for your political aims. The work of mercy that he does, he does for justice and for humanity.'

'And for sport,' said de Batz with a sneer, 'so I've been told.'

'He is English,' assented St Just, 'and as such will never own to sentiment. Whatever be the motive, look at the result!'

'Yes! a few lives stolen from the guillotine.'

'Women and children – innocent victims who would have perished but for his devotion.'

'The more innocent they were, the more helpless, the more pitiable, the louder would their blood have cried for reprisals against the wild beasts who sent them to their death.'

St Just made no reply. It was obviously useless to attempt to argue with this man, whose political aims were as far apart from those of the Scarlet Pimpernel as was the North Pole from the South.

'If any of you have influence over that hot-headed leader of yours,' continued de Batz, unabashed by the silence of his friend, 'I wish to God you would exert it now.'

'In what way?' queried St Just, smiling in spite of himself at the thought of his or anyone else's control over Blakeney and his plans.

It was de Batz' turn to be silent. He paused for a moment or two, then he asked abruptly:

'Your Scarlet Pimpernel is in Paris now, is he not?'

'I cannot tell you,' replied Armand.

'Bah! there is no necessity to fence with me, my friend. The moment I set eyes on you this afternoon I knew that you had not come to Paris alone.'

'You are mistaken, my good de Batz,' rejoined the young man earnestly; 'I came to Paris alone.'

'Clever parrying, on my word – but wholly wasted on my unbelieving ears. Did I not note at once that you did not seem overpleased today when I accosted you?'

'Again you are mistaken. I was very pleased to meet you, for I had felt singularly lonely all day, and was glad to shake a friend by the hand. What you took for displeasure was only surprise.'

'Surprise? Ah yes! I don't wonder that you were surprised to see me walking unmolested and openly in the streets of Paris – whereas you had heard of me as a dangerous conspirator, eh? – and as a man who has the entire police of his country at his heels – on whose head there is a price – what?'

'I knew that you had made several noble efforts to rescue the unfortunate King and Queen from the hands of these brutes.'

'Yes, my friend, I made several efforts to rescue King Louis and Queen Marie Antoinette from the scaffold, and every time I was foiled, and yet here I am, you see, unscathed and free. I walk about the streets boldly, and talk to my friends as I meet them.'

'You are lucky,' said St Just, not without a tinge of sarcasm.

'I have been prudent,' retorted de Batz. 'I have taken the trouble to make friends there where I thought I needed them most.'

'Yes, I know,' rejoined St Just, with the tone of sarcasm still more apparent in his voice now. 'You have Austrian money at your disposal.'

'Any amount,' said the other complacently, 'and a great deal of it sticks to the grimy fingers of these patriotic makers of revolutions. Thus do I ensure my own safety. I buy it with the Emperor's money, and thus I am able to work for the restoration of the monarchy in France.'

'We advance slowly, but step by step, my good St Just,' he said. 'I have not been able to save the monarchy in the person of the King or the Queen, but I may yet do it in the person of the Dauphin.'

'The Dauphin,' murmured St Just involuntarily.

That involuntary murmur, scarcely audible so soft was it, seemed in some way to satisfy de Batz, for the keenness of his gaze relaxed, and his fat fingers ceased their nervous, intermittent tattoo on the ledge of the box.

'Yes! the Dauphin,' he said, nodding his head as if in answer to his own thoughts, 'or rather, let me say, the reigning King of France – Louis XVII, by the grace of God – the most precious life at present upon the whole of this earth.'

'You are right there, friend de Batz,' assented Armand fervently, 'the most precious life, as you say, and one that must be saved at all costs.'

'Yes,' said de Batz calmly, 'but not by your friend the Scarlet Pimpernel.'

'Why not?'

Scarce were those two little words out of St Just's mouth than he repented of them. He bit his lip, and with a dark frown upon his face he turned almost defiantly towards his friend.

But de Batz smiled with easy *bonhomie*.

'Ah, friend Armand,' he said, 'you were not cut out for diplomacy, nor yet for intrigue. So then,' he added more seriously, 'that gallant hero, the Scarlet Pimpernel, has hopes of rescuing our young King from the clutches of Simon the cobbler and of the herd of hyenas on the watch for his attenuated little corpse, eh?'

'I did not say that,' retorted St Just sullenly.

'No. But I say it. Nay! nay! do not blame yourself, my over-loyal young friend. When I met you so luckily today I guessed at once that you were here under the banner of the enigmatical little red flower, and, thus guessing, I even went a step further in my conjecture. The Scarlet Pimpernel is in Paris now in the hope of rescuing Louis XVII from the Temple prison.'

'If that is so, you must not only rejoice but should be able to help.'

'And yet, my friend, I do neither the one now nor mean to do the other in the future,' said de Batz placidly. 'I happen to be a Frenchman, you see.'

'What has that to do with such a question?'

'Everything; though you, Armand, despite that you are a Frenchman too, do not look through my spectacles. Louis XVII is King of France, my good St Just; he must owe his freedom and his life to us Frenchmen, and to no one else.'

'That is sheer madness, man,' retorted Armand. 'Would you have the child perish for the sake of your own selfish ideas?'

'You may call them selfish if you will; all patriotism is in a measure selfish. What does the rest of the world care if we are a republic or a monarchy, an oligarchy or hopeless anarchy? We work for ourselves and to please ourselves, and I for one will not brook foreign interference.'

'Yet you work with foreign money!'

'That is another matter. I cannot get money in France, so I get it where I can; but I can arrange for the escape of Louis XVII from the Temple prison, and to us Royalists of France should belong the honour and glory of having saved our King.'

Even a less astute man of the world than was Armand St Just

17

would easily have guessed that de Batz' desire to be the only instrument in the rescue of the poor little Dauphin from the Temple was not actuated by patriotism, but solely by greed. Obviously there was a rich reward waiting for him in Vienna the day that he brought Louis XVII safely into Austrian territory; that reward he would miss if a meddlesome Englishman interfered in this affair. Whether in this wrangle he risked the life of the child-King or not mattered to him not at all. It was de Batz who was to get the reward, and whose welfare and prosperity mattered more than the most precious life in Europe.

CHAPTER III

The demon Chance

St Just would have given much to be back in his lonely squalid lodgings now. Too late did he realize how wise had been the dictum which had warned him against making or renewing friendships in France.

The curtain had descended on the first act, and traditionally, as the works of M. de Molière demanded it, the three knocks were heard again without any interval. St Just rose ready with a pretext for parting with his friend. The curtain was being slowly drawn up on the second act, and disclosed Alceste in wrathful conversation with Célimène. Then it was that the wayward demon Chance intervened. The excuse hovered on his lips, de Batz reluctantly was preparing to bid him goodbye, when Célimène, speaking commonplace words enough in answer to her quarrelsome lover, caused him to drop the hand which he was holding out to his friend, and to turn back towards the stage.

It was an exquisite voice that had spoken – a voice mellow and tender, with deep tones in it that betrayed latent power. The voice had caused Armand to look, the lips that spoke forged the first tiny link of that chain which riveted him for ever after to the speaker.

There, no doubt, the matter would have ended; a young man fascinated by a pretty woman on the stage – 'tis a small matter, and one from which there doth not often spring a weary trail of tragic circumstances. But de Batz was a man who never allowed an opportunity to slip by, if that opportunity led towards the furtherance of his own desires.

He waited quietly until the fall of the curtain at the end of Act II; then, as Armand, with a sigh of delight, leaned back in his chair, and closing his eyes appeared to be living the last half-hour all over again, de Batz remarked with well-assumed indifference:

'Mlle Lange is a promising young actress. Do you not think so, my friend?'

'She has a perfect voice – it was exquisite melody to the ear,' replied Armand. 'I was conscious of little else.'

'She is a beautiful woman, nevertheless,' continued de Batz with a smile. 'During the next act, my good St Just, I would suggest that you opened your eyes as well as your ears.'

Armand did as he was bidden. The whole appearance of Mlle Lange seemed in harmony with her voice. She was not very tall, but eminently graceful, with a small, oval face and slender almost childlike figure.

At the end of the fourth act de Batz said casually to his friend:

'I have the honour of personal acquaintanceship with Mlle Lange. An you care for an introduction to her, we can go round to the green-room after the play.'

Armand St Just was not five-and-twenty, and Mlle Lange's melodious voice spoke louder than the whisperings of prudence or even than the call of duty.

He thanked de Batz warmly, and during the last half-hour while the misanthropical lover spurned repentant Célimène, he was conscious of a curious sensation of impatience, a tingling of his nerves, a wild, mad longing to hear those full, moist lips pronounce his name, and to see those large brown eyes throw their half-veiled look into his own.

*　　*　　*

The green-room was crowded when de Batz and St Just arrived there after the performance. The older man cast a hasty glance through the open door. The crowd did not suit his purpose, and he dragged his companion hurriedly away from the contemplation of Mlle Lange, sitting in a far corner of the room, surrounded by an admiring throng, and by innumerable floral tributes offered to her beauty and to her success.

The best part of an hour had gone by since the fall of the curtain before Mlle Lange finally dismissed her many admirers, and de Batz had the satisfaction of seeing her running down the passage, turning back occasionally in order to bid gay 'good-nights' to the loiterers who were loath to part from her. She was a child in all her movements, quite unconscious of self or of her own charms, but frankly delighted with her success.

Having at last said the positively final adieu, Mlle Lange with a happy little sigh turned to continue down the passage.

She came face to face with Armand, and gave a sudden little gasp of terror. It was not good these days to come on any loiterer unawares.

But already de Batz had quickly joined his friend, and his smooth, pleasant voice, and podgy, beringed hand extended towards Mlle Lange, were sufficient to reassure her.

'You were so surrounded in the green-room, mademoiselle,' he said courteously, 'I did not venture to press in among the crowd of your admirers. Yet I had the great wish to present my respectful congratulations in person.'

'*Ah! c'est ce cher de Batz!*' exclaimed mademoiselle gaily, in that exquisitely rippling voice of hers. 'And where in the world do you spring from, my friend?'

'Hush-sh-sh!' he whispered, holding her small bemittened hand in his, and putting one finger to his lips with an urgent entreaty for discretion; 'not my name, I beg of you, fair one.'

'Bah!' she retorted lightly, even though her full lips trembled now as she spoke and belied her very words. 'You need have no fear while you are in this part of the house. It is an understood thing that the Committee of General Security does not send his spies behind the curtain of a theatre. Why, if all of us actors and actresses were sent to the guillotine there would be no play on the morrow. Artistes are not replaceable in a few hours; those that are in existence must perforce be spared, or the citizens who govern us now would not know where to spend their evenings.'

But though she spoke so airily and with her accustomed gaiety, it was easily perceived that even on this childish mind the dangers which beset everyone these days had already imprinted their mark of suspicion and of caution.

'Come into my dressing-room,' she said. 'I must not tarry here any longer, for they will be putting out the lights. But I have a room to myself, and we can talk there quite agreeably.'

She led the way across the stage towards the wooden stairs. Armand, who during this brief colloquy between his friend and the young girl had kept discreetly in the background, felt undecided what to do. But at a peremptory sign from de Batz, he, too, turned in the wake of the gay little lady, who ran swiftly up the rickety steps, humming snatches of popular songs the while, and not turning to see if indeed the two men were following her.

She had the sheaf of narcissi still in her arms, and the door of her tiny dressing-room being open, she ran straight in and threw the flowers down in a confused, sweet-scented mass upon the small table that stood at one end of the room, littered with pots and bottles, letters, mirrors, powder-puffs, silk stockings, and cambric handkerchiefs.

Then she turned and faced the two men, a merry look of unalterable gaiety dancing in her eyes.

'Shut the door, *mon ami*,' she said to de Batz, 'and after that sit down where you can, so long as it is not on my most precious pot of unguent or a box of costliest powder.'

While de Batz did as he was told, she turned to Armand and said with a pretty tone of interrogation in her melodious voice:

'Monsieur?'

'St Just, at your service, mademoiselle,' said Armand, bowing very low in the most approved style obtaining at the English Court.

'St Just?' she repeated, a look of puzzlement in her brown eyes. 'Surely —'

'A kinsman of citizen St Just, whom no doubt you know, mademoiselle,' he explained.

'My friend Armand St Just,' interposed de Batz, 'is practically a newcomer in Paris. He lives in England habitually.'

'In England?' she exclaimed. 'Oh! do tell me all about England. I would love to go there. Perhaps I may have to go some day. Oh! do sit down, de Batz,' she continued, talking rather volubly, even as a delicate blush heightened the colour in her cheeks under the look of obvious admiration from Armand St Just's expressive eyes.

Armand was vexed that de Batz was sitting there. He felt he could have told this dainty little lady quite a good deal about England if only his pompous, fat friend would have had the good sense to go away.

As it was, he felt unusually timid and *gauche*, not quite knowing what to say, a fact which seemed to amuse Mlle Lange not a little.

'I am very fond of England,' he said lamely; 'my sister is married to an Englishman, and I myself have taken up my permanent residence there.'

'Among the society of *émigrés*?' she queried.

Then, as Armand made no reply, de Batz interposed quickly:

'Oh! you need not fear to admit it, my good Armand; Mademoiselle Lange has many friends among the *émigrés* – have you not, mademoiselle?'

'Yes, of course,' she replied lightly; 'I have friends everywhere. Their political views have nothing to do with me. Artistes, I think, should have naught to do with politics. You see, citizen St Just, I never inquired of you what were your views.'

'He is no partisan of citizen Robespierre,' again interposed de Batz; 'in fact, mademoiselle, I may safely tell you, I think, that my friend has but one ideal on this earth, whom he has set up in a shrine, and whom he worships with all the ardour of a Christian for his God.'

'How romantic!' she said, and she looked straight at Armand. 'Tell me, monsieur, is your ideal a woman or a man?'

His look answered her, even before he boldly spoke the two words:

'A woman.'

'That was well turned, friend Armand,' de Batz said lightly; 'but I assure you, mademoiselle, that before I brought him here tonight his ideal was a man.'

'A man!' she exclaimed, with a contemptuous little pout. 'Who was it?'

'I know no other name for him but that of a small, insignificant flower – the Scarlet Pimpernel,' replied de Batz.

'The Scarlet Pimpernel!' she ejaculated, dropping the flowers suddenly, and gazing on Armand with wide, wondering eyes. 'And do you know him, monsieur?'

Again he felt that if only he could have been alone with mademoiselle he could have told her all about the Scarlet Pimpernel, knowing that in her he would find a ready listener, a helping and a loving heart; but as it was he merely replied tamely enough:

'Yes, mademoiselle, I do know him.'

'You have seen him?' she queried eagerly; 'spoken to him?'

'Yes.'

'Oh! do tell me all about him. You know quite a number of us in France have the greatest possible admiration for your national hero. Monsieur, tell me, what is he like?'

'That, mademoiselle,' he replied, 'I am not at liberty to tell you.'

'Not at liberty to tell me!' she exclaimed; 'but, monsieur, if I command you —'

'At risk of falling for ever under the ban of your displeasure, mademoiselle, I would still remain silent on that subject.'

She gazed on him with obvious astonishment. It was quite an unusual thing for this spoilt darling of an admiring public to be thus openly thwarted in her whims.

'How tiresome and pedantic!' she said, with a shrug of her pretty shoulders and a *moue* of discontent. 'And, oh! how ungallant!'

She said nothing more about the Scarlet Pimpernel or about England just then, but after a while she began talking of more indifferent subjects: the state of the weather, the price of food, the discomforts of her own house, now that the servants had been put on perfect equality with their masters.

Armand soon gathered that the burning questions of the day, the horrors of massacres, the raging turmoil of politics, had not affected her very deeply as yet. She had not troubled her pretty head very much about the social and humanitarian aspect of the present seething revolution. She did not really wish to think about it at all. An artist to her finger-tips, she was spending her young life in earnest work, striving to attain perfection in her art, absorbed in study during the day, and in the expression of what she had learnt in the evenings.

Once de Batz mentioned the Dauphin, but mademoiselle put up her hand quickly, and said in a trembling voice, while the tears gathered in her eyes:

'Do not speak of the child to me, de Batz. What can I, a lonely, hard-working woman, do to help him? I try not to think of him, for if I did, knowing my own helplessness, I feel that I could hate my countrymen, and speak my bitter hatred of them across the footlights; which would be more than foolish,' she added naïvely, 'for it would not help the child, and I should be sent to the guillotine.'

Soon after this she dismissed her two visitors.

'You will come and see me again, citizen St Just?' she asked.

'At your service, mademoiselle,' he replied with alacrity.

'How long do you stay in Paris?'

'I may be called away at any time.'

'Well, then, come tomorrow. I shall be free towards four o'clock. Square du Roule. You cannot miss the house. Anyone there will tell you where lives citizeness Lange.'

'At your service, mademoiselle,' he replied again.

CHAPTER IV

The Temple prison

IT was close on midnight when the two friends finally parted company outside the doors of the theatre. The night air struck with biting keenness against them when they emerged from the stuffy, overheated building, and both wrapped their caped cloaks tightly round their shoulders.

Looking neither to right nor left, Armand made his way very quickly up the Rue Richelieu towards the Montmartre quarter, where he lodged. De Batz stood and watched him for as long as the dim lights of the street lamps illuminated his slim, soberly clad figure; then he turned on his heel and walked off in the opposite direction.

'So my pretty Scarlet Pimpernel,' he muttered between his closed lips, 'you wish to meddle in my affairs, to have for yourself and your friends the credit and glory of snatching the golden prize from the clutches of these murderous brutes. Well, we shall see! We shall see which is the wiliest – the French ferret or the English fox.'

He walked deliberately away from the busy part of the town, turning his back on the river, stepping out briskly straight before him, and swinging his gold-headed cane as he walked.

The streets which he had to traverse were silent and deserted, save occasionally where a drinking or an eating house had its swing-doors still invitingly open.

We may take it that he did not philosophize overmuch on what went on around him. He had walked swiftly up the Rue St Martin, then turning sharply to his right he found himself beneath the tall, frowning walls of the Temple prison, the grim guardian of so many secrets, such terrible despair, such unspeakable tragedies.

The sentinel challenged him, but he had the password, and explained that he desired to have speech with citizen Héron.

With a surly gesture the guard pointed to the heavy bell-pull up against the gate, and de Batz pulled it with all his might. The long clang of the brazen bell echoed and re-echoed round the solid stone walls. Anon a tiny judas in the gate was cautiously pushed open, and an arrogant voice once again challenged the midnight intruder.

De Batz, more peremptorily this time, asked for citizen Héron, with whom he had immediate and important business, and a glimmer of a piece of silver which he held up close to the judas secured him the necessary admittance.

The massive gates slowly swung open on their creaking hinges, and as de Batz passed beneath the archway they closed again behind him.

The concierge's lodge was immediately on his left. Again he was challenged, and again gave the password. But his face was apparently known here, for no serious hindrance to proceed was put in his way.

A man, whose wide, lean frame was but ill-covered by a threadbare coat and ragged breeches, and with soleless shoes on his feet, was told off to direct the citoyen to citizen Héron's rooms.

A winding, narrow stone stair, another length or two of corridor, and his guide's shuffling footsteps paused beside a low iron-studded door let into the solid stone. De Batz dismissed his ill-clothed guide and pulled the iron bell-handle which hung beside the door.

The bell gave forth a dull and broken clang, which seemed like an echo of the wails of sorrow that peopled the huge building with their weird and monotonous sounds.

'Enter!' said Héron curtly.

He banged the heavy door to behind his visitor; and de Batz, who seemed to know his way about the place, walked straight across the narrow landing to where a smaller door stood invitingly open.

There was but little furniture; two or three chairs, a table which was littered with papers, and a corner-cupboard – the open doors of which revealed a miscellaneous collection – bundles of papers, a tin saucepan, a piece of cold sausage, and a couple of pistols.

Héron pointed to one of the chairs, and then sat down on the other, close to the table, on which he rested his elbow. He picked up a short-stemmed pipe, which he had evidently laid aside at the sound of the bell, and having taken several deliberate long-drawn puffs from it, he said abruptly :

'Well, what is it now? Out with it! What do you want? Why have you come at this hour of the night – to compromise me, I suppose – bring your own d—d neck and mine into the same noose – what?'

'Easy, easy, my friend,' responded de Batz imperturbably;

'waste not so much time in idle talk. Why do I usually come to see you? Surely you have had no cause to complain hitherto of the unprofitableness of my visits to you?'

'They will have to be still more profitable to me in the future,' growled the other across the table. 'I have more power now.'

'I know you have,' said de Batz suavely. 'The new decree? What? You may denounce whom you please, search whom you please, arrest whom you please, and send whom you please to the Supreme Tribunal without giving them the slightest chance of escape.'

'Is it in order to tell me all this that you have come to see me at this hour of the night?' queried Héron with a sneer.

'No; I came at this hour of the night because I surmised that in the future you and your hell-hounds would be so busy all day "beating up game for the guillotine" that the only time you would have at the disposal of your friends would be the late hours of the night. I saw you at the theatre a couple of hours ago, friend Héron; I didn't think to find you yet abed.'

'Well, what do you want?'

'Rather,' retorted de Batz blandly, 'shall we say, whom do you want, citizen Héron?'

'For what?'

'For my continued immunity at the hands of yourself and your pack?'

'I don't know,' he said slowly, 'that I am prepared to treat with you any longer. You are an intolerable bit of vermin that has annoyed the Committee of General Security for over two years now. It would be excessively pleasant to crush you once and for all, as one would a buzzing fly.'

'Pleasant, perhaps, but immeasurably foolish,' rejoined de Batz coolly; 'you would only get thirty-five livres for my head, and I offer you ten times that amount for the self-same commodity.'

'I know, I know; but the whole thing has become too dangerous.'

'Why? I am very modest. I don't ask a great deal. Let your hounds keep off my scent.'

'You have too many d—d confederates.'

'Oh! never mind about the others. I am not bargaining about them. Let them look after themselves.'

'Every time we get a batch of them, one or the other denounces you.'

'Under torture, I know,' rejoined de Batz placidly, holding his

26

podgy hands to the warm glow of the fire. 'For you have started torture in your house of Justice now, eh, friend Héron? You and your friend the Public Prosecutor have gone the whole gamut of devilry – eh?'

'What's that to you?' retorted the other gruffly.

'Oh, nothing, nothing! I was even proposing to pay you three thousand five hundred livres for the privilege of taking no further interest in what goes on inside this prison!'

'Three thousand five hundred!' ejaculated Héron involuntarily, and this time even his eyes lost their cruelty; they joined issue with the mouth in an expression of hungry avarice.

'Two little zeros added to the thirty-five, which is all you would get for handing me over to your accursed Tribunal,' said de Batz, and, as if thoughtlessly, his hand wandered to the inner pocket of his coat, and a slight rustle as of thin crisp paper brought drops of moisture to the lips of Héron.

'Leave me alone for three weeks and the money is yours,' concluded de Batz pleasantly.

There was silence in the room now. Through the narrow barred window the steely rays of the moon fought with the dim yellow light of the oil lamp, and lit up the pale face of the Committee's agent with its lines of cruelty in sharp conflict with those of greed.

'Well! is it a bargain?' asked de Batz at last in his usual smooth, oily voice, as he half drew from out of his pocket that tempting little bundle of crisp printed paper. 'You have only to give me the usual receipt for the money and it is yours.'

Héron gave a vicious snarl.

'It is dangerous, I tell you. That receipt, if it falls into some cursed meddler's hands, would send me straight to the guillotine.'

'The receipt could only fall into alien hands,' rejoined de Batz blandly, 'if I happened to be arrested, and even in that case they could but fall into those of the chief agent of the Committee of General Security, and he hath name Héron. You must take some risks, my friend. I take them too. We are each in the other's hands. The bargain is quite fair.'

For a moment or two longer Héron appeared to be hesitating, while de Batz watched him with keen intentness. He had no doubt himself as to the issue. He had tried most of the patriots in his own golden crucible, and had weighed their patriotism against Austrian money, and had never found the latter wanting. He had not been here tonight if he were not quite sure. This

27

inveterate conspirator in the Royalist cause never took personal risks. He looked on Héron now, smiling to himself the while with perfect satisfaction.

'Very well,' said the Committee's agent with sudden decision, 'I'll take the money. But on one condition.'

'What is it?'

'That you leave little Capet alone.'

'The Dauphin!'

'Call him what you like,' said Héron, taking a step nearer to de Batz, and from his great height glowering down in fierce hatred and rage upon his accomplice; 'call the young devil what you like, but leave us to deal with him. I am just going on my usual nocturnal round,' he added abruptly. 'Come with me, citizen de Batz.'

A certain grim humour was apparent in his face as he proffered this invitation, which sounded like a rough command. As de Batz seemed to hesitate he nodded peremptorily to him to follow. Already he had gone into the hall and picked up his lanthorn. From beneath his waistcoat he drew forth a bunch of keys, which he rattled impatiently, calling to his friend to come.

'Come, citizen,' he said roughly. 'I wish to show you the one treasure in this house which your d—d fingers must not touch.'

Mechanically de Batz rose at last. He tried to be master of the terror which was invading his very bones. He would not own to himself even that he was afraid, and almost audibly he kept murmuring to himself that he had no cause for fear.

CHAPTER V

The most precious life in Europe

ONCE more he was being led through the interminable corridors of the gigantic building. Once more from the narrow, barred windows close by him he heard the heart-breaking sighs, the moans, the curses which spoke of tragedies that he could only guess.

Héron was recognized everywhere the moment he appeared, and though in these days of equality no one presented arms, nevertheless every guard stood aside to let him pass, or when necessary opened a gate for the powerful chief agent of the Committee of General Security.

Indeed, de Batz had no keys such as these to open the way for him to the presence of the martyred little King.

Thus the two men wended their way on in silence, one preceding the other. De Batz walked leisurely, thoughtfully, taking stock of everything he saw – the gates, the barriers, the positions of sentinels and warders, of everything in fact that might prove a help or a hindrance presently, when the great enterprise would be hazarded. At last – still in the wake of Héron – he found himself once more behind the main entrance gate, underneath the archway on which gave the *guichet* of the concierge.

Héron rapped with his keys against the door of the concierge's lodge, then, as it was not immediately opened from within, he pushed it open with his foot.

'The concierge?' he queried peremptorily.

From a corner of the small panelled room there came a grunt and a reply:

'Gone to bed, *quoi*!'

The man who previously had guided de Batz to Héron's door slouched forward now still carrying a boot in one hand and a blacking brush in the other.

'Take this lanthorn, then,' said the chief agent, 'and come along. Why are you still here?' he added.

'The citizen concierge was not satisfied with the way I had done his boots,' muttered the man. 'A hell of a place this ... twenty cells to sweep out every day ... and boots to clean for every aristo of a concierge or warder who demands it. ... Is that work for a free born patriot, I ask?'

'Well, if you are not satisfied, citoyen Dupont,' retorted Héron dryly, 'you may go when you like, you know ... there are plenty of others ready to do your work....'

'Nineteen hours a day, and nineteen sous by way of payment. ... I have had fourteen days of this convict work....'

He continued to mutter under his breath, while Héron turned abruptly towards a group of soldiers stationed outside.

'*En avant*, corporal!' he said; 'bring four men with you.... we go up to the tower.'

The small procession was formed. On ahead the lanthorn-bearer, with arched spine and shaking knees, dragging shuffling footsteps along the corridor, then the corporal with two of his soldiers, then Héron closely followed by de Batz, and two more soldiers bringing up the rear.

Héron had given the bunch of keys to the man Dupont. The latter, on ahead, holding the lanthorn aloft, opened one gate after another. At each gate he waited for the little procession to file through, then he relocked the gate and passed on.

Up two or three flights of winding stairs set in the solid stone, and the final heavy door was reached.

At a sign from the chief agent the soldiers stood at attention. He then called de Batz and the lanthorn-bearer to him.

He took a key from his breeches-pocket, and with his own hand unlocked the heavy door. He curtly ordered the lanthorn-bearer and de Batz to go through, then he himself went in, and finally once more relocked the door behind him, the soldiers remaining on guard on the landing outside.

Now the three men were standing in a square ante-chamber, dank and dark, devoid of furniture save for a large cupboard that filled the whole length of one wall; the others, mildewed and stained, were covered with a greyish paper, which here and there hung away in strips.

Héron crossed this ante-chamber, and with his knuckles rapped against a small door opposite.

'*Holà!*' he shouted. 'Simon, *mon vieux, tu es là?*'

From the inner room came the sound of voices, a man's and a woman's, and now, as if in response to Héron's call, the shrill tones of a child. There was shuffling, too, of footsteps, and some pushing about of furniture, then the door was opened, and a gruff voice invited the belated visitors to enter.

The atmosphere in this further room was so thick that at first de Batz was only conscious of the evil smells that pervaded it; smells which were made up of the fumes of tobacco, of burning coke, of a smoky lamp, and of stale food, and mingling through it all the pungent odour of raw spirits.

Héron had stepped briskly in, closely followed by de Batz. The man Dupont with a mutter of satisfaction put down his lanthorn and curled himself up in a corner of the ante-chamber. His interest in the spectacle so favoured by citizen Héron had apparently been exhausted by constant repetition.

'How is it Capet is not yet in bed?' queried Héron.

'He wouldn't say his prayers this evening,' replied Simon with a coarse laugh, 'and wouldn't drink his medicine. Bah!' he added with a snarl, 'this is a place for dogs and not for human folk.'

'If you are not satisfied, *mon vieux*,' retorted Héron curtly, 'you can send in your resignation when you like. There are plenty who will be glad of the place.'

The ex-cobbler gave another surly growl and expectorated on the floor in the direction where stood the child.

'Little vermin,' he said, 'he is more trouble than man or woman can bear.'

The boy in the meanwhile seemed to take but little notice of the vulgar insults put upon him by his guardian. He stood, a quaint, impassive little figure, his pale young face wearing the air of sullen indifference, and an abject desire to please, which would have appeared heart-breaking to any spectator less self-seeking and egotistic than was this Gascon conspirator.

Madame Simon had called him to her while her man and the citizen Héron were talking, and the child went readily enough, without any sign of fear. She took the corner of her coarse dirty apron in her hand, and wiped the boy's mouth and face with it.

'I can't keep him clean,' she said with an apologetic shrug of the shoulders and a look at de Batz. 'There now,' she added, speaking once more to the child, 'drink like a good boy, and say your lesson to please *maman*, and then you shall go to bed.'

She took a glass from the table, which was filled with a clear liquid that de Batz at first took to be water, and held it to the boy's lips. He turned his head away and began to whimper.

'Take it now,' she said. 'You know it makes papa angry if you don't have at least half a glass now and then.'

And thus did de Batz see the descendant of St Louis quaffing a glass of raw spirit at the bidding of a rough cobbler's wife, whom he called by the fond and foolish name sacred to childhood, *maman*!

Selfish egotist though he was, de Batz turned away in loathing. Simon had watched the little scene with obvious satisfaction. He chuckled audibly when the child drank the spirit, and called Héron's attention to him, while a look of triumph lit up his wide, pale eyes.

'And now, *mon petit*,' he said jovially, 'let the citizen hear you say your prayers!'

He winked towards de Batz, evidently anticipating a good deal of enjoyment for the visitor from what was coming. From a heap of litter in a corner of the room he fetched out a greasy red bonnet adorned with a tricolour cockade, and a soiled and tattered flag, which had once been white, and had golden fleur-de-lys embroidered upon it.

The cap he set on the child's head, and the flag he threw upon the floor.

'Now, Capet – your prayers!' he said with another chuckle of amusement.

Obediently, quite mechanically it seemed, the boy trod on the flag which Henri IV had borne before him at Ivry, and *le Roi Soleil* had flaunted in the face of the armies of Europe. The son of the Bourbons was spitting on their flag, and wiping his shoes upon its tattered folds. With shrill cracked voice he sang the Carmagnole, '*Ça ira! ça ira! les aristos à la lanterne!*' until de Batz himself felt inclined to stop his ears and to rush from the place in horror. Whatever the man's private character was, he had been born a gentleman, and his every instinct revolted against what he saw and heard. The scene had positively sickened him. He turned precipitately towards the door.

As to the lad, the intensity of excitement in him was immediately followed by an overwhelming desire for sleep. Without any preliminary of undressing or of washing, he tumbled, just as he was, on to the sofa. Madame Simon, with quite pleasing solicitude, arranged a pillow under his head, and the very next moment the child was fast asleep.

'That is the way we conduct our affairs, citizen,' said Héron gruffly, as he once more led his guests back into his office.

It was his turn to be complacent now. De Batz, for once in his life cowed by what he had seen, still wore a look of horror and disgust upon his florid face.

'What devils you all are!' he said at last.

'We are good patriots,' retorted Héron, 'and the tyrant's spawn leads but the life that hundreds of thousands of children led while his father oppressed the people. Nay! what am I saying? He leads a far better, far happier life. He gets plenty to eat and plenty of warm clothes. Thousands of innocent children, who have not the crimes of a despot father upon their consciences, have to starve while he grows fat.'

And de Batz knew that even with millions or countless money at his command he could not purchase from this brute the life and liberty of the son of King Louis. No amount of bribery would accomplish that; it would have to be ingenuity pitted against animal force, the wiliness of the fox against the power of the wolf.

De Batz thought it well at this point to finger once more nonchalantly the bundle of crisp paper in the pocket of his coat.

'Only on that one condition,' reiterated Héron in a hoarse voice; 'if you try to get at Capet, I'll drag you to the Tribunal with my own hands.'

He picked up his short-stemmed pipe and pulled savagely at it

32

for a while. De Batz was meditating.

'My friend,' he said after a little while, 'you are agitating yourself quite unnecessarily, and gravely jeopardizing your prospects of getting a comfortable little income through keeping your fingers off my person. Who said I wanted to meddle with the child?'

'You had best not,' growled Héron.

'Exactly. You have said that before. But do you not think that you would be far wiser, instead of directing your undivided attention to my unworthy self, to turn your thoughts a little to one whom, believe me, you have far greater cause to fear?'

'Who is that?'

'The Englishman.'

'You mean the man they call the Scarlet Pimpernel?'

'Himself. Have you not suffered from his activity, friend Héron? I fancy that citizen Chauvelin and citizen Collot would have quite a tale to tell about him.'

'They ought both to have been guillotined for that blunder last autumn at Boulogne.'

'Take care that the same accusation be not laid at your door this year, my friend,' commented de Batz placidly.

'Bah!'

'The Scarlet Pimpernel is in Paris even now.'

'The devil he is!'

'And on what errand, think you?'

There was a moment's silence, and then de Batz continued with slow dramatic emphasis:

'That of rescuing your most precious prisoner from the Temple.'

'How do you know?' Héron queried savagely.

'I guessed.'

'How?'

'I saw a man in the Théâtre National today ...'

'Well?'

'Who is a member of the League of the Scarlet Pimpernel.'

'D— him! Where can I find him?'

'Will you sign a receipt for the three thousand five hundred livres, which I am pining to hand over to you, my friend, and I will tell you?'

'Where's the money?'

'In my pocket.'

Without further words Héron dragged the inkhorn and a sheet of paper towards him, took up a pen, and wrote a few words rapidly in a loose, scrawly hand. He strewed sand over the writing, then handed it across the table to de Batz.

'Will that do?' he asked briefly.

The other was reading the note through carefully.

'I see you only grant me a fortnight,' he remarked casually.

'For that amount of money it is sufficient. If you want an extension you must pay more.'

'So be it,' assented de Batz coolly, as he folded the paper across. 'On the whole a fortnight's immunity in France these days is quite a pleasant respite. And I prefer to keep in touch with you, friend Héron. I'll call on you again this day fortnight.'

He took out a letter-case from his pocket. Out of this he drew a packet of bank-notes, which he laid on the table in front of Héron, then he placed the receipt carefully into the letter-case, and this back into his pocket.

Héron in the meanwhile was counting over the bank-notes. The light of ferocity had entirely gone from his eyes; momentarily the whole expression of the face was one of satisfied greed.

'Well!' he said at last when he had assured himself that the number of notes was quite correct, and he had transferred the bundle of crisp papers into an inner pocket of his coat – 'well, what about your friend?'

'I knew him years ago,' rejoined de Batz coolly; 'he is a kinsman of citizen St Just. I know that he is one of the confederates of the Scarlet Pimpernel.'

'Where does he lodge?'

'That is for you to find out. I saw him at the theatre, and afterwards in the green-room; he was making himself agreeable to the citizeness Lange. I heard him ask for leave to call on her tomorrow at four o'clock. You know where she lodges, of course!'

CHAPTER VI

What love can do

'YESTERDAY you were unkind and ungallant. How could I smile when you seemed so stern?'

'Yesterday I was not alone with you. How could I say what lay next my heart, when indifferent ears could catch the words that were meant only for you?'

'Ah, monsieur, do they teach you in England how to make pretty speeches?'

'No, mademoiselle, that is an instinct that comes to birth by the fire of a woman's eyes.'

Mademoiselle Lange was sitting upon a small sofa of antique design, with cushions covered in faded silks heaped round her pretty head. Armand thought that she looked like that carved cameo which his sister Marguerite possessed.

She told Armand all about her early life, her childhood in the back-shop of Maître Mézière, the jeweller, who was a relative of her mother's; of her desire for an artistic career, her struggles with the middle-class prejudices of her relations, her bold defiance of them, and final independence.

She made no secret of her humble origin, her want of education in those days; on the contrary, she was proud of what she had accomplished for herself. She was only twenty years of age, and already held a leading place in the artistic world of Paris.

She asked him a good deal about himself, and about his beautiful sister Marguerite, who, of course, had been the most brilliant star in that most brilliant constellation, the Comédie Française.

Thus the conversation drifted naturally back to England. Mademoiselle professed a vast interest in the citizen's country of adoption.

'I had always,' she said, 'thought it an ugly country, with the noise and bustle of industrial life going on everywhere, and smoke and fog to cover the landscape and to stunt the trees.'

'Then, in future, mademoiselle,' he replied, 'must you think of it as one carpeted with verdure, where in the spring the orchard trees covered with delicate blossom would speak to you of fairyland, where the dewy grass stretches its velvety surface in the shadow of ancient monumental oaks, and ivy-covered towers rear their stately crowns to the sky.'

'And the Scarlet Pimpernel? Tell me about him, monsieur.'

'Ah, mademoiselle, what can I tell you that you do not already know? The Scarlet Pimpernel is a man who has devoted his entire existence to the benefit of suffering mankind. He has but one thought, and that is for those who need him; he hears but one sound – the cry of the oppressed.'

'They fear him in France, monsieur. He has saved so many whose death had been decreed by the Committee of Public Safety.'

'Please God, he will save many yet.'

'Ah, monsieur, the poor little boy in the Temple prison!'

'He has your sympathy, mademoiselle?'

'Of every right-minded woman in France, monsieur. Oh!' she added with a pretty gesture of enthusiasm, clasping her hands together, and looking at Armand with large eyes filled with tears, 'if your noble Scarlet Pimpernel will do aught to save that poor innocent lamb, I would indeed bless him in my heart, and help him with all my humble might if I could.'

She did not restrain her tears; with her they came very easily, just as with a child, and as they gathered in her eyes and rolled down her fresh cheeks they in no way marred the charm of her face. One hand lay in her lap fingering a diminutive bit of cambric, which from time to time she pressed to her eyes. The other she had almost unconsciously yielded to Armand.

If Armand had been allowed to depart from here now, without having been the cause as well as the chief actor in the events that followed, no doubt that Mademoiselle Lange would always have remained a charming memory with him.

But they yielded to one another, to the springtime of their life, calling for Love, which would come presently hand in hand with his grim attendant. Sorrow. He was kneeling at her feet.

Even as Armand's glowing face was at last lifted up to hers asking with mute lips for that first kiss which she already was prepared to give, there came the loud noise of men's heavy footsteps tramping up the old oak stairs, then some shouting, a woman's cry, and the next moment Madame Belhomme, her old housekeeper and duenna, trembling, wide-eyed, and in obvious terror, came rushing into the room.

'Jeanne! Jeanne! My child! It is awful! It is awful! *Mon Dieu – mon Dieu!* What is to become of us?'

She was moaning and lamenting even as she ran in, and now she threw her apron over her face and sank into a chair.

They heard the brief words of command: 'Open in the name of the people!' and knew quite well what it all meant; they had not wandered so far in the realms of romance that reality – the grim, horrible reality of the moment – had not the power to bring them back to earth.

'Open in the name of the people!' came in a loud harsh voice once more from the other side of the front door.

'Aunt Marie, as you value your life and mine, pull yourself together,' said Jeanne firmly.

'What shall we do? Oh! what shall we do?' moaned Madame Belhomme. But she had dragged the apron away from her face, and was looking with some puzzlement at meek, gentle little Jeanne, who had suddenly become so strange, so dictatorial, all unlike her habitual somewhat diffident self.

'You need not have the slightest fear, Aunt Marie, if you will only do as I tell you,' resumed Jeanne quietly; 'if you give way to fear, we are all of us undone. As you value your life and mine,' she now repeated authoritatively, 'pull yourself together, and do as I tell you.'

The girl's firmness, her perfect quietude had the desired effect. Madame Belhomme, though still shaken up with sobs of terror, made a great effort to master herself; she stood up, smoothed down her apron, passed her hand over her ruffled hair, and said in a quaking voice:

'What do you think we had better do?'

'Go quietly to the door and open it.'

Madame Belhomme, impressed and cowed, obeyed like an automaton. She turned and marched fairly straight out of the room. It was not a minute too soon. From outside had already come the third and final summons:

'Open in the name of the people!'

After that a crowbar would break open the door.

Madame Belhomme's heavy footsteps were heard crossing the ante-chamber. Armand still knelt at Jeanne's feet, holding her trembling little hands in his.

'A love-scene,' she whispered rapidly, 'a love scene – quick – do you know one?'

And even as he had tried to rise she held him back, down on his knees.

He thought that fear was making her distracted.

'Mademoiselle —' he murmured, trying to soothe her.

'Try and understand,' she said with wonderful calm, 'and do as I tell you. Aunt Marie has obeyed. Will you do likewise?'

'To the death!' he whispered eagerly.

'Then a love-scene,' she entreated. 'Surely you know one.

Rodrigue and Chimène! Surely – surely,' she urged, even as tears of anguish rose into her eyes, 'you must, or, if not that, something else. Quick! The very seconds are precious!'

They were indeed! Madame Belhomme, obedient as a frightened dog, had gone to the door and opened it; even her well-feigned grumblings could now be heard and the rough interrogations from the soldiery.

'Citizeness Lange!' said a gruff voice.

'In her boudoir, *quoi*!'

Madame Belhomme, braced up apparently by fear, was playing her part remarkably well.

'Bothering good citizens! On baking day, too!' she went on grumbling and muttering.

'Oh, think – think!' murmured Jeanne now in an agonized whisper, her hot little hand grasping his so tightly that her nails were driven into his flesh. 'You must know something that will do – anything – for dear life's sake. . . . Armand!'

His name – in the tense excitement of this terrible moment – had escaped her lips.

All in a flash of sudden intuition he understood what she wanted, and even as the door of the boudoir was thrown violently open Armand – still on his knees, but with one hand pressed to his heart, the other stretched upwards to the ceiling in the most approved dramatic style, was loudly declaiming:

> 'Pour venger son honneur il perdit son amour,
> Pour venger sa maîtresse il quitté le jour!'

Whereupon Mademoiselle Lange feigned the most perfect impatience.

'No, no, my good cousin,' she said with a pretty *moue* of disdain, 'that will never do! You must not thus emphasize the end of every line; the verses should flow more evenly, as thus . . .'

Héron had paused at the door. 'What does this mean?' he asked gruffly, striding forward into the room and glaring first at mademoiselle, then at Armand.

Mademoiselle gave a little cry of surprise.

'Why, if it isn't citizen Héron!' she cried, jumping up with a dainty movement of coquetry and embarrassment. 'Why did not Aunt Marie announce you? . . . It is indeed remiss of her, but she is so ill-tempered on baking days I dare not even rebuke her. Won't you sit down, citizen Héron? And you, cousin,' she added, looking down airily on Armand, 'I pray you maintain no longer that foolish attitude.'

'Cousin,' she said to Armand, who in the meanwhile had risen from his knees, 'this is citizen Héron, of whom you have heard me speak. My cousin Belhomme,' she continued, once more turning to Héron, 'is fresh from the country, citizen. He hails from Orléans, where he has played leading parts in the tragedies of the late citizen Corneille. But, ah me! I fear that he will find Paris audiences vastly more critical than the good Orléanese. Did you hear him, citizen, declaiming those beautiful verses just now? He was murdering them, say I – yes, murdering them – the gaby!'

Then only did it seem as if she realized that there was something amiss, that citizen Héron had come to visit her, not as an admirer of her talent who would wish to pay his respects to a successful actress, but as a person to be looked on with dread.

She gave a quaint, nervous little laugh, and murmured in the tones of a frightened child :

'La, citizen, how glum you look! I thought you had come to compliment me on my latest success. I saw you at the theatre last night, though you did not afterwards come to see me in the green-room. Why! I had a regular ovation! Look at my flowers!' she added more gaily, pointing to several bouquets in vases about the room. 'Citizen Danton brought me the violets himself, and citizen Santerre the narcissi, and that laurel wreath – is it not charming? – that was a tribute from citizen Robespierre himself.'

She was so artless, so simple, and so natural that Héron was completely taken off his usual balance.

'So that is a cousin from Orléans, is it?' he asked, throwing his lanky body into an arm-chair, which creaked dismally under his weight.

'Yes! a regular gaby – what?' she said archily. 'Now, citizen Héron, you must stay and take coffee with me. Aunt Marie will be bringing it in directly. Hector,' she added, turning to Armand, 'come down from the clouds and ask Aunt Marie to be quick.'

This certainly was the first time in the whole of his experience that Héron had been asked to stay and drink coffee with the quarry he was hunting down. Mademoiselle's innocent little ways, her desire for the prolongation of his visit, further addled his brain. De Batz had undoubtedly spoken of an Englishman, and the cousin from Orléans was certainly a Frenchman every inch of him.

He jumped to his feet, curtly declining mademoiselle's offers of hospitality. He wanted to get away at once. Actors and actresses were always, by tacit consent of the authorities, more immune than the rest of the community. They provided the only amusement in the intervals of the horrible scenes around the scaffolds; they were irresponsible, harmless creatures who did not meddle in politics.

Jeanne the while was gaily prattling on, her luminous eyes fixed upon the all-powerful enemy, striving to read his thoughts, to understand what went on behind those cruel, prominent eyes, the chances that Armand had of safety and of life.

She knew, of course, that the visit was directed against Armand – someone had betrayed him, that odious de Batz may-hap – and she was fighting for Armand's safety, for his life. Her armoury consisted of her presence of mind, her cool courage, her self-control; she used all these weapons for his sake, though at times she felt as if the strain on her nerves would snap the thread of life in her. The effort seemed more than she could bear.

But she kept up the part, rallying Héron for the shortness of his visit, begging him to tarry for another five minutes at least, throwing out – with subtle feminine intuition – just those very hints anent little Capet's safety that were most calculated to send him flying back towards the Temple.

'I felt so honoured last night, citizen,' she said coquettishly, 'that you even forgot little Capet in order to come and watch my *début* as Célimène.'

'Forget him!' retorted Héron, smothering a curse, 'I never forget the vermin. I must go back to him; there are too many cats nosing round my mouse. Good day to you, citizeness. I ought to have brought flowers, I know; but I am a busy man – a harassed man.'

He walked out, closely followed by his two men. Then at last she closed the door behind them. The tension on her nerves relaxed; there was the inevitable reaction. Her knees were shaking under her, and she literally staggered back into the room.

But Armand was already near her, down on both his knees this time, his arms clasping the delicate form that swayed like the slender stems of narcissi in the breeze.

'Oh! you must go out of Paris at once – at once,' she said through sobs which no longer would be kept back. 'He'll return – I know that he will return – and you will not be safe until you are back in England.'

But he could not think of himself or of anything in the future. He had forgotten Héron, Paris, the world; he could only think of her.

'I owe my life to you!' he murmured. 'Oh, how beautiful you are – how brave! How I love you!'

Armand the idealist had found his ideal in a woman. He found in her all that he had admired most, all that he had admired in the leader who hitherto had been the only personification of his ideal. But Jeanne possessed all those qualities which had roused his enthusiasm in the noble hero he revered. Her pluck, her ingenuity, her calm devotion which had averted the threatened danger from him!

What had he done that she should have risked her own sweet life for his sake?

But Jeanne did not know. She could not tell. Her nerves now were somewhat unstrung, and the tears that always came so readily to her eyes flowed quite unchecked.

Armand rose from his knees. Her eyes were calling to him, her lips were ready to yield.

'Tu m'aimes?' he whispered.

And like a tired child she sank upon his breast.

He kissed her hair, her eyes, her lips; her skin was fragrant as the flowers of spring, the tears on her cheeks glistened like morning dew.

Aunt Marie came in at last, carrying the lamp. She found them sitting side by side, like two children, hand in hand, mute with the eloquence which comes from boundless love. They were under a spell, forgetting even that they lived, knowing nothing except that they loved.

The lamp broke the spell, and Aunt Marie's still trembling voice:

'Oh, my dear! how did you manage to rid youself of those brutes?'

But she asked no other question, even when the lamp showed up quite clearly the glowing cheeks of Jeanne and the ardent eyes of Armand. In her heart, long since atrophied, there were a few memories, carefully put away in a secret cell, and those memories caused the old woman to understand.

Neither Jeanne nor Armand noticed what she did; the spell had been broken, but the dream lingered on; they did not see Aunt Marie putting the room tidy, and then quietly tiptoeing out by the door.

But through the dream, reality was struggling for recognition. After Armand had asked for the hundredth time: '*Tu m'aimes?*' and Jeanne for the hundredth time had replied mutely with her eyes, her fears for him suddenly returned.

Something had awakened her from her trance – a heavy foot-step, mayhap, in the street below, the distant roll of a drum, or only the clash of saucepans in Aunt Marie's kitchen. But suddenly Jeanne was alert, and with her alertness came terror for the beloved.

'Your life,' she said – for he had called her his life just then, 'your life – and I was forgetting that it is still in danger ... your dear, your precious life!'

'Doubly dear now,' he replied, 'since I owe it to you.'

'Then I pray you, I entreat you, guard it well for my sake – make all haste to leave Paris ... oh, this I beg of you!' she continued more earnestly, seeing a look of demur in his eyes; 'every hour you spend in it brings danger nearer to your door.'

'I could not leave Paris while you are here.'

'But I am safe here,' she urged; 'quite, quite safe, I assure you. I am only a poor actress, and the Government takes no heed of us mimes. Men must be amused, even between the intervals of killing one another. Indeed, indeed, I should be far safer here now, waiting quietly for a while, while you make preparations to go.... My hasty departure at this moment would bring disaster on us both.'

There was logic in what she said. And yet how could he leave her?

'Listen, sweetheart,' he said after a while, when presently reason struggled back for first place in his mind. 'Will you allow me to consult with my chief, with the Scarlet Pimpernel, who is in Paris at the present moment? I am under his orders; I could not leave France just now. My life, my entire person are at his disposal. I and my comrades are here under his orders, for a great undertaking which he has not yet unfolded to us, but which I firmly believe is framed for the rescue of the Dauphin from the Temple.'

She gave an involuntary exclamation of horror.

'You must not be afraid for me, Jeanne,' he urged. 'The Scarlet Pimpernel cares for all his followers; he would never allow me to run unnecessary risks.'

She was unconvinced, almost jealous now of his enthusiasm for that unknown man. Already she had taken full possession of Armand; she had purchased his life, and he had given her his love. She would share neither treasure with that nameless leader who held Armand's allegiance.

'It is only for a little while, sweetheart,' he reiterated again and again. 'I could not, anyhow, leave Paris while I feel that you are here, maybe in danger. The thought would be horrible. I should go mad if I had to leave you.'

Then he talked again of England, of his life there, of the happiness and peace that were in store for them both.

'We will go to England together,' he whispered, 'and there we will be happy together, you and I. You will come, sweetheart, will you not?'

'If you still wish it, Armand,' she murmured.

Still wish it! He would gladly go tomorrow, if she would come with him. But, of course, that could not be arranged. She had her contract to fulfil at the theatre, then there would be her house and furniture to dispose of, and there was Aunt Marie. . . .

At last she promised him that she would take the advice of his chief; they would both be guided by what he said. Armand would confide in him tonight, and if it could be arranged she would hurry on her preparations, and, mayhap, be ready to join him in a week.

'In the meanwhile, that cruel man must not risk your dear life,' she said. 'Remember, Armand, your life belongs to me. Oh, I could hate him for the love you bear him.'

'Sh – sh – sh!' he said earnestly. 'Dear heart, you must not speak like that of the man whom, next to your perfect self, I love most upon earth.'

'You think of him more than of me. I shall scarce live until I know that you are safely out of Paris.'

Though it was horrible to part, yet it was best, perhaps, that he should go back to his lodgings now, in case Héron sent his spies back to her door, and since he meant to consult with his chief.

Thus this perfect hour was past; the most pure, the fullest of joy that these two young people were ever destined to know. Perhaps they felt within themselves the consciousness that their great love would rise anon to yet greater, fuller perfection when Fate had crowned it with his halo of sorrow. Perhaps, too, it was that consciousness that gave to their kisses now the solemnity of a last farewell.

CHAPTER VII

The League of the Scarlet
Pimpernel

ARMAND never could say definitely afterwards whither he went when he left the Square de Roule that evening. No doubt he wandered about the streets for some time in an absent, mechanical way, paying no heed to the passers-by, none to the direction in which he was going.

His mind was full of Jeanne, her beauty, her courage, her attitude in face of the hideous bloodhound who had come to pollute that charming old-world boudoir by his loathsome presence. He recalled every word she uttered, every gesture she made.

At length he hurried on; he was anxious to be among his own comrades, to hear his chief's pleasant voice, to feel assured that by all the sacred laws of friendship Jeanne henceforth would become the special care of the Scarlet Pimpernel and his league.

Blakeney lodged in a small house situated on the Quai de l'École, at the back of St Germain l'Auxerrois, from whence he had a clear and uninterrupted view across the river, as far as the irregular block of buildings of the Châtelet prison and the house of Justice.

The same tower-clock that two centuries ago had tolled the signal for the massacre of the Huguenots was even now striking nine. Armand slipped through the half-open *porte-cochère*, crossed the narrow dark courtyard, and ran up two flights of winding stone stairs. At the top of these, a door on his right allowed a thin streak of light to filtrate between its two folds. An iron bell handle hung beside it; Armand gave it a pull.

Two minutes later he was among his friends. He heaved a great sigh of content and relief. The very atmosphere here seemed to be different. As far as the lodging itself was concerned, it was as bare, as devoid of comfort as those sort of places – so-called *chambres garnies* – usually were in those days. The chairs looked rickety and uninviting, the sofa was of black horsehair, the carpet was threadbare, and in places in actual holes; but there was a certain something in the air which revealed, in the midst of all this squalor, the presence of a man of fastidious taste.

To begin with, the place was spotlessly clean; the stove,

highly polished, gave forth a pleasing warm glow, even while the window, slightly open, allowed a modicum of fresh air to enter the room. In a rough earthenware jug on the table stood a large bunch of Christmas roses, and to the educated nostrils the slight scent of perfume that hovered in the air was doubly pleasing after the fetid air of the narrow streets.

Sir Andrew Ffoulkes was there, also my Lord Tony, and Lord Hastings. They greeted Armand with wholehearted cheeriness.

'Where is Blakeney?' asked the young man as soon as he had shaken his friends by the hand.

'Present!' came in loud, pleasant accents from the door of an inner room on the right.

And there he stood under the lintel of the door, the man against whom was raised the giant hand of an entire nation – the man for whose head the revolutionary government of France would gladly pay out all the savings of its Treasury – the man whom human bloodhounds were tracking, hot on the scent – for whom the nets of a bitter revenge and relentless reprisals were constantly being spread.

'I am rather late, I fear,' Armand said. 'I wandered about the streets in the late afternoon and lost my way in the dark. I hope I have not kept you all waiting.'

They all pulled chairs closely round the fire, except Blakeney, who preferred to stand. He waited a while until they were all comfortably settled, and all ready to listen, then:

'It is about the Dauphin,' he said abruptly without further preamble.

They understood. All of them had guessed it, almost before the summons came that had brought them to Paris two days ago. Sir Andrew Ffoulkes had left his young wife because of that, and Armand had demanded it as a right to join hands in this noble work. Blakeney had not left France for over three months now. Backwards and forwards between Paris, or Mantes, or Orléans to the coast, where his friends would meet him to receive those unfortunates whom one man's whole-hearted devotion had rescued from death: Now it was about the Dauphin. They all waited, breathless and eager.

'Everything, I think, is prepared,' resumed Sir Percy after a slight pause. 'The Simons have been summarily dismissed; I learned that today. They remove from the Temple on Sunday next, the nineteenth. Obviously that is the one day most likely to help us in our operations. As far as I am concerned, I cannot make any hard-and-fast plans. Chance at the last moment will have to dictate. But from every one of you I must have co-operation, and it can only be by your following my directions implicitly that we can ever remotely hope to succeed.'

'The way, I think, in which we could best succeed would be this,' he resumed after a while, sitting now on the edge of the table and directly facing his four friends. The light from the lamp which stood upon the table behind him fell full upon those four glowing faces fixed eagerly upon him, but he himself was in shadow, a massive silhouette broadly cut out against the light-coloured map on the wall beyond.

'I remain here, of course, until Sunday,' he said, 'and will closely watch my opportunity, when I can with the greatest amount of safety enter the Temple building and take possession of the child. I shall, of course, choose the moment when the Simons are actually on the move, with their successors probably coming in at about the same time. God alone knows,' he added earnestly, 'how I shall contrive to get possession of the child; at the moment I am just as much in the dark about that as you are.'

He paused a moment, and suddenly his grave face seemed flooded with sunshine, a kind of lazy merriment danced in his eyes, effacing all trace of solemnity within them.

'La!' he said lightly, 'on one point I am not at all in the dark, and that is that His Majesty Louis XVII will come out of that ugly house in my company next Sunday, the nineteenth day of January in this year of grace seventeen hundred and ninety-four: and this, too, do I know – that those murderous blackguards shall not lay hands on me while that precious burden is in my keeping. So I pray you, my good Armand, do not look so glum,' he added with his pleasant, merry laugh; 'you'll need all your wits about you to help us in our undertaking.'

'What do you wish me to do, Percy?' said the young man simply.

'In one moment I will tell you. I want you all to understand the situation first. The child will be out of the Temple on Sunday, but at what hour I know not. The later it will be the better would it suit my purpose, for I cannot get out of Paris before evening with any chance of safety. Here we must risk nothing; the child is far better off as he is now than he would be if he were dragged back after an abortive attempt at rescue. But at this hour of the night, between nine and ten o'clock, I can arrange to get him out of Paris by the Villette gate, and that is where I want you, Ffoulkes, and you, Tony, to be, with some

46

kind of covered cart, yourselves in any disguise your ingenuity will suggest. Here are a few certificates of safety; I have been making a collection of them for some time, as they are always useful.'

He dived into the wide pocket of his coat and drew forth a number of cards, greasy, much-fingered documents of the usual pattern which the Committee of General Security delivered to the free citizens of the new republic, and without which no one could enter or leave any town or country commune without being detained as 'suspect'. He glanced at them and handed them over to Ffoulkes.

'Choose your own identity for the occasion, my good friend,' he said lightly; 'and you too, Tony. You may be stonemasons or coal-carriers, chimney-sweeps or farm-labourers, I care not which so long as you look sufficiently grimy and wretched to be unrecognizable, and so long as you can procure a cart without arousing suspicions, and can wait for me punctually at the appointed spot.'

Ffoulkes turned over the cards, and with a laugh handed them over to Lord Tony. The two fastidious gentlemen discussed for a while the respective merits of a chimney-sweep's uniform as against that of a coal-carrier.

'You can carry more grime if you are a sweep,' suggested Blakeney; 'and if the soot gets into your eyes it does not make them smart like coal does.'

'But soot adheres more closely,' argued Tony solemnly, 'and I know that we shan't get a bath for at least a week afterwards.'

At last the question of the disguise was effectually dismissed. Sir Andrew Ffoulkes and Lord Anthony Dewhurst had settled their differences of opinion by solemnly agreeing to represent two over-grimy and over-heated coal-heavers. They chose two certificates of safety that were made out in the names of Jean Lepetit and Achille Grospierre, labourers.

'Though you don't look at all like an Achille, Tony,' was Blakeney's parting shot to his friend.

Then without any transition from this schoolboy nonsense to the serious business of the moment, Sir Andrew Ffoulkes said abruptly :

'Tell us exactly, Blakeney, where you will want the cart to stand on Sunday.'

Blakeney rose and turned to the map against the wall, Ffoulkes and Tony following him. They stood close to his elbow while his slender, nervy hand wandered along the shiny surface of the varnished paper. At last he placed his finger on one spot.

'Here you see,' he said, 'is the Villette gate. Just outside it a narrow street on the right leads down in the direction of the canal. It is just at the bottom of that narrow street at its junction with the tow-path there that I want you two and the cart to be. It had better be a coal-cart by the way; they will be unloading coal close by there tomorrow,' he added with one of his sudden irrepressible outbursts of merriment. 'You and Tony can exercise your muscles coal-heaving, and incidentally make yourselves known in the neighbourhood as good if somewhat grimy patriots.'

'We had better take up our parts at once then,' said Tony. 'I'll take a fond farewell of my clean shirt tonight.'

'Yes, you will not see one again for some time, my good Tony. After your hard day's work tomorrow you will have to sleep either inside your cart, if you have already secured one, or under the arches of the canal bridge, if you have not.'

'I hope you have an equally pleasant prospect for Hastings,' was my Lord Tony's grim comment.

It was easy to see that he was as happy as a schoolboy about to start for a holiday. Lord Tony was a true sportsman. Perhaps there was in him less sentiment for the heroic work which he did under the guidance of his chief than an inherent passion for dangerous adventures. Sir Andrew Ffoulkes, on the other hand, thought perhaps a little less of the adventure, but a great deal of the martyred child in the Temple. He was just as buoyant, just as keen as his friend, but the leaven of sentiment raised his sporting instincts to perhaps a higher plane of self-devotion.

'Well, now, to recapitulate,' he said, in turn following with his finger the indicated route on the map. 'Tony and I and the coal-cart will await you on this spot, at the corner of the towpath on Sunday evening at nine o'clock.'

'And your signal, Blakeney?' asked Tony.

'The usual one,' replied Sir Percy, 'the seamew's cry thrice repeated at brief intervals. But now,' he continued, turning to Armand and Hastings, who had taken no part in the discussion hitherto, 'I want your help a little farther afield.'

'I thought so,' nodded Hastings.

'The coal-cart, with its usual miserable nag, will carry us a distance of fifteen or sixteen kilometres, but no more. My purpose is to cut along the north of the city, and to reach St Germain, the nearest point where we can secure good mounts. There is a farmer just outside the commune; his name is Achard.

He has excellent horses, which I have borrowed before now; we shall want five, of course, and he has one powerful beast that will do for me, as I shall have, in addition to my own weight, which is considerable, to take the child with me on the pillion. Now you, Hastings and Armand, will have to start early tomorrow morning, leave Paris by the Neuilly gate, and from there make your way to St Germain by any conveyance you can contrive to obtain. At St Germain you must at once find Achard's farm; disguised as labourers you will not arouse suspicion by so doing. You will find the farmer quite amenable to money, and you must secure the best horses you can get for our own use, and, if possible, the powerful mount I spoke of just now. You are both excellent horsemen, therefore I selected you among the others for this special errand, for you two, with the five horses, will have to come and meet our coal-cart seventeen kilometres out of St Germain, to where the first signpost indicates the road to Courbevoie. Some two hundred metres down this road on the right there is a small spinney, which will afford splendid shelter for yourselves and your horses. We hope to be there at about one o'clock after midnight of Monday morning. Now, is all that quite clear, and are you both satisfied?'

'It is quite clear,' exclaimed Hastings placidly; 'but I, for one, am not at all satisfied.'

'And why not?'

'Because it is all too easy. We get none of the danger.'

'Oho! I thought that you would bring that argument forward, you incorrigible grumbler,' laughed Sir Percy, good-humouredly. 'Let me tell you that if you start tomorrow from Paris in that spirit you will run your head and Armand's into a noose long before you reach the gate of Neuilly. I cannot allow either of you to cover your faces with too much grime; an honest farm labourer should not look over-dirty, and your chances of being discovered and detained are, at the outset, far greater than those which Ffoulkes and Tony will run —'

Armand had said nothing during this time. While Blakeney was unfolding his plan for him and for Lord Hastings – a plan which practically was a command – he had sat with his arms folded across his chest, his head sunk upon his breast. When Blakeney had asked if they were satisfied, he had taken no part in Hastings' protest nor responded to his leader's good-humoured banter.

Though he did not look up now, yet he felt that Percy's eyes were fixed upon him, and they seemed to scorch into his soul.

He made a great effort to appear eager like the others, and yet from the first a chill had struck at his heart. He could not leave Paris before he had seen Jeanne.

He looked up suddenly, trying to seem unconcerned; he even looked his chief fully in the face.

'When ought we to leave Paris?' he asked calmly.

'You MUST leave at daybreak,' replied Blakeney with a slight, almost imperceptible emphasis on the word of command. 'When the gates are first opened, and the work-people go to and fro at their work, that is the safest hour. And you must be at St Germain as soon as may be, or the farmer may not have a sufficiency of horses available at a moment's notice. I want you to be spokesman with Achard, so that Hastings' British accent should not betray you both. Also you might not get a conveyance for St Germain immediately. We must think of every eventuality, Armand. There is so much at stake.'

Armand made no further comment just then. But the others looked astonished. Armand had but asked a simple question, and Blakeney's reply seemed almost like a rebuke – so circumstantial too, and so explanatory.

Silence had fallen on them all. They all sat round the fire buried in thought. Through the open window there came from the quay beyond the hum of life in the open-air camp; the tramp of the sentinels around it, the words of command from the drill-sergeant, and through it all the moaning of the wind and the beating of the sleet against the window-panes.

A whole world of wretchedness was expressed by those sounds! Blakeney gave a quick, impatient sigh, and going to the window he pushed it further open, and just then there came from afar the muffled roll of drums, and from below the watch-man's cry that seemed such dire mockery :

'Sleep, citizens! Everything is safe and peaceful.'

'Sound advice,' said Blakeney lightly. 'Shall we also go to sleep? What say you all – eh?'

He had, with that sudden rapidity characteristic of his every action, already thrown off the serious air, which he had worn a moment ago when giving instructions to Hastings. His usual *débonnaire* manner was on him once again, his laziness, his careless *insouciance*. He was even at this moment deeply engaged in flicking off a grain of dust from the immaculate Mechlin cuff at his wrist. The heavy lids had fallen over the tell-tale eyes as if weighted with fatigue, the mouth appeared ready for the laugh which never was absent from it very long.

It was only Ffoulkes's devoted eyes that were sharp enough to pierce the mask of light-hearted gaiety which enveloped the soul of his leader at the present moment. He saw – for the first time in all the years that he had known Blakeney – a frown across the habitually smooth brow, and though the lips were parted for a laugh, the lines round mouth and chin were hard and set.

With that intuition born of whole-hearted friendship Sir Andrew guessed what troubled Percy. He had caught the look which the latter had thrown on Armand, and knew that some explanation would have to pass between the two men before they parted tonight. Therefore he gave the signal for the breaking up of the meeting.

'There is nothing more to say, is there, Blakeney?' he asked.

'No, my good fellow, nothing,' replied Sir Percy. 'I do not know how you all feel, but I am demmed fatigued.'

'What about the rags for tomorrow?' queried Hastings.

'You know where to find them. In the room below. Ffoulkes has the key. Wigs and all are there. But don't use false hair if you can help it – it is apt to shift in a scrimmage.'

He spoke jerkily, more curtly than was his wont. Hastings and Tony thought that he was tired. They rose to say good night. Then the three men went away together, Armand remaining behind.

'Well now, Armand, what is it?' asked Blakeney, the moment the footsteps of his friends had died away down the stone stairs, and their voices had ceased to echo in the distance.

'You guessed, then, that there was ... something?' said the younger man, after a slight hesitation.

'Of course.'

Armand rose, pushing the chair away from him with an impatient nervy gesture. Burying his hands in the pockets of his breeches, he began striding up and down the room, a dark, troubled expression in his face, a deep frown between his eyes.

Suddenly the young man paused in his restless walk and stood in front of his friend – an earnest, solemn, determined figure.

'Blakeney,' he said, 'I cannot leave Paris tomorrow.'

Sir Percy made no reply. He was contemplating the polish which he had just succeeded in producing on his thumbnail.

'I must stay here for a while longer,' continued Armand firmly. 'I may not be able to return to England for some weeks. You have the three others here to help you in your enterprise outside Paris. I am entirely at your service within the compass of its walls.'

Blakeney was apparently satisfied at last with the result of his polishing operations. He rose, gave a slight yawn, and turned towards the door.

'Good night, my dear fellow,' he said pleasantly; 'it is time we were all abed. I am so demmed fatigued.'

'Percy, you cannot go and leave me like this!' exclaimed Armand.

'Like what, my dear fellow?' queried Sir Percy with good-humoured impatience.

'Without a word – without a sign. What have I done that you should treat me like a child, unworthy even of attention?'

Blakeney had turned back and was now facing him, towering above the slight figure of the younger man. His face had lost none of its gracious air, and beneath their heavy lids his eyes looked down not unkindly on his friend.

'Would you have preferred it, Armand,' he said quietly, 'if I had said the word that your ears have heard even though my lips have not uttered it?'

'I don't understand,' murmured Armand defiantly.

'What sign would you have had me make?' continued Sir Percy, his pleasant voice falling calm and mellow on the younger man's supersensitive consciousness: 'That of branding you, Marguerite's brother, as a liar and a cheat?'

'Blakeney!' retorted the other, as with flaming cheeks and wrathful eyes he took a menacing step towards his friend; 'had any man but you dared to speak such words to me —'

'I pray to God, Armand, that no man but I has the right to speak them.'

'You have no right.'

'Every right, my friend. Do I not hold your oath? ... Are you not prepared to break it?'

'I ii not break my oath to you. I'll serve and help you in every way you can command ... my life I'll give to the cause ... give me the most dangerous – the most difficult task to perform ... I'll do it – I'll do it gladly.'

'I have given you an over-difficult and dangerous task.'

'Bah! To leave Paris in order to engage horses, while you and the others do all the work. That is neither difficult nor dangerous.'

'It will be difficult for you, Armand, because your head is not sufficiently cool to foresee serious eventualities and to prepare against them. It is dangerous, because you are a man in love, and a man in love is apt to run his head – and that of his friends – blindly into a noose.'

'Who told you that I was in love?'

'You yourself, my good fellow. Had you not been so transparent at the outset,' he continued, still speaking very deliberately and never raising his voice, 'I would even now be standing over you, dog-whip in hand, to thrash you as a defaulting coward and a perjurer. ... Bah!' he added with a return to his habitual *bonhomie*, 'I would no doubt even have lost my temper with you. Which would have been purposeless, and excessively bad form. Eh?'

A violent retort had sprung to Armand's lips. But fortunately at that very moment his eyes, glowing with anger, caught those of Blakeney fixed with lazy good-nature upon his. Something of that irresistible dignity which pervaded the whole personality of the man checked Armand's hot-headed words on his lips.

'I cannot leave Paris tomorrow,' he reiterated more calmly.

'Because you have arranged to see her again?'

'Because she saved my life today, and is herself in danger.'

'She is in no danger,' said Blakeney simply, 'since she saved the life of my friend.'

The words he said – simple though they were – sent a thrill through Armand's veins. He felt himself disarmed. His resistance fell before the subtle strength of an unbendable will; nothing remained in his heart but an overwhelming sense of shame and of impotence.

He sank into a chair and rested his elbows on the table, burying his face in his hands.

'Percy, cannot you release me? I would not hinder you if I stayed.'

'God knows you have hindered us enough already.'

'How?'

'You say she saved your life ... then you were in danger. ... Héron and his spies have been on your track ... your track leads to mine, and I have sworn to save the Dauphin. ... A man in love, Armand, is a deadly danger among us. ... Therefore at daybreak you must leave Paris with Hastings on your difficult and dangerous task.'

'And if I refuse?' retorted Armand.

'You would be offering a tainted name and tarnished honour to the woman you pretend to love.'

'And you insist upon my obedience?'

'By the oath which I hold from you.'

'But this is cruel – inhuman!'

'Honour, my good Armand, is often cruel and seldom human.

He is a godlike taskmaster, and we who call ourselves men are all of us his slaves.'

'The tyranny comes from you alone. You could release me an you would.'

'And to gratify the selfish desire of immature passion you would wish to see me jeopardize the life of those who place infinite trust in me.'

'God knows how you have gained their allegiance, Blakeney. To me now you are selfish and callous.'

'There is the difficult task you craved for, Armand,' was all the answer that Blakeney made to the taunt — 'to obey a leader whom you no longer trust.'

But this Armand could not brook. He had spoken hotly, impetuously, but his heart was loyal to the chief whom he had reverenced for so long.

'Forgive me, Percy,' he said humbly; 'I am distracted. I don't think I quite realized what I was saying. I trust you, of course ... implicitly ... and you need not even fear ... I shall not break my oath, though your orders now seem to me needlessly callous and selfish. ... I will obey ... you need not be afraid.'

'I was not afraid of that, my good fellow.'

'Of course, you do not understand ... you cannot. ... To you, your honour, the task which you have set yourself, has been your only fetish. ... Love in its true sense does not exist for you. ... I see it now ... you do not know what it is to love.'

Blakeney made no reply for the moment. At Armand's words his lips had imperceptibly tightened, his eyes had narrowed as if they tried to see something that was beyond the range of their focus.

Suddenly a sigh escaped the man's tightly pressed lips. With a strange gesture, wholly unusual to him, he passed his hand right across his eyes.

'Mayhap you are right, Armand,' he said quietly; 'mayhap I do not know what it is to love.'

Armand turned to go. There was nothing more to be said. He knew Percy well enough by now to realize the finality of his pronouncements. His heart felt sore, but he was too proud to show his hurt again to a man who did not understand. All thoughts of disobedience he had put resolutely aside; he had never meant to break his oath. All that he had hoped to do was to persuade Percy to release him from it for a while.

That by leaving Paris he risked to lose Jeanne he was quite convinced, but it is nevertheless a true fact that in spite of this he did not withdraw his love and trust from his chief. He was under the influence of that same magnetism which enchained all his comrades to the will of this man; and though his enthusiasm for the great cause had somewhat waned, his allegiance to its leader was no longer tottering.

But he would not trust himself to speak again on the subject. 'I will find the others downstairs,' was all he said, 'and will arrange with Hastings for tomorrow. Good night, Percy.'

'Good night, my dear fellow. By the way, you have not told me yet who she is.'

'Her name is Jeanne Lange,' said St Just half reluctantly. He had not meant to divulge his secret quite so fully as yet.

CHAPTER VIII

Then everything was dark

THE night that Armand St Just spent tossing about on a hard, narrow bed was the most miserable, agonizing one he had ever passed in his life. A kind of fever ran through him, causing his teeth to chatter, and the veins in his temples to throb until he thought that they must burst.

Physically he certainly was ill; the mental strain caused by two great conflicting passions had attacked his bodily strength, and while his brain and heart fought their battles together, his aching limbs found no repose.

His love for Jeanne! His loyalty to the man to whom he owed his life, and to whom he had sworn allegiance and implicit obedience!

He rose long before daybreak, with tired back and burning eyes, but unconscious of any pain save that which tore at his heart. One thought – and one alone – was clear in his mind : he must see Jeanne before he left Paris.

He did not pause to think how he could accomplish that at this hour of the day. All he knew was that he must obey his chief, and that he must see Jeanne. He would see her, explain to her that he must leave Paris immediately, and beg her to make her preparations quickly, so that she might meet him as soon as maybe, and accompany him to England straight away.

No one challenged Armand when he turned into the square, and though the darkness was intense, he made his way fairly straight for the house where lodged Mademoiselle Lange.

He pulled the concierge's bell, and the latch of the outer door, manipulated from within, duly sprang open in response. He entered, and from the lodge the concierge's voice challenged him with an oath at the unseemliness of the hour.

'Mademoiselle Lange,' said Armand boldly.

'At this hour of the morning?' queried the man with a sneer.

'I desire to see her.'

'Then you have come to the wrong house, citizen,' said the concierge with a rude laugh.

'The wrong house? What do you mean?' stammered Armand, a little bewildered.

'She is not here — *quoi!*' retorted the concierge, who now turned deliberately on his heel. 'Go and look for her, citizen; it'll take you some time to find her.'

He shuffled off in the direction of the stairs. Armand, vainly trying to shake himself free from a sudden, an awful sense of horror, gripped him peremptorily by the arm.

'Where is Mademoiselle Lange?' he asked.

His voice sounded quite strange in his own ear; his throat felt parched, and he had to moisten his lips with his tongue before he was able to speak.

'Arrested,' replied the man.

'Arrested? When? Where? How?'

'When — late yesterday evening. Where? — here in her room. How? — by the agents of the Committee of General Security. She and the old woman! *Basta!* that's all I know. Now I am going back to bed, and you clear out of the house. You are making a disturbance, and I shall be reprimanded. I ask you, is this a decent time for rousing honest patriots out of their morning sleep?'

Armand stood like a man who has been stunned by a blow on the head. His limbs were paralysed. He could not for the moment have moved or spoken if his life had depended on a sign or on a word.

Jeanne had been arrested! Jeanne was in prison — she would be tried, condemned, and all because of him.

Like a wild creature driven forth he started to run, out by the front door and into the street. In a moment he was out of the little square; then like a hunted hare he still ran down the Rue St Honoré, along its narrow, interminable length. His hat had fallen from his head, his hair was wild all round his face, the rain weighted the cloak upon his shoulders; but still he ran.

It was still dark, but Armand St Just was a born Parisian, and

he knew every inch of this quarter. He had kept just a sufficiency of reason – or was it merely blind instinct? – to avoid the
places where the night patrols of the National Guard might be
on the watch. He avoided the Place du Carrousel, also the quay,
and struck sharply to his right until he reached the façade of St
Germain l'Auxerrois.

Another effort; round the corner, and there was the house at
last. He was like the hunted creature now that has run to earth.
Up the two flights of stone stairs, and then the pull at the bell; a
moment of tense anxiety, while panting, gasping, almost choked
with the sustained effort and the strain of the past half-hour, he
leaned against the wall, striving not to fall.

Then the well-known firm step across the rooms beyond, the
open door, the hand upon his shoulder.

After that he remembered nothing more.

He had not actually fainted, but the exertion of that long run
had rendered him partially unconscious. He knew now that he
was safe, that he was sitting in Blakeney's room, and that something hot and vivifying was being poured down his throat.

'Percy, they have arrested her!' he said, panting, as soon as
speech returned to his paralysed tongue.

'All right. Don't talk now. Wait till you are better.'

With infinite care and gentleness Blakeney arranged some
cushions under Armand's head, turned the sofa towards the fire,
and anon brought his friend a cup of hot coffee, which the latter
drank with avidity.

He roused himself with one vigorous effort from his lethargy,
feeling quite ashamed of himself and of this breakdown of his
nervous system. He looked with frank admiration on Sir Percy,
who stood immovable and silent by the window – a perfect
tower of strength, serene and impassive, yet kindly in distress.

'Percy,' said the young man, 'I ran all the way from the top of
the Rue St Honoré. I was only breathless. I am quite all right.
May I tell you all about it?'

Without a word Blakeney closed the window and came across
to the sofa; he sat down beside Armand, and to all outward
appearances he was nothing now but a kind and sympathetic
listener to a friend's tale of woe. Not a line in his face or look in
his eyes betrayed the thoughts of the leader who had been
thwarted at the outset of a dangerous enterprise, or of the man,
accustomed to command, who had been so flagrantly disobeyed.

Armand, unconscious of all save of Jeanne and of her immediate need, put an eager hand on Percy's arm.

'Héron and his hell-hounds went back to her lodgings last night,' he said, speaking as if he were still a little out of breath. 'They hoped to get me, no doubt; not finding me there, they took her. Oh, my God!'

It was the first time that he had put the whole terrible circumstance into words, and it seemed to gain in reality by the recounting. The agony of mind which he endured was almost unbearable; he hid his face in his hands lest Percy should see how terribly he suffered.

'I knew that,' said Blakeney quietly.

Armand looked up in surprise.

'How? When did you know it?' he stammered.

'Last night when you left me. I went down to the Square du Roule. I arrived there just too late.'

'Percy!' exclaimed Armand, whose pale face had suddenly flushed scarlet, 'you did that – last night you —'

'Of course,' interposed the other calmly; 'had I not promised you to keep watch over her? When I heard the news it was already too late to make further inquiries, but when you arrived just now I was on the point of starting out, in order to find out in what prison Mademoiselle Lange is being detained. I shall have to go soon, Armand, before the guard is changed at the Temple and the Tuileries. This is the safest time, and God knows we are all of us sufficiently compromised already.'

In a moment now Armand realized all the harm which his recklessness had done, was still doing to the work of the League. Every one of his actions since his arrival in Paris two days ago had jeopardized a plan or endangered a life: his friendship with de Batz, his connexion with Mademoiselle Lange, his visit to her yesterday afternoon, the repetition of it this morning, culminating in that wild run through the streets of Paris, when at any moment a spy lurking round a corner might either have barred his way, or, worse still, have followed him to Blakeney's door. Armand, without a thought of anyone save of his beloved, might easily this morning have brought an agent of the Committee of General Security face to face with his chief.

'Percy,' he murmured, 'can you ever forgive me?'

'Pshaw, man!' retorted Blakeney lightly; 'there is naught to forgive, only a great deal that should no longer be forgotten; your duty to the others, for instance, your obedience, and your honour.'

'What do you wish me to do?'

'Firstly, you must be outside Paris within the hour. Every minute that you spend inside the city now is full of danger – oh no! not for you,' added Blakeney, checking with a good-humoured gesture Armand's words of protestation, 'danger for the others – and for our scheme tomorrow.'

'How can I go to St Germain, Percy, knowing that she —'

'Is under my charge?' interposed the other calmly. 'That should not be so difficult. Come,' he added, placing a kindly hand on the other's shoulder, 'you shall not find me such an inhuman monster after all. But I must think of the others, you see, and of the child whom I have sworn to save. But I won't send you as far as St Germain. Go down to the room below and find a good bundle of rough clothes that will serve you as a disguise, for I imagine that you have lost those which you had. In a tin box with the clothes downstairs you will find the packet of miscellaneous certificates of safety. Take an appropriate one, and then start out immediately for Villette. You understand?'

'Yes, yes!' said Armand eagerly. 'You want me to join Ffoulkes and Tony.'

'Yes. You'll find them probably unloading coal by the canal. Try and get private speech with them as early as may be, and tell Tony to set out at once for St Germain, and to join Hastings there, instead of you, while you take his place with Ffoulkes.'

'Yes, I understand; but how will Tony reach St Germain?'

'La, my good fellow,' said Blakeney gaily, 'you may safely trust Tony to go where I send him. Do you but do as I tell you, and leave him to look after himself. And now,' he added, speaking more earnestly. 'the sooner you get out of Paris the better it will be for us all. As you see, I am only sending you to La Villette, because it is not too far for me to keep in personal touch with you. Remain close to the gates for an hour after nightfall. I will contrive before they close to bring you news of Mademoiselle Lange.'

Armand said no more. The sense of shame in him deepened with every word spoken by his chief. He felt how untrustworthy he had been, how undeserving of the selfless devotion which Percy was showing him even now. The words of gratitude died on his lips; he knew that they would be unwelcome. These Englishmen were so devoid of sentiment, he thought, and his brother-in-law, with all his unselfish and heroic deeds, was, he felt, absolutely callous in matters of the heart.

But Armand was a noble-minded man, and with the true sporting instinct in him, despite the fact that he was a creature of nerves, highly strung and imaginative. He could give ungrudging admiration to his chief, even while giving himself up entirely to sentiment for Jeanne.

So he braced up his nerves, trying his best to look cool and unconcerned, but he could not altogether hide from his friend the burning anxiety which was threatening to break his heart.

'I have given you my word, Armand,' said Blakeney in answer to the unspoken prayer; 'cannot you try and trust me – as the others do?'

Then with sudden transition he pointed to the map behind him.

'Remember the gate of Villette, and the corner by the tow-path. Join Ffoulkes as soon as maybe and send Tony on his way, and wait for news of Mademoiselle Lange some time tonight.'

'God bless you, Percy!' said Armand involuntarily. 'Goodbye!'

'Goodbye, my dear fellow. Slip on your disguise as quickly as you can, and be out of the house in a quarter of an hour.'

He accompanied Armand through the ante-room, and finally closed the door on him. Then he went back to his room and walked up to the window, which he threw open to the humid morning air. Now that he was alone the look of trouble on his face deepened to a dark, anxious frown, and as he looked out across the river a sigh of bitter impatience and disappointment escaped his lips.

*   *   *

The gate of La Villette, at the north-east corner of the city, was about to close. Armand, dressed in the rough clothes of a labouring man, was leaning against a low wall, from which point of vantage he could command a view of the gate and of the life and bustle around it.

He was dog-tired, after a day's hard manual toil, and felt lonely and desperately anxious. The more he thought of it, the more impossible did it seem that Blakeney could find anything out. In his fevered fancy he saw Jeanne standing in the tumbril – being led to the guillotine. And Percy had not come. A town clock inside the city struck six – and still no sign of Percy.

Resolution was not slow in coming. Surely, he argued with himself, it was not for Percy, who did not know her, to save Jeanne; the task was his – Armand's – who worshipped her.

The certificate of safety in his hand, Armand walked boldly up to the gate, and, after five minutes of tense anxiety, was allowed to cross back into the city, but his certificate of safety was detained. He would have to get another from the Committee of General Security before he would be allowed to leave Paris again.

The lion had closed his jaws.

CHAPTER IX

The weary search

BLAKENEY was not at his lodgings when Armand arrived there that evening, nor did he return, while the young man haunted the precincts of St Germain l'Auxerrois and wandered along the quays hours and hours at a stretch.

He dragged his weary footsteps back to his own lodgings on the heights of Montmartre. He had not found Percy, he had no news of Jeanne; it seemed as if hell itself could hold no worse tortures than this intolerable suspense.

He threw himself down on the narrow palliasse and, tired Nature asserting herself, at last fell into a heavy dreamless torpor, like the sleep of a drunkard, deep but without the beneficent aid of rest.

It was broad daylight when he awoke. The pale light of a damp wintry morning filtered through the grimy panes of the window. Armand jumped out of bed, aching of limb but resolute of mind. There was no doubt that Percy had failed in discovering Jeanne's whereabouts; but where a mere friend had failed a lover was more likely to succeed.

The rough clothes which he had worn yesterday were the only ones he had. They would, of course, serve his purpose better than his own, which he had left at Blakeney's lodgings yesterday. In half an hour he was dressed, looking a fairly good imitation of a labourer out of work.

It was quite a usual thing these days for relatives and friends of prisoners to go wondering about from prison to prison to find out where the loved ones happened to be detained. The prisons were overfull just now; convents, monasteries, and public institutions had all been requisitioned by the Government for the housing of the hundreds of so-called traitors who had been arrested on the barest suspicion, or at the mere denunciation of an evil-wisher.

There were the Abbaye and the Luxembourg, the erstwhile convents of the Visitation and the Sacré-Coeur, the cloister of the Oratorians, the Salpêtrière, and the St Lazare hospitals, and there was, of course, the Temple, and, lastly, the Conciergerie.

Persons under arrest at some of the other prisons did sometimes come out of them alive, but the Conciergerie was only the ante-chamber of the guillotine.

Therefore Armand's idea was to visit the Conciergerie first.

If Jeanne was not there, then there might be some hope that she was only being temporarily detained, and through Armand's excited brain there had already flashed the thought that mayhap the Committee of General Security would release her if he gave himself up.

He reached the Quai de l'Horloge soon after nine, skirted the square clock-tower, and passed through the monumental gateways of the house of Justice.

He knew that his best way to the prison would be through the halls and corridors of the Tribunal, to which the public had access whenever the court was sitting. The sittings began at ten, and already the usual crowd of idlers was assembling – men and women who apparently had no other occupation save to come day after day to this theatre of horrors and watch the different acts of the heartrending dramas that were enacted here with a kind of awful monotony.

Armand mingled with the crowd that stood about the courtyard, and anon moved slowly up the gigantic flight of stone steps talking lightly on indifferent subjects. There was quite a goodly sprinkling of working-men among this crowd, and Armand in his toil-stained clothes attracted no attention.

Suddenly a word reached his ear – just a name flippantly spoken by spiteful lips – and it changed the whole trend of his thoughts. Since he had risen that morning he had thought of nothing but of Jeanne, and – in connexion with her – of Percy and his vain quest of her. Now that name spoken by someone unknown brought his mind back to more definite thoughts of his chief.

'Capet!' the name whereby the uncrowned little King of France was designated by the revolutionary party.

Armand suddenly recollected that today was Sunday, the 19th of January. He had lost count of days and of dates lately, but the name 'Capet', had brought everything back; the child in the Temple; the conference in Blakeney's lodgings; the plans for the rescue of the boy. That was to take place today – Sunday, the 19th. The Simons would be moving from the Temple, at what hour Blakeney did not know, but it would be today, and he

62

would be watching his opportunity.

Now Armand understood everything; a great wave of bitterness swept over his soul. Percy had forgotten Jeanne! He was busy thinking of the child in the Temple, and while Armand had been eating out his heart with anxiety, the Scarlet Pimpernel, true only to his mission, and impatient of all sentiment that interfered with his schemes, had left Jeanne to pay with her life for the safety of the uncrowned King.

But the bitterness did not last long; on the contrary, a kind of wild exultation took its place. If Percy had forgotten, then Armand could stand by Jeanne alone. It was better so! He would save the loved one; it was his duty and his right to work for her sake. Never for a moment did he doubt that he could save her, that his life would be readily accepted in exchange for hers.

The crowd around him was moving up the monumental steps, and Armand went with the crowd. It lacked but a few minutes to ten now; soon the court would begin to sit. In the olden days, when he was studying for the law, Armand had often wandered about at will along the corridors of the house of Justice, He knew exactly where the different prisons were situated about the buildings, and how to reach the courtyards where the prisoners took their daily exercise.

To watch those aristos who were awaiting trial and death taking their recreation in these courtyards had become one of the sights of Paris, and Armand joined a knot of idlers who were drifting leisurely towards the corridors. He followed in their wake and soon found himself in the long Galerie des Prisonniers.

At first he could scarcely distinguish one woman from another among the crowd that thronged the courtyard, and the close ironwork hindered his view considerably. The women looked almost like phantoms in the grey misty air, gliding slowly along with noiseless tread on the flagstones.

The sentinel, who had stood aside for him, chaffed him for his intentness.

'Have you a sweetheart among those aristos, citizen?' he asked. 'You seem to be devouring them with your eyes.'

Armand, with his rough clothes soiled with coal-dust, his face grimy and streaked with sweat, certainly looked to have but little in common with the *ci-devant* aristos who formed the bulk of the groups in the courtyards. He looked up; the soldier was regarding him with obvious amusement, and at sight of Armand's wild, anxious eyes he gave vent to a coarse jest.

'Have I made a shrewd guess, citizen?' he said. 'Is she among that lot?'

'I do not know where she is,' said Armand almost involuntarily.

'Then why don't you find out?' queried the soldier.

The man was not speaking altogether unkindly. Armand devoured with the maddening desire to know, threw the last fragment of prudence to the wind. He assumed a more careless air, trying to look as like a country bumpkin in love as he could.

'I would like to find out,' he said, 'but I don't know where to inquire. My sweetheart has certainly left her home,' he added lightly; 'some say that she has been false to me, but I think that, mayhap, she has been arrested.'

'Well, then, you gaby,' said the soldier good-humouredly, 'go straight to La Tournelle; you know where it is?'

Armand knew well enough, but thought it more prudent to keep up the air of the ignorant lout.

'Straight down that first corridor on your right,' explained the other, pointing in the direction which he had indicated, 'you will find the *guichet* of la Tournelle exactly opposite to you. Ask the concierge for the register of female prisoners – every freeborn citizen of the Republic has the right to inspect prison registers. It is a new decree framed for safeguarding the liberty of the people. But if you do not press half a livre in the hand of the concierge,' he added, speaking confidentially, 'you will find that the register will not be quite ready for your inspection.'

'Half a livre!' exclaimed Armand, striving to play his part to the end. 'How can a poor devil of a labourer have half a livre to give away?'

'Well! a few sous will do in that case; a few sous are always welcome these hard times.'

Armand took the hint, and as the crowd had drifted away momentarily to a farther portion of the corridor, he contrived to press a few copper coins into the hand of the obliging soldier.

Of course, he knew his way to La Tournelle, and at last found himself in front of the *guichet* – a narrow wooden box, wherein the clerk in charge of the prison registers sat nominally at the disposal of the citizens of this free republic.

But to Armand's almost overwhelming chagrin he found the place entirely deserted. The *guichet* was closed down; there was not a soul in sight.

After much fruitless inquiry, Armand at last was informed by a *bon bourgeois*, who was wandering about the house of Justice and who seemed to know its multifarious rules, that the prison registers all over Paris could only be consulted by the public between the hours of six and seven in the evening.

How he contrived to kill those long, weary hours he could not afterwards have said. Once he felt very hungry and turned almost mechanically into an eating-house, and tried to eat and drink. But most of the day he wandered through the streets, restlessly, unceasingly, feeling neither chill nor fatigue. The hour before six o'clock found him on the Quai de l'Horloge in the shadow of the great towers of the Hall of Justice, listening for the clang of the clock that would sound the hour of his deliverance from this agonizing torture of suspense.

He found his way to La Tournelle without any hesitation. There before him was the wooden box, with its *guichet* open at last, and two stands upon its ledge, on which were placed two huge leather-bound books.

Though Armand was nearly an hour before the appointed time, he saw when he arrived a number of people standing round the *guichet*. Two soldiers were there keeping guard and forcing the patient, long-suffering inquirers to stand in a queue, each waiting his or her turn at the books.

From inside his box the clerk disputed every inquirer's right to consult the books; he made as many difficulties as he could, demanding the production of certificates of safety, or permits from the section. He was as insolent as he dared, and Armand from where he stood could see that a continuous if somewhat thin stream of coppers flowed from the hands of the inquirers into those of the official.

It was quite dark in the passage where the long queue continued to swell with amazing rapidity. Only on the ledge in front of the *guichet* there was a guttering tallow candle at the disposal of the inquirers.

Now it was Armand's turn at last. By this time his heart was beating so strongly and so rapidly that he could not have trusted himself to speak. He fumbled in his pocket, and without unnecessary preliminaries he produced a small piece of silver, and pushed it towards the clerk, then he seized on the register marked '*Femmes*' with voracious avidity.

The clerk had with stolid indifference pocketed the half livre; he looked on Armand over a pair of large bone-rimmed spectacles, with the air of an old hawk that sees a helpless bird and yet is too satiated to eat. He was apparently vastly amused at Armand's trembling hands, and the clumsy, aimless way with which he fingered the book, and held up the tallow candle.

'What date?' he asked curtly in a piping voice.

'What date?' reiterated Armand vaguely.

'What day and hour was she arrested?' said the man, thrusting his beak-like nose closer to Armand's face. Evidently the piece of silver had done its work well; he meant to be helpful to this country lout.

'On Friday evening,' murmured the young man.

The clerk's hands did not in character gainsay the rest of his appearance; they were long and thin, with nails that resembled the talons of a hawk. Armand watched them fascinated as from above they turned over rapidly the pages of the book; then one long, grimy finger pointed to a row of names down a column.

'If she is here,' said the man curtly, 'her name should be among these.'

Armand's vision was blurred. He could scarcely see. The row of names was dancing a wild dance in front of his eyes; perspiration stood out on his forehead, and his breath came in quick stertorous gasps.

He never knew afterwards whether he actually saw Jeanne's name there in the book, or whether his fevered brain was playing his aching senses a cruel and mocking trick. Certain it is that suddenly among a row of indifferent names hers suddenly stood clearly on the page, and to him it seemed as if the letters were writ out in blood.

582. Belhomme, Louise, aged sixty. Discharged.

And just below, the other entry:

583. Lange, Jeanne, aged twenty, actress. Square du Roule No. 5. Suspected of harbouring traitors and *ci-devants*. Transferred 29th Nivôse to the Temple, cell 29.

He saw nothing more, for suddenly it seemed to him as if someone held a vivid scarlet veil in front of his eyes, while a hundred claw-like hands were tearing at his heart and at his throat.

Jeanne was a prisoner in the Temple; then his place was in the prison of the Temple, too. It could not be very difficult to run one's head into the noose that caught so many necks these days. A few cries of '*Vive le roi!*' or '*A bas la république*' and more than one prison door would gape invitingly to receive another guest.

The hot blood had rushed into Armand's head. He did not see clearly before him, nor did he hear distinctly. There was a buzzing in his ears as of myriads of mocking birds' wings, and there was a veil in front of his eyes – a veil through which he saw faces and forms flitting ghost-like in the gloom, men and women jostling or being jostled, soldiers, sentinels; then long, interminable corridors, more crowd and more soldiers, winding stairs, courtyards and gates; finally the open street, the quay, and the river beyond.

An incessant hammering went on in his temples, and that veil never lifted from before his eyes. Now it was lurid and red, as if stained with blood; anon it was white like a shroud, but it was always there.

Through it he saw the Pont-au-Change, which he crossed, then far down on the Quai de l'École to the left the corner house behind St Germain l'Auxerrois, where Blakeney lodged – Blakeney, who for the sake of a stranger had forgotten all about his comrade and Jeanne.

Through it he saw the network of streets which separated him from the neighbourhood of the Temple, the gardens of ruined habitations, the closely-shuttered and barred windows of ducal houses, then the mean streets, the crowded drinking bars, the tumble-down shops with their dilapidated awnings.

He saw with eyes that did not see, heard the tumult of daily life round him with ears that did not hear. Jeanne was in the Temple prison, and when its grim gates closed finally for the night, he – Armand, her chevalier, her lover, her defender – would be within its walls as near to cell No. 29 as bribery, entreaty, promises would help him to attain.

Ah! there at last loomed the great building, the pointed bastions cut through the surrounding gloom as with a sable knife.

Armand reached the gate; the sentinels challenged him; he replied:

'*Vive le roi!*' shouting wildly like one who is drunk.

He was hatless, and his clothes were saturated with moisture. He tried to pass, but crossed bayonets barred the way. Still he shouted:

'*Vive le roi!*' and '*A bas la république!*'

'*Allons!* the fellow is drunk!' said one of the soldiers.

Armand fought like a madman; he wanted to reach that gate. He shouted, he laughed, and he cried, until one of the soldiers in a fit of rage struck him heavily on the head.

Armand fell backwards, stunned by the blow; his foot slipped on the wet pavement. Was he indeed drunk, or was he dreaming? He put his hand up to his forehead; it was wet, but whether with the rain or with blood he did not know; but for the space of one second he tried to collect his scattered wits.

'Citizen St Just!' said a quiet voice at his elbow.

Then, as he looked round dazed, feeling a firm pleasant grip on his arm, the same quiet voice continued calmly:

'Perhaps you do not remember me, citizen St Just. I had not the honour of the same close friendship with you as I had with your charming sister. My name is Chauvelin. Can I be of any service to you?'

CHAPTER X

Chauvelin

CHAUVELIN! The presence of this man here at this moment made the events of the past few days seem more absolutely like a dream. Chauvelin! – the most deadly enemy he, Armand, and his sister Marguerite had in the world. Chauvelin! – the evil genius that presided over the Secret Service of the Republic. Chauvelin! the aristocrat turned revolutionary, the diplomat turned spy, the baffled enemy of the Scarlet Pimpernel.

'I had an idea, somehow,' continued Chauvelin calmly, 'that you and I would meet during your sojourn in Paris. I heard from my friend Héron that you had been in the city; he, unfortunately, lost your track almost as soon as he had found it, and I, too, had begun to fear that our mutual and ever-enigmatical friend, the Scarlet Pimpernel, had spirited you away, which would have been a great disappointment to me.'

Then he once more took hold of Armand by the elbow, but quite gently, more like a comrade who is glad to have met another, and is preparing to enjoy a pleasant conversation for a while. He led the way back to the gate, the sentinel saluting at sight of the tricolour scarf which was visible underneath his cloak. Under the stone rampart Chauvelin paused and shook the damp off his cloak, talking all the time in his own peculiar, gently ironical manner.

'Lady Blakeney?' he was saying – 'I hope that she is well!'

'I thank you, sir,' murmured Armand mechanically.

'And my dear friend, Sir Percy Blakeney? I had hoped to meet him in Paris. Ah! but no doubt he has been busy – very busy; but I live in hopes – I live in hopes. See how kindly Chance has treated me,' he continued in the same bland and mocking tones. 'I was taking a stroll in these parts, scarce hoping to meet a friend, when, passing the postern-gate of this charming hostelry, whom should I see but my amiable friend St Just striving to gain admission. But, la! here am I talking of myself and I am not reassured as to your state of health. You felt faint just now, did you not? The air about this building is very dank and close. I hope you feel better now. Command me, pray, if I can be of service to you in any way.'

While Chauvelin talked he had drawn Armand after him into the lodge of the concierge. The young man now made a great effort to pull himself vigorously together and to steady his nerves.

He had his wish. He was inside the Temple prison now, not far from Jeanne, and though his enemy was older and less vigorous than himself, and the door of the concierge's lodge stood wide open, he knew that he was indeed as effectually a prisoner already as if the door of one of the numerous cells in this gigantic building had been bolted and barred upon him.

'Citizen Chauvelin,' he said, as soon as he felt quite sure of the steadiness of his voice and the calmness of his manner, 'I wonder if you are quite certain that that light grip which you have on my arm is sufficient to keep me here walking quietly by your side instead of knocking you down, as I certainly feel inclined to do, for I am a younger, more athletic man than you.'

'H'm!' said Chauvelin, who made pretence to ponder over this difficult problem; 'like you, citizen St Just, I wonder —'

'It could easily be done, you know.'

'Fairly easily,' rejoined the other; 'but there is the guard; it is numerous and strong in this building, and —'

'The gloom would help me; it is dark in the corridors, and a desperate man takes risks, remember —'

'Quite so! And you, citizen St Just, are a desperate man just now.'

'My sister Marguerite is not here, citizen Chauvelin. You cannot barter my life for that of your enemy.'

'No! no! no!' rejoined Chauvelin blandly; 'not for that of my enemy, I know, but —'

Armand caught at his words like a drowning man at a reed.

'For hers!' he exclaimed.

'For hers?' queried the other with obvious puzzlement.

'Mademoiselle Lange,' continued Armand with all the egoistic ardour of the lover who believes that the attention of the entire world is concentrated upon his beloved. 'Mademoiselle Lange! You will set her free now that I am in your power?'

Chauvelin smiled, his usual suave, enigmatical smile.

'Ah yes!' he said. 'Mademoiselle Lange. I had forgotten.'

'Forgotten, man? – forgotten that those murderous dogs have arrested her? – the best, the purest, this vile, degraded country has ever produced. She sheltered me one day just for an hour. I am a traitor to the Republic – I own it. I'll make full confession; but she knew nothing of this. I deceived her; she is quite innocent, you understand? I'll make full confession, but you must set her free.'

He had gradually worked himself up again to a state of feverish excitement. Through the darkness which hung about in this small room he tried to peer in Chauvelin's impassive face.

'Easy, easy, my young friend,' said the other placidly, 'you seem to imagine that I have something to do with the arrest of the lady in whom you take so deep an interest. You forget that now I am but a discredited servant of the Republic whom I failed to serve in her need. My life is only granted me out of pity for my efforts, which were genuine if not successful. I have no power to set anyone free.'

'Nor to arrest me now, in that case!' retorted Armand.

Chauvelin paused a moment before he replied with a deprecating smile:

'Only to denounce you, perhaps. I am still an agent of the Committee of General Security.'

'Then all is for the best!' exclaimed St Just eagerly. 'You shall denounce me to the Committee. They will be glad of my arrest, I assure you. I have been a marked man for some time. I had intended to evade arrest and to work for the rescue of Mademoiselle Lange; but I will give up all thought of that – I will deliver myself into your hands absolutely; nay, more, I will give you my most solemn word of honour that not only will I make no attempt to escape, but that I will not allow anyone to help me to do so. I will be a passive and willing prisoner if you, on the other hand, will effect Mademoiselle Lange's release.'

'H'm!' mused Chauvelin again; 'it sounds feasible.'

'It does! it does!' rejoined Armand, whose excitement was at fever-pitch. 'My arrest, my condemnation, my death, will be of vast deal more importance to you than that of a young and innocent girl against whom unlikely charges would have to be tricked up, and whose acquittal mayhap public feeling might demand. As for me, I shall be an easy prey; my known counter-revolutionary principles, my sister's marriage with a foreigner —'

'Your connexion with the Scarlet Pimpernel,' suggested Chauvelin blandly.

'Quite so. I should not defend myself —'

'And your enigmatical friend would not attempt your rescue. *C'est entendu*,' said Chauvelin with his wonted blandness. 'Then, my dear enthusiastic young friend, shall we adjourn to the office of my colleague, citizen Héron, who is chief agent of the Committee of General Security, and will receive your — did you say confession? — and note the conditions under which you place yourself absolutely in the hands of the Public Prosecutor and subsequently of the executioner? Is that it?'

Armand just then had absolutely forgotten his chief, his friends, the league of mercy and help to which he belonged.

Enthusiasm and the spirit of self-sacrifice were carrying him away. He watched his enemy with glowing eyes as one who looks on the arbiter of his fate.

Chauvelin, without another word, beckoned to him to follow. He led the way out of the lodge, then, turning sharply to his left, he reached the wide quadrangle with the covered passage running right round it, the same which de Batz had traversed two evenings before, when he went to visit Héron.

Armand, with a light heart and springy step, followed him as if he were going to a feast where he would meet Jeanne, where he would kneel at her feet, kiss her hands, and lead her triumphantly to freedom and to happiness.

CHAPTER XI

'It is about the Dauphin'

HERON was not at his lodgings when, at last, after vigorous pulls at the bell, a great deal of waiting and much cursing, Chauvelin closely followed by Armand, was introduced in the chief agent's office.

The soldier who acted as servant said that citizen Héron had gone out to sup, but would surely be home again by eight o'clock. Armand by this time was so dazed with fatigue that he sank on a chair like a log, and remained there staring into the fire, unconscious of the flight of time.

Anon Héron came home. He nodded to Chauvelin, and threw but a cursory glance on Armand.

'Five minutes, citizen,' he said, with a rough attempt at an apology. 'I am sorry to keep you waiting, but the new commissaries have arrived who are to take charge of Capet. The Simons have just gone, and I want to assure myself that everything is all right in the Tower. Cochefer has been in charge, but I like to cast an eye over the brat every day myself.'

The heat from the stove had made Armand drowsy; his head fell forward on his chest. Chauvelin, with his hands held behind his back, paced ceaselessly up and down the narrow room.

Suddenly Armand started – wide awake now. Hurried footsteps on the flagstones outside, a hoarse shout, a banging of heavy doors, and the next moment Héron stood once more on the threshold of the room. Armand, with wide-open eyes, gazed on him in wonder. The whole appearance of the man had changed. He looked ten years older, with lank, dishevelled hair hanging matted over a moist forehead, the cheeks ashen-white, the full lips bloodless and hanging flabby and parted, displaying both rows of yellow teeth that shook against each other. The whole figure looked bowed, as if shrunk within itself.

Chauvelin had paused in his restless walk. He gazed on his colleague, a frown of puzzlement on his pale, set face.

'Capet!' he exclaimed, as soon as he had taken in every detail of Héron's altered appearance, and seen the look of wild terror that literally distorted his face.

Héron could not speak; his teeth were chattering in his mouth, and his tongue seemed paralysed. Chauvelin went up to him. He was several inches shorter than his colleague, but at this moment he seemed to be towering over him like an avenging spirit. He placed a firm hand on the other's bowed shoulder.

'Capet has gone – is that it?' he queried peremptorily.

The look of terror increased in Héron's eyes, giving its mute reply.

'How? When?'

But for the moment the man was speechless. An almost maniacal fear seemed to hold him in its grip. With an impatient oath Chauvelin turned away from him.

'Brandy!' he said curtly, speaking to Armand.

A bottle and glass were found in the cupboard. It was St Just who poured out the brandy and held it to Héron's lips. Chauvelin was once more pacing up and down the room in angry impatience.

'Pull yourself together, man,' he said roughly after a while, 'and try and tell me what has occurred.'

Héron had sunk into a chair. He passed a trembling hand once or twice over his forehead.

'Capet has disappeared,' he murmured; 'he must have been spirited away while the Simons were moving their furniture. That accursed Cochefer was completely taken in.'

Héron spoke in a toneless voice, hardly above a whisper, and like one whose throat is dry and mouth parched. But the brandy had revived him somewhat, and his eyes lost their former glassy look.

'How?' asked Chauvelin curtly.

'I was just leaving the Tower when he arrived. I spoke to him at the door. I had seen Capet safely installed in the room, and gave orders to the woman Simon to let citizen Cochefer have a look at him too, and then to lock up the brat in the inner room and install Cochefer in the ante-chamber on guard. I stood talking to Cochefer for a few moments in the ante-chamber. The woman Simon and the man-of-all-work, Dupont – whom I know well – were busy with the furniture. There could not have been anyone else concealed about the place – that I'll swear. Cochefer, after he took leave of me, went straight into the room; he found the woman Simon in the act of turning the key in the door of the inner chamber. "I have locked Capet in there," she said, giving the key to Cochefer; "he will be quite safe until tonight, when the other commissaries come."'

'Didn't Cochefer go into the room and ascertain whether the woman was lying?'

'Yes, he did! He made the woman reopen the door, and peeped in over her shoulder. She said the child was asleep. He vows that he saw the child lying fully dressed on a rug in the further corner of the room. The room, of course, was quite empty of furniture and only lighted by one candle, but there was the rug and the child asleep on it. Cochefer swears he saw him, and now – when I went up –'

'Well!'

'The commissaries were all there – Cochefer and Lasnière, Lorinet and Legrand. We went into the inner room, and I had a candle in my hand. We saw the child lying on the rug, just as Cochefer had seen him, and for a while we took no notice of it. Then someone – I think it was Lorinet – went to have a closer look at the brat. He took up the candle and went up to the rug. Then he gave a cry, and we all gathered round him. The sleeping

73

child was only a bundle of hair and of clothes, a dummy – what?'

There was silence now in the narrow room, while the white-faced clock continued to tick off each succeeding second of time. Héron had once more buried his head in his hands; a trembling – like an attack of ague – shook his wide, bony shoulders. Armand had listened to the narrative with glowing eyes and a beating heart.

'Have you any suspicions?' asked Chauvelin now, pausing in his walk, and once more placing a firm, peremptory hand on his colleague's shoulder.

'Suspicions!' exclaimed the chief agent with a loud oath. 'Suspicions! Certainties, you mean. The man sat here but two days ago, in that very chair, and bragged of what he would do. I told him then that if he interfered with Capet I would wring his neck with my own hands.'

And his long, talon-like fingers, with their sharp, grimy nails, closed and unclosed like those of feline creatures when they hold the coveted prey.

'Of whom do you speak?' queried Chauvelin curtly.

'Of whom? Of whom but that accursed de Batz? His pockets are bulging with Austrian money, with which, no doubt, he has bribed the Simons and Cochefer and the sentinels —'

'And Lorinet and Lasnière and you,' interposed Chauvelin dryly.

'It is false!' roared Héron, who already at the suggestion was foaming at the mouth and had jumped up from his chair, standing at bay as if prepared to fight for his life.

'False, is it?' retorted Chauvelin calmly; 'then be not so quick, friend Héron, in slashing out with senseless denunciations right and left. You'll gain nothing by denouncing anyone just now. This is too intricate a matter to be dealt with with a sledge-hammer. Is anyone up in the Tower at this moment?' he asked in quiet, business-like tones.

'Yes. Cochefer and the others are still there. They are making wild schemes to cover their treachery. Cochefer is aware of his own danger, and Lasnière and the others know that they arrived at the Tower several hours too late. They are all at fault, and they know it. As for that de Batz,' he continued with a voice rendered raucous with bitter passion, 'I swore to him two days ago that he should not escape me if he meddled with Capet. I'm on his track already. I'll have him before the hour of midnight, and I'll torture him – yes! I'll torture him – the Tribunal shall give me leave. We have a dark cell down below here where my men know how to apply tortures worse than the rack – where they know just how to prolong life long enough to make it unendurable. I'll torture him! I'll torture him!'

But Chauvelin abruptly silenced the wretch with a curt command; then without another word he walked straight out of the room.

In thought Armand followed him. The wild desire was suddenly born in him to run away at this moment, while Héron, wrapped in his own meditations, was paying no heed to him. He rose softly from his chair and crossed the room. Héron paid no attention to him. Now he had traversed the ante-chamber and unlatched the outer door.

Immediately a couple of bayonets were crossed in front of him, two more further on ahead scintillated feebly in the flickering light. Chauvelin had taken his precautions. There was no doubt that Armand St Just was effectively a prisoner now.

With a sigh of disappointment he went back to his place beside the fire. Héron had not even moved while he had made this futile attempt at escape. Fifteen minutes later Chauvelin re-entered the room.

CHAPTER XII

The certificate of safety

'You can leave de Batz and his gang alone, citizen Héron,' said Chauvelin, as soon as he had closed the door behind him; 'he had nothing to do with the escape of the Dauphin.'

Héron growled out a few words of incredulity. But Chauvelin shrugged his shoulders and looked with unutterable contempt on his colleague. Armand, who was watching him closely, saw that in his hand he held a small piece of paper, which he had crushed into a shapeless mass.

'Do not waste your time, citizen,' he said, 'in raging against an empty wind-bag. Arrest de Batz if you like, or leave him alone as you please – we have nothing to fear from that braggart.'

With nervous, slightly shaking fingers he set to work to smooth out the scrap of paper which he held. His hot hands had soiled it and pounded it until it was a mere rag and the writing on it illegible. But, such as it was, he threw it down with a blasphemous oath on the desk in front of Héron's eyes.

'It is that accursed Englishman who has been at work again,' he said more calmly; 'I guessed it the moment I heard your story. Set your whole army of sleuth-hounds on his track, citizen; you'll need them all.'

Héron picked up the scrap of torn paper and tried to decipher the writing on it by the light of the lamp. He seemed almost dazed now with the awful catastrophe that had befallen him, and the fear that his own wretched life would have to pay the penalty for the disappearance of the child.

As for Armand – even in the midst of his own troubles, and of his own anxiety for Jeanne, he felt a proud exultation in his heart. The Scarlet Pimpernel had succeeded; Percy had not failed in his self-imposed undertaking. Chauvelin, whose piercing eyes were fixed on him at the moment, smiled with contemptuous irony.

'As you will find your hands overfull for the next few hours, citizen Héron,' he said, speaking to his colleague and nodding in the direction of Armand, 'I'll not trouble you with the voluntary confession this young citizen desired to make to you. All I need tell you is that he is an adherent of the Scarlet Pimpernel – I believe one of his most faithful, most trusted officers.'

Héron roused himself from the maze of gloomy thoughts that were again paralysing his tongue. He turned bleary, wild eyes on Armand.

'We have got one of them, then?' he murmured incoherently, babbling like a drunken man.

'M'yes!' replied Chauvelin lightly; 'but it is too late now for a formal denunciation and arrest. He cannot leave Paris anyhow, and all that your men need do is to keep a close watch on him. But I should send him home tonight if I were you.'

Héron muttered something more, which, however, Armand did not understand. Chauvelin's words were still ringing in his ear. Was he, then, to be set free tonight? Free in a measure, of course, since spies were to be set to watch him – but free, nevertheless? He could not understand Chauvelin's attitude, and his own self-love was not a little wounded at the thought that he was of such little account that these men could afford to give him even this provisional freedom. And, of course, there was still Jeanne.

'I must, therefore, bid you goodnight, citizen,' Chauvelin was saying in his bland, gently ironical manner. 'You will be glad to return to your lodgings. As you see, the chief agent of the Committee of General Security is too much occupied just now to accept the sacrifice of your life which you were prepared so generously to offer him.'

'I do not understand you, citizen,' retorted Armand coldly, 'nor do I desire indulgence at your hands. You have arrested an innocent woman on the trumped-up charge that she was har-bouring me. I came here tonight to give myself up to justice so that she might be set free.'

'But the hour is somewhat late, citizen,' rejoined Chauvelin urbanely. 'The lady in whom you take so fervent an interest is no doubt asleep in her cell at this hour. It would not be fitting to disturb her now. She might not find shelter before morning, and the weather is quite exceptionally unpropitious.'

'Then, sir,' said Armand, a little bewildered, 'am I to under-stand that if I hold myself at your disposition Mademoiselle Lange will be set free as early tomorrow morning as may be?'

'No doubt, sir – no doubt,' replied Chauvelin with more than his accustomed blandness; 'if you will hold yourself entirely at our disposition, Mademoiselle Lange will be set free tomorrow. I think that we can safely promise that, citizen Héron, can we not?' he added, turning to his colleague.

But Héron, overcome with the stress of emotions, could only murmur vague, unintelligible words.

'Your word on that, citizen Chauvelin?' asked Armand.

'My word on it and you will accept it.'

'No, I will not do that. Give me an unconditional certificate of safety and I will believe you.'

'Of what use were that to you?' asked Chauvelin.

'I believe my capture to be of more importance to you than that of Mademoiselle Lange,' said Armand quietly. 'I will use the certificate of safety for myself or one of my friends if you break your word to me anent Mademoiselle Lange.'

'H'm! the reasoning is not illogical, citizen,' said Chauvelin, while a curious smile played round the corners of his thin lips. 'You are quite right. You are a more valuable asset to us than the charming lady who, I hope, will for many a day and year to come delight pleasure-loving Paris with her talent and her grace.'

'Amen to that, citizen,' said Armand fervently.

'Well, it will all depend on you, sir! Here,' he added, coolly turning over some papers on Héron's desk until he found what he wanted, 'is an absolutely unconditional certificate of safety. The Committee of General Security issue very few of these. It is worth the cost of a human life. At no barrier or gate of any city can such a certificate be disregarded, nor even can it be detained.

Allow me to hand it to you, citizen, as a pledge of my own good faith.'

Smiling, urbane, with a curious look that almost expressed amusement, lurking in his shrewd, pale eyes, Chauvelin handed the momentous document to Armand.

The young man studied it very carefully before he slipped it into the inner pocket of his coat.

'How soon shall I have news of Mademoiselle Lange?' he asked finally.

'In the course of tomorrow. I myself will call on you and redeem that precious document in person. You, on the other hand, will hold yourself at my disposition. That's understood, is it not?'

'I shall not fail you. My lodgings are —'

'Oh! do not trouble,' interposed Chauvelin with a polite bow; 'we can find that out for ourselves.'

Héron had taken no part in this colloquy. Now that Armand prepared to go he made no attempt to detain him, or to question his colleague's actions. He sat by the table like a log; his mind was obviously a blank to all else save to his own terrors engendered by the events of this night.

With bleary, half-veiled eyes he followed Armand's progress through the room, and seemed unaware of the loud slamming of the outside door. Chauvelin escorted the young man past the first line of sentries, then he took cordial leave of him.

'Your certificate will, you will find, open every gate to you. Good night, citizen. À demain.'

'Good night.'

Armand's slim figure disappeared in the gloom. Chauvelin watched him for a few moments until even his footsteps had died away in the distance; then he turned back towards Héron's lodgings.

'À nous deux,' he muttered between tightly clenched teeth; 'à nous deux one more, my enigmatical Scarlet Pimpernel.'

CHAPTER XIII

Back to Paris

IT was an exceptionally dark night, and the rain was falling in torrents. Sir Andrew Ffoulkes, wrapped in a piece of sacking, had taken shelter right underneath the coal-cart; even then he was getting wet through to the skin.

He had worked hard for two days coal-heaving, and the night before he had found a cheap, squalid lodging where at any rate he was protected from the inclemencies of the weather; but tonight he was expecting Blakeney at the appointed hour and place. He had secured a cart of the ordinary ramshackle pattern used for carrying coal. Unfortunately there were no covered ones to be obtained in the neighbourhood, and equally unfortunately the thaw had set in with blustering wind and driving rain, which made waiting in the open air for hours at a stretch and in complete darkness excessively unpleasant.

But for all these discomforts Sir Andrew Ffoulkes cared not one jot. Here tonight in the rough and tattered clothes of a coal-heaver, drenched to the skin, and crouching under the body of a cart that hardly sheltered him from the rain, he was as happy as a schoolboy out for a holiday.

Then he heard the cry – a seamew's call – repeated thrice at intervals, and five minutes later something loomed out of the darkness quite close to the hind wheels of the cart.

'Hist! Ffoulkes!' came in a soft whisper, scarce louder than the wind.

'Present!' came in quick response.

'Here, help me to lift the child into the cart. He is asleep, and has been a dead weight on my arm for close on an hour now. Have you a dry bit of sacking or something to lay him on?'

'Not very dry, I am afraid.'

With tender care the two men lifted the sleeping little King of France into the rickety cart. Blakeney laid his cloak over him, and listened for a while to the slow regular breathing of the child.

'St Just is not here – you knew that?' said Sir Andrew after a while.

'Yes, I knew it,' replied Blakeney curtly.

It was characteristic of these two men that not a word about the adventure itself, about the terrible risks and dangers of the past few hours, was exchanged between them. The child was here and was safe, and Blakeney knew the whereabouts of St Just – that was enough for Sir Andrew Ffoulkes, the most devoted follower, the most perfect friend the Scarlet Pimpernel would ever know.

Ffoulkes now went to the horse, detached the nose-bag, and undid the nooses of the hobble and of the tether.

'Will you get in now, Blakeney?' he said; 'we are ready.'

And in unbroken silence they both got into the cart; Blakeney sitting on its floor beside the child, and Ffoulkes gathering the reins in his hands.

The wheels of the cart and the slow jog-trot of the horse made scarcely any noise in the mud of the roads; what noise they did make was effectually drowned by the soughing of the wind in the bare branches of the stunted acacia trees that edged the towpath along the line of the canal.

Past Clichy, they had to cross the river by the rickety wooden bridge that was unsafe even in broad daylight. They were not far from their destination now. Ffoulkes got down in order to make sure of the way. He walked at the horse's head now, fearful lest he should miss the crossroads and the signpost.

The horse was getting overtired; it had covered fifteen kilometres, and it was close on three o'clock of Monday morning.

Another hour went by in absolute silence. Ffoulkes and Blakeney took turns at the horse's head. Then at last they reached the crossroads; even through the darkness the signpost showed white against the surrounding gloom.

'This looks like it,' murmured Sir Andrew. He turned the horse's head sharply towards the left, down a narrower road, and leaving the signpost behind him, he walked slowly along for another quarter of an hour; then Blakeney called a halt.

'The spinney must be sharp on our right now,' he said.

He got down from the cart, and while Ffoulkes remained beside the horse, he plunged into the gloom. A moment later the cry of the seamew rang out three times into the air. It was answered almost immediately.

Blakeney lifted the sleeping child out of the cart. Then he called to Sir Andrew and led the way across the road and into the spinney.

Five minutes later Hastings received the uncrowned King of France in his arms.

Unlike Ffoulkes, my Lord Tony wanted to hear all about the adventure of this afternoon. A thorough sportsman, he loved a good story of hairbreadth escapes, of dangers cleverly avoided, risks taken and conquered.

'Just in ten words, Blakeney,' he urged entreatingly; 'how did you actually get the boy away?'

Sir Percy laughed – despite himself – at the young man's eagerness.

'Next time we meet, Tony,' he begged; 'I am so demmed fatigued, and there's this beastly rain —'

'No, no – now while Hastings sees to the horses! I could not exist long without knowing, and we are well sheltered from the rain under this tree.'

'Well, then, since you will have it,' began Blakeney with a laugh, which despite the weariness and anxiety of the past twenty-four hours had forced itself to his lips, 'I have been sweeper and man-of-all-work at the Temple for the past few weeks, you must know —'

'No!' ejaculated Lord Tony lustily. 'By gum!'

'Indeed, you old sybarite, while you were enjoying yourself heaving coal on the canal wharf, I was scrubbing floors, lighting fires, and doing a number of odd jobs for a lot of demmed murdering villains, and' – he added under his breath – 'incidentally, too, for our league. Whenever I had an hour or two off duty I spent them in my lodgings, and asked you all to come and meet me there.'

'By Gad, Blakeney! Then the day before yesterday? – when we all met —'

'I had just had a bath – sorely needed, I can tell you. I had been cleaning boots half the day, but I had heard that the Simons were removing from the Temple on the Sunday, and had obtained an order from them to help them shift their furniture.'

'Cleaning boots!' murmured my Lord Tony with a chuckle. 'Well! And then?'

'Well, then everything worked out splendidly. You see by that time I was a well-known figure in the Temple. Héron knew me well. I used to be his lanthorn-bearer when at nights he visited that poor mite in his prison. It was "Dupont here! Dupont there!" all day long. "Light the fire in the office, Dupont! Dupont, brush my coat! Dupont, fetch me a light!" When the Simons wanted to move their household goods they called loudly for Dupont. I got a covered laundry cart, and I brought a dummy with me to substitute for the child. Simon himself knew nothing of this, but Madame was in my pay. The dummy was just splendid, with real hair on its head; Madame helped me to substitute it for the child; we laid it down and covered it over with a rug, even while those brutes Héron and Cochefer were on the landing outside, and we stuffed His Majesty the King of France into a linen basket. The room was badly lighted and anyone would have been deceived. No one was suspicious of that type of trickery, so it went off perfectly. I moved the furniture of the Simons out of the Tower. His Majesty King Louis XVII was still concealed in the linen basket. I drove the Simons to their new lodgings – the man still suspects nothing, and there I helped them to unload the furniture – with the exception of the linen basket, of course. After that I drove my laundry cart to a house I knew of, and collected a number of linen baskets, which I had arranged should be in readiness for me. Thus loaded up I left Paris by the Vincennes gate, and drove as far as Bagnolet, where there is no road except past the octroi, where the officials might have proved unpleasant. So I lifted His Majesty out of the basket and we walked on hand in hand in the darkness and the rain until the poor little feet gave out. Then the little fellow – who has been wonderfully plucky throughout, indeed, more a Capet than a Bourbon – snuggled up in my arms and went fast asleep, and – and – well, I think that's all, for here we are, you see.'

The daring, the pluck, the ingenuity, and, above all, the super-human heroism and endurance rendered the hearers of this simple narrative, simply told, dumb with admiration.

'How soon was the hue and cry for the child about the streets?' asked Tony after a moment's silence.

'It was not out when I left the gates of Paris,' said Blakeney meditatively; 'so quietly has the news of the escape been kept, that I am wondering what devilry that brute Héron can be after. And now no more chattering,' he continued lightly; 'all to horse, and you, Hastings, have a care. The destinies of France, mayhap, will be lying asleep in your arms.'

'But you, Blakeney?' exclaimed the three men almost simultaneously.

'I am not going with you. I entrust the child to you. For God's sake guard him well! Ride with him to Mantes. You should arrive there about ten o'clock. One of you then go straight to No. 9 Rue la Tour. Ring the bell; an old man will answer it. Say the one word to him, "Enfant"; he will reply, "De roi!" Give him the child, and may Heaven bless you all for the help you have given me this night!'

'But you, Blakeney?' reiterated Tony with a note of deep anxiety in his fresh young voice.

'I am straight for Paris,' he said quietly.

'Impossible!'

'Therefore feasible.'

'But why? Percy, in the name of Heaven, do you realize what you are doing?'

'Perfectly.'

'They'll not leave a stone unturned to find you – they know by now, believe me, that your hand did this trick.'

'I know that.'

'And yet you mean to go back?'

'And yet I am going back.'

'Blakeney!'

'It's no use, Tony. Armand is in Paris. I saw him in the corridor of the Temple prison in the company of Chauvelin.'

'Great God!' exclaimed Lord Hastings.

The others were silent. What was the use of arguing? One of themselves was in danger. Armand St Just, the brother of Marguerite Blakeney! Was it likely that Percy would leave him in the lurch?

'One of us will stay with you, of course?' asked Sir Andrew after a while.

'Yes! I want Hastings and Tony to take the child to Mantes, then to make all possible haste for Calais, and there to keep in close touch with the *Daydream*; the skipper will contrive to open communication. Tell him to remain in Calais waters. I hope I may have need of him soon. And now to horse, both of you,' he added gaily. 'Hastings, when you are ready, I will hand up the child to you. He will be quite safe with a strap round him and you.'

Nothing more was said after that. The orders were given, there was nothing to do but to obey; and the uncrowned King of France was not yet out of danger. Hastings and Tony led two of the horses out of the spinney; at the roadside they mounted, and then the little lad for whose sake so much heroism, such selfless devotion had been expended, was hoisted up, still half asleep, in front of my Lord Hastings.

'Keep your arm round him,' admonished Blakeney; 'your horse looks quiet enough. But put on speed as far as Mantes, and may Heaven guard you both!'

The two men pressed their heels to their horses' flanks, the beasts snorted and pawed the ground anxious to start. There were a few whispered farewells, two loyal hands were stretched out at the last, eager to grasp the leader's hand.

Then horses and riders disappeared in the utter darkness which comes before the dawn.

Blakeney and Ffoulkes stood side by side in silence for as long as the pawing of hoofs in the mud could reach their ears, then Ffoulkes asked abruptly :

'What do you want me to do, Blakeney ?'

'Well, for the present, my dear fellow, I want you to take one of the three horses we have left in the spinney, and put him into the shafts of our old friend the coal-cart; then I am afraid that you must go back by the way we came.'

'Yes ?'

'Continue to heave coal on the canal wharf by La Villette; it is the best way to avoid attention. After your day's work keep your cart and horse in readiness against my arrival, at the same spot where you were last night. If after having waited for me like this for three consecutive nights you neither see nor hear anything from me, go back to England and tell Marguerite that in giving my life for her brother I gave it for her !'

'Blakeney —!'

'I spoke differently to what I usually do, is that it?' he interposed, placing his firm hand on his friend's shoulder. 'I am degenerating, Ffoulkes – that's what it is. Pay no heed to it. I suppose that carrying that sleeping child in my arms last night softened some nerves in my body. I was so infinitely sorry for the poor mite, and vaguely wondered if I had not saved it from one misery only to plunge it in another. There was such a fateful look on that wan little face, as if destiny had already writ its veto there against happiness. It came on me then how futile were our actions, if God chooses to interpose His will between us and our desires.'

Almost as he left off speaking the rain ceased to patter down against the puddles in the road. Overhead the clouds flew by at terrific speed, driven along by the blustering wind. It was less dark now, and Sir Andrew, peering through the gloom could see his leader's face. It was singularly pale and hard, and the deep-set lazy eyes had in them just that fateful look which he himself had spoken of just now.

'You are anxious about Armand, Percy ?' asked Ffoulkes softly.

'Yes. He should have trusted me, as I had trusted him. He missed me at the Villette gate on Friday, and without a thought left me – left us all in the lurch; he threw himself into the lion's jaws, thinking that he could help the girl he loved. I knew that I could save her. She is in comparative safety even now. The old woman, Madame Belhomme, was released the day after her arrest, and Jeanne Lange is in a house in the Rue St Germain l'Auxerrois, close to my own lodgings. I got her there early this morning. It was easy for me, of course: '*Holá*, Dupont! my boots, Dupont!' "One moment, citizen; my daughter —" "Curse thy daughter; bring me my boots!" and Jeanne Lange walked out of the Temple prison, her hand in that of that lout Dupont.'

'But Armand does not know that she is in safety?'

'No. I have not seen him since that early morning on Saturday when he came to tell me that she had been arrested. Having sworn that he would obey me, he went to meet you and Tony at La Villette, but returned to Paris a few hours later, and drew the undivided attention of all the committees on Jeanne Lange by his senseless, foolish inquiries. But for his action throughout the whole of yesterday I could have smuggled Jeanne out of Paris, got her to join you at Villette, or Hastings in St Germain. But the barriers were being closely watched for her, and I had the Dauphin to think of. She is in comparative safety; the people in the Rue St Germain l'Auxerrois are friendly for the moment; but for how long? Who knows? I must look after her of course. And Armand! Poor old Armand! The lion's jaws have snapped over him, and they hold him tight. Chauvelin and his gang are using him as a decoy to trap me, of course. All that had not happened if Armand had trusted me.'

He uttered a quick sigh of impatience, almost of regret. Ffoulkes was the one man who could guess the bitter disappointment that this had meant. Percy had longed to be back in England soon, back to Marguerite, to a few days of unalloyed happiness and a few days of peace.

'And you, Blakeney – how will you go back to that awful Paris?' he said.

'I don't know yet,' replied Blakeney; 'but it would not be safe to ride. I'll reach one of the gates on this side of the city and contrive to slip in somehow. I have a certificate of safety in my pocket in case I need it.'

'We'll leave the horses here,' he said presently, while he was helping Sir Andrew to put the horse in the shafts of the coal-cart; 'they cannot come to much harm. Some poor devil might steal them, in order to escape from those vile brutes in the city. If so, God speed him, say I. I'll compensate my friend the farmer of St Germain for their loss at an early opportunity. And now, goodbye, my dear fellow! Some time tonight, if possible, you shall hear direct news of me – if not, then tomorrow or the day after that. Goodbye, and Heaven guard you!'

'God guard you, Blakeney!' said Sir Andrew fervently.

CHAPTER XIV

Of that there could be no question

BLAKENEY was a man of abnormal physique and iron nerve, else he could never have endured the fatigues of the past twenty-four hours, from the moment when on the Sunday afternoon he began to play his part of furniture-remover at the Temple, to that when at last on Monday at noon he succeeded in persuading the sergeant at the Maillot gate that he was an honest stone-mason residing at Neuilly, who was come to Paris in search of work.

After that matters became more simple. Terribly footsore, though he would never have admitted it, hungry and weary, he turned into an unpretentious eating-house and ordered some dinner. The place when he entered was occupied mostly by labourers and workmen, dressed very much as he was himself, and quite as grimy as he had become after having driven about for hours in a laundry-cart and in a coal-cart, and having walked twelve kilomètres, some of which he had covered while carrying a sleeping child in his arms.

Thus, Sir Percy Blakeney, Bart., the friend and companion of the Prince of Wales, the most fastidious fop the salons of London and Bath had ever seen, was in no way distinguishable outwardly from the tattered, half starved, dirty, and out-at-elbows products of this fraternizing and equalizing Republic.

He was so hungry that the ill-cooked, badly served meal tempted him to eat; and he ate on in silence, seemingly more interested in boiled beef than in the conversation that went on around him. But he would not have been the keen and daring adventurer that he was if he did not all the while keep his ears open for any fragment of news that the desultory talk of his fellow-diners was likely to yield to him.

Politics were, of course, discussed; the tyranny of the sections, the slavery that this free Republic had brought on its citizens. The names of the chief personages of the day were all mentioned in turns: Foucquier-Tinville, Santerre, Danton, Robespierre. Héron and his sleuth-hounds were spoken of with execrations quickly suppressed, but of little Capet not one word.

Blakeney could not help but infer that Chauvelin, Héron and the commissaries in charge were keeping the escape of the child a secret for as long as they could.

In the afternoon he started off in search of lodgings for the night. He found what would suit him in the Rue de l'Arcade, which was equally far from the house of Justice as it was from his former lodgings. Here he would be safe for at least twenty-four hours, after which he might have to shift again.

Having taken possession of his new quarters and snatched a few hours of sound, well-deserved rest, until the time when the shades of evening and the darkness of the streets would make progress through the city somewhat more safe, Blakeney sallied forth at about six o'clock, having a threefold object in view.

Primarily, of course, the threefold object was concentrated on Armand. There was the possibility of finding out at the young man's lodgings in Montmartre what had become of him; then there were the usual inquiries that could be made from the registers of the various prisons; and, thirdly, there was the chance that Armand had succeeded in sending some kind of message to Blakeney's former lodgings in the Rue St Germain l'Auxerrois.

His next objective, then, was Armand's former lodging, and from six o'clock until close upon eight Sir Percy haunted the slopes of Montmartre, and more especially the neighbourhood of the Rue de la Croix Blanche, where Armand St Just had lodged. At the house itself he could not inquire as yet; obviously it would not have been safe; tomorrow, perhaps, when he knew more, but not tonight. His keen eyes had already spied at least two figures clothed in the rags of out-of-work labourers like himself who had hung with suspicious persistence in this same neighbourhood, and who during the two hours that he had been watching had never strayed out of sight of the house in the Rue de la Croix Blanche.

That these were two spies on the watch was, of course, obvious; but whether they were on the watch for St Just or for some other unfortunate wretch it was at this stage impossible to conjecture.

Then, as from the Tour des Dames close by the clock solemnly struck the hour of eight, and Blakeney prepared to wend his way back to another part of the city, he suddenly saw Armand walking slowly up the street.

The young man did not look either right or left; he held his head forward on his chest, and his hands were hidden underneath his cloak. When he passed immediately under one of the street lamps Blakeney caught sight of his face; it was pale and drawn. Then he turned his head, and for the space of two seconds his eyes crossed the narrow street encountered those of his chief. He had the presence of mind not to make a sign or to utter a sound; he was obviously being followed, but in that brief moment Sir Percy had seen in the young man's eyes a look that reminded him of a hunted creature.

'What have those brutes been up to with him, I wonder?' he muttered between clenched teeth.

Armand soon disappeared under the doorway of the same house where he had been lodging all along. Even as he did so Blakeney saw the two spies gather together like a pair of slimy lizards, and whisper excitedly one to another. A third man, who obviously had been dogging Armand's footsteps, came up and joined them after a while.

Blakeney could have sworn loudly and lustily, had it been possible to do so without attracting attention. The whole of Armand's history in the past twenty-four hours was perfectly clear to him. The young man had been made free that he might prove a decoy for more important game.

His every step was being watched, and he still thought Jeanne Lange in immediate danger of death. The look of despair in his face proclaimed these two facts, and Blakeney's heart ached for the mental torture which his friend was enduring. He longed to let Armand know that the woman he loved was in comparative safety.

Jeanne Lange first, and then Armand himself; and the odds would be very heavy against the Scarlet Pimpernel! But Marguerite should not have to mourn an only brother, of that Sir Percy made oath.

He now turned his steps towards his own former lodgings by St Germain l'Auxerrois. It was just possible that Armand had succeeded in leaving a message there for him. It was, of course, equally possible that when he did so Héron's men had watched his movements, and that spies would be stationed there, too, on the watch.

But that risk must, of course, be run. Blakeney's former lodging was the one place that Armand would know of to which he could send a message to his chief, if he wanted to do so. Of course, the unfortunate young man could not have known until just now that Percy would come back to Paris, but he might guess it, or wish it, or only vaguely hope for it; he might want to send a message, he might long to communicate with his brother-in-law, and, perhaps, feel sure that the latter would not leave him in the lurch.

Still keeping up the slouching gait peculiar to the out-at-elbows working man of the day, hugging the houses as he walked along the streets, Blakeney made slow progress across the city. But at last he reached the façade of St Germain l'Auxerrois, and turning sharply to his right he soon came in sight of the house which he had only quitted twenty-four hours previously.

Blakeney made his way cautiously right round the house; he peered up and down the quay, and his keen eyes tried to pierce the dense gloom that hung at the corners of the Pont Neuf immediately opposite. Soon he assured himself that for the present, at any rate, the house was not being watched.

Armand presumably had not yet left a message for him here; but he might do so at any time now that he knew that his chief was in Paris and on the look-out for him.

Blakeney made up his mind to keep this house in sight. This art of watching he had acquired to a masterly extent, and could have taught Héron's watch-dogs a remarkable lesson in it. At night, of course, it was a comparatively easy task. There were a good many unlighted doorways along the quay, while a street lamp was fixed on a bracket in the wall of the very house which he kept in observation.

It was close on midnight when at last he thought it best to give up his watch and to go back to his lodgings for a few hours' sleep; but at seven o'clock the next morning he was back again at his post.

He had not very long to wait. Soon the *porte-cochère* of the house was opened, and the concierge came out with his broom, making a show of cleaning the pavement in front of the door. Five minutes later a lad, whose clothes consisted entirely of rags, and whose feet and head were bare, came rapidly up the street from the quay, and walked along looking at the houses as he went, as if trying to decipher their number. The cold grey dawn was just breaking, dreary and damp, as all the past days had been. Blakeney watched the lad as he approached, the small naked feet falling noiselessly on the cobblestones of the road. When the boy was quite close to him and to the house, Blakeney shifted his position and took the pipe out of his mouth.

'Up early, my son!' he said gruffly.

'Yes,' said the pale-faced little creature; 'I have a message to deliver at No. 9 Rue St Germain l'Auxerrois. It must be some-where near here.'

With an instinct which he somehow felt could not err at this moment, Blakeney knew that the message was one from Armand to himself, a written message, too, since – instinctively when he spoke – the boy had clutched at his thin shirt, as if trying to guard something precious that had been entrusted to him.

'I will deliver the message myself, sonny,' said Blakeney gruffly. 'I know the citizen for whom it is intended. He would not like the concierge to see it.'

'Oh! I would not give it to the concierge,' said the boy. 'I would take it upstairs myself.'

'My son,' retorted Blakeney, 'let me tell you this. You are going to give that message up to me and I will put five whole livres into your hand.'

Blakeney, with all his sympathy aroused for this poor pale-faced lad, put on the airs of a ruffianly bully. He did not wish that message to be taken indoors by the lad, for the concierge might get hold of it, despite the boy's protests and tears, and after that Blakeney would perforce have to disclose himself before it would be given up to him.

'*Allons!*' he said gruffly, 'give me the letter, or that five livres goes back into my pocket.'

'Five livres!' exclaimed the child with pathetic eagerness. 'Oh, citizen!'

The thin little hand fumbled under the rags, but it reappeared again empty, while a faint blush spread over the hollow cheeks.

'The other citizen also gave me five livres,' he said humbly. 'He lodges in the house where my mother is concierge. It is in the Rue de la Croix Blanche. He has been very kind to my mother. I would rather do as he bade me.'

'Bless the lad,' murmured Blakeney under his breath; 'his loyalty redeems many a crime of this God-forsaken city. Now I suppose I shall have to bully him, after all.'

He took his hand out of his breeches pocket; between two very dirty fingers he held a piece of gold. The other hand he placed quite roughly on the lad's chest.

'Give me the letter,' he said harshly, 'or —'

He pulled at the ragged blouse, and a scrap of soiled paper soon fell into his hand. The lad began to cry.

'Here,' said Blakeney, thrusting the piece of gold into the thin small palm, 'take this home to your mother and tell your lodger that a big, rough man took the letter away from you by force. Now run, before I kick you out of the way.'

The lad, terrified out of his poor wits, did not wait for further commands; he took to his heels and ran, his small hand clutching the piece of gold. Soon he had disappeared round the corner of the street.

Blakeney did not at once read the paper; he thrust it quickly into his breeches pocket and slouched slowly down the street, and thence across the Place du Carrousel, in the direction of his new lodgings in the Rue de l'Arcade.

It was only when he found himself alone in the narrow squalid room which he was occupying that he took the scrap of paper from his pocket and read it slowly through. It said:

'Percy, you cannot forgive me, nor can I ever forgive myself, but if you only knew what I have suffered for the past two days you would, I think, try and forgive. I am free and yet a prisoner; my every footstep is dogged. What they ultimately mean to do with me I do not know. And when I think of Jeanne I long for the power to end my own miserable existence. Percy! she is still in the hands of those fiends ... I saw the prison register; her name written there has been like a burning brand on my heart ever since. She was still in prison the day that you left Paris; tomorrow, tonight mayhap, they will try her, condemn her, torture her, and I dare not go to see you, for I would only be bringing spies to your door. But will you come to me, Percy? It should be safe in the hours of the night, and the concierge is devoted to me. Tonight at ten o'clock she will leave the *porte-cochère* unlatched. If you find it so, and if on the ledge of the window immediately on your left as you enter you find a candle alight, and beside it a scrap of paper with your initial S.P. traced on it, then it will be quite safe for you to come up to my room. It is on the second landing – a door on your right – that too I will leave on the latch. But in the name of the woman you love best in all the world come at once to me then, and bear in mind, Percy, that the woman I love is threatened with immediate death, and that I am powerless to save her. Indeed, believe me, I would gladly die even now but for the thought of Jeanne, whom I should be leaving in the hands of those fiends. For God's sake, Percy, remember that Jeanne is all the world to me.'

'Poor old Armand,' murmured Blakeney with a kindly smile

directed at the absent friend, 'he won't trust me even now. He won't trust his Jeanne in my hands. Well,' he added after a while, 'after all, I would not entrust Marguerite to anybody else either.'

PART II

CHAPTER XV

The news

THE grey January day was falling, drowsy and dull, into the arms of night.

Marguerite, sitting in the dusk beside the fire in her small boudoir, shivered a little as she drew her scarf closer round her shoulders.

Edwards, the butler, entered with the lamp. The room looked particularly cheery now, with the delicate white panelling of the walls glowing under the soft kiss of the flickering firelight and the steadier glow of the rose-shaded lamp.

'Has the courier not arrived yet, Edwards?' asked Marguerite, fixing the impassive face of the well-drilled servant with her large purple-rimmed eyes.

'Not yet, m'lady,' he replied placidly.

'It is his day, is it not?'

'Yes, m'lady. And the forenoon is his time. But there have been heavy rains, and the roads must be rare muddy. He must have been delayed, m'lady.'

'Yes, I suppose so,' she said listlessly. 'That will do, Edwards. No, don't close the shutters. I'll ring presently.'

The man went out of the room as automatically as he had come. He closed the door behind him, and Marguerite was once more alone.

She picked up the book which she had fingered idly before the light gave out. She tried once more to fix her attention on this tale of love and adventure written by Mr Fielding; but she had lost the thread of the story, and there was a mist between her eyes and the printed pages.

With an impatient gesture she threw down the book and passed her hand across her eyes, then seemed astonished to find that her hand was wet.

She felt unaccountably restless, and could she but have analysed her feelings – had she dared so to do – she would have realized that the weight which oppressed her heart so that she could hardly breathe was one of vague yet dark foreboding.

She closed the window and returned to her seat by the fire, taking up her book with the strong resolution not to allow her nerves to get the better of her. But it was difficult to fix one's attention on the adventures of Master Tom Jones when one's mind was fully engrossed with those of Sir Percy Blakeney.

The sound of carriage wheels on the gravelled forecourt in the front of the house suddenly awakened her drowsy senses. She threw down the book, and with trembling hands clutched the arms of her chair, straining her ears to listen. A carriage at this hour – and on this damp winter's evening! She racked her mind wondering who it could be.

Lady Ffoulkes was in London, she knew. Sir Andrew, of course, was in Paris. His Royal Highness, ever a faithful visitor, would surely not venture out to Richmond in this inclement weather – and the courier always came on horseback.

There was a murmur of voices; that of Edwards, mechanical and placid, could be heard quite distinctly saying:

'I'm sure that her ladyship will be at home to you, m'lady. But I'll go and ascertain.'

Marguerite ran to the door and with joyful eagerness tore it open.

'Suzanne!' she called – 'my little Suzanne! I thought you were in London. Come up quickly! In the boudoir – yes. Oh! what good fortune has brought you?'

Suzanne flew into her arms, holding the friend whom she loved so well closer and closer to her heart, trying to hide her face, which was wet with tears, in the folds of Marguerite's kerchief.

'Come inside, my darling,' said Marguerite. 'Why, how cold your little hands are!'

She was on the point of turning back to her boudoir drawing Lady Ffoulkes by the hand, when suddenly she caught sight of Sir Andrew, who stood at a little distance from her, at the top of the stairs.

'Sir Andrew!' she exclaimed with unstinted gladness.

Then she paused. The cry of welcome died on her lips, leaving them dry and parted. She suddenly felt as if some fearful talons had gripped her heart and were tearing at it with sharp, long nails; the blood flew from her cheeks and from her limbs, leaving her with a sense of icy numbness.

She backed into the room, still holding Suzanne's hand, and drawing her in with her. Sir Andrew followed them, then closed the door behind him. At last the word escaped Marguerite's parched lips:

'Percy! Something has happened to him! He is dead?'

'No, no!' exclaimed Sir Andrew quickly.

Suzanne put her loving arms round her friend and drew her down into the chair by the fire. She knelt at her feet on the hearthrug, and pressed her own burning lips on Marguerite's icy-cold hands. Sir Andrew stood silently by, a world of loving friendship, of heart-broken sorrow, in his eyes.

There was silence in the pretty white-panelled room for a while. Marguerite sat with her eyes closed, bringing the whole armoury of her will-power to bear her up outwardly now.

'Tell me!' she said at last, and her voice was toneless and dull, like one that came from the depths of a grave – 'tell me – exactly – everything. Don't be afraid. I can bear it. Don't be afraid.'

Sir Andrew remained standing, with bowed head and one hand resting on the table. In a firm, clear voice he told her the events of the past few days as they were known to him. All that he tried to hide was Armand's disobedience, which, in his heart, he felt was the primary cause of the catastrophe. He told of the rescue of the Dauphin from the Temple, the midnight drive in the coal-cart, the meeting with Hastings and Tony in the spinney. He only gave vague explanations of Armand's stay in Paris, which caused Percy to go back to the city, even at the moment when his most daring plan had been so successfully carried through.

'Armand, I understand, has fallen in love with a beautiful woman in Paris, Lady Blakeney,' he said, seeing that a strange, puzzled look had appeared in Marguerite's pale face. 'She was arrested a day or two before the rescue of the Dauphin from the Temple. Armand could not join us. He felt that he could not leave her. I am sure that you will understand.'

Then, as she made no comment, he resumed his narrative:

'I had been ordered to go back to La Villette, and there to resume my duties as a labourer in the day-time, and to wait for Percy during the night. The fact that I had received no message from him for two days had made me somewhat worried, but I have such faith in him, such belief in his good luck and his ingenuity, that I would not allow myself to be really anxious. Then on the third day I heard the news.'

'What news?' asked Marguerite mechanically.

'That the Englishman who was known as the Scarlet Pimpernel had been captured in a house in the Rue de la Croix Blanche, and had been inprisoned in the Conciergerie.'

'The Rue de la Croix Blanche? Where is that?'

'In the Montmartre quarter. Armand lodged there. Percy, I imagine, was working to get him away; and those brutes captured him.'

'Having heard the news, Sir Andrew, what did you do?'

'I went into Paris and ascertained its truth.'

'And there is no doubt of it?'

'Alas, none! I went to the house in the Rue de la Croix Blanche. Armand had disappeared. I succeeded in inducing the concierge to talk. She seems to have been devoted to her lodger. Amidst tears she told me some of the details of the capture. Can you bear to hear them, Lady Blakeney?'

'Yes – tell me everything – don't be afraid,' she reiterated with the same dull monotony.

'It appears that early on the Tuesday morning the son of the concierge – a lad about fifteen – was sent off by her lodger with a message to No. 9 Rue St Germain l'Auxerrois. That was the house where Percy was staying all last week, where he kept disguises and so on for us all, and where some of our meetings were held. Percy evidently expected that Armand would try and communicate with him at that address, for when the lad arrived in front of the house he was accosted – so he says – by a big, rough workman, who browbeat him into giving up the lodger's letter, and finally pressed a piece of gold into his hand. The workman was Blakeney, of course. I imagine that Armand, at the time that he wrote the letter, must have been under the belief that Mademoiselle Lange was still in prison; he could not know then that Blakeney had already got her into comparative safety. In the letter he must have spoken of the terrible plight in which he stood, and also of his fears for the woman he loved. Percy was not the man to leave a comrade in the lurch! He would not be the man whom we all love and admire, whose word we all obey, for whose sake we would gladly all of us give our life – he would not be that man if he did not brave even the certain dangers in order to be of help to those who call on him. Armand called and Percy went to him. He must have known that Armand was being spied upon, for Armand, alas! was already a marked man, and the watch-dogs of those infernal committees were already on his heels. Whether these sleuth-hounds had followed the son of the concierge and seen him give the letter to the workman in the Rue St Germain l'Auxerrois, or

96

whether the concierge in the Rue de la Croix Blanche was nothing but a spy of Héron's, or, again whether the Committee of General Security kept a company of soldiers on constant guard in that house, we shall, of course, never know. All that I do know is that Percy entered that fatal house at half-past ten, and that a quarter of an hour later the concierge saw some of the soldiers descending the stairs, carrying a heavy burden. She peeped out of her lodge, and by the light in the corridor she saw that that heavy burden was the body of a man bound closely with ropes: his eyes were closed, his clothes were stained with blood. He was seemingly unconscious. The next day the official organ of the Government proclaimed the capture of the Scarlet Pimpernel, and there was a public holiday in honour of the event.'

Marguerite had listened to this terrible narrative dry-eyed and silent. Now she still sat there, hardly conscious of what went on around her – of Suzanne's tears, that fell unceasingly upon her fingers – of Sir Andrew, who had sunk into a chair, and buried his head in his hands. She was hardly conscious that she lived; the universe seemed to have stood still before this awful, monstrous cataclysm.

But, nevertheless, she was the first to return to the active realities of the present.

'Sir Andrew,' she said after a while, 'tell me, where are my Lords Tony and Hastings?'

'At Calais, madam,' he replied. 'I saw them there on my way hither. They had delivered the Dauphin safely into the hands of his adherents at Mantes, and were awaiting Blakeney's further orders, as he had commanded them to do.'

'Will they wait for us there, think you?'

'For us, Lady Blakeney?' he exclaimed in puzzlement.

'Yes, for us, Sir Andrew,' she replied, while the ghost of a smile flitted across her drawn face; 'you had thought of accompanying me to Paris, had you not?' I cannot let him die alone; he will be longing for me, and – and, after all, there are you, and my Lord Tony, and Lord Hastings and the others; surely – surely we are not going to let him die, not like that, and not alone.'

'You are right, Lady Blakeney,' said Sir Andrew earnestly; 'we are not going to let him die, if human agency can do aught to save him. Already Tony, Hastings and I have agreed to return to Paris. There are one or two hidden places in and around the city known only to Percy and to the members of the League where he must find one or more of us if he succeeds in getting away. All the way between Paris and Calais we have places of refuge, places where any of us can hide at a given moment; where we can find disguises when we want them, or horses in an emergency. No! no! we are not going to despair, Lady Blakeney; there are nineteen of us prepared to lay down our lives for the Scarlet Pimpernel. Already I, as his lieutenant, have been selected as the leader of as determined a gang as ever entered on a work of rescue before. We leave for Paris tomorrow, and if human pluck and devotion can destroy mountains, then we'll destroy them. Our watchword is: "God save the Scarlet Pimpernel!"'

He knelt beside her chair and kissed the cold fingers which, with a sad little smile, she held out to him.

'And God bless you all!' she murmured.

Suzanne had risen to her feet when her husband knelt; now he stood up beside her. The dainty young woman – hardly more than a child – was doing her best to restrain her tears.

'See how selfish I am,' said Marguerite. 'I talk calmly of taking your husband from you, when I myself know the bitterness of such partings.'

'My husband will go where his duty calls him,' said Suzanne with charming and simple dignity. 'I love him with all my heart, because he is brave and good. He could not leave his comrade, who is also his chief, in the lurch. God will protect him, I know. I would not ask him to play the part of a coward.'

Her brown eyes glowed with pride. She was the true wife of a soldier, and with all her dainty ways and childlike manners she was a splendid woman and a staunch friend. Sir Percy Blakeney had saved her entire family from death; and Comte and Comtesse de Tournai, the Vicomte, her brother, and she herself all owed their lives to the Scarlet Pimpernel.

This she was not likely to forget.

'There is but little danger to us, I fear me,' said Sir Andrew lightly; 'the revolutionary Government only wants to strike at a head, it cares nothing for the limbs. Perhaps it feels that without our leader we are enemies not worthy of persecution. If there are any dangers, so much the better,' he added; 'but I don't anticipate any, unless we succeed in freeing our chief; and having freed him, we fear nothing more.'

'The same applies to me, Sir Andrew,' rejoined Marguerite earnestly. 'Now that they have captured Percy, those human fiends will care naught for me. If you succeed in freeing Percy I, like you, will have nothing more to fear, and if you fail —'

She paused and put her small, white hand on Sir Andrew's arms.

'Take me with you, Sir Andrew,' she entreated.

Sir Andrew turned to his wife, a mute query in his eyes.

'You would do an inhuman and a cruel act,' said Suzanne with seriousness that sat quaintly on her baby face, 'if you did not afford your protection to Marguerite, for I do believe that if you did not take her with you tomorrow she would go to Paris alone.'

*　　*　　*

They had been in Paris three days now, and it was six days since Blakeney had been arrested. Sir Andrew and Marguerite had found temporary lodgings inside Paris, Tony and Hastings were just outside the gates, and all along the route between Paris and Calais, at St Germain, at Mantes, in the villages between Beauvais and Amiens, wherever money could obtain friendly help, members of the devoted League of the Scarlet Pimpernel lay in hiding waiting to aid their chief.

Ffoulkes had ascertained that Percy was kept a close prisoner in the Conciergerie, in the very rooms occupied by Marie Antoinette during the last months of her life. He left poor Marguerite to guess how closely that elusive Scarlet Pimpernel was being guarded, the precautions surrounding him being even more minute than those which had made the unfortunate Queen's closing days a martyrdom for her.

But of Armand he could glean no satisfactory news, only the negative probability that he was not detained in any of the larger prisons of Paris, as no register which he, Ffoulkes, so laboriously consulted bore record of the name of St Just.

Haunting the restaurants and drinking booths where the most advanced Jacobins and Terrorists were wont to meet, he had learned one or two details of Blakeney's incarceration which he could not possibly impart to Marguerite. The capture of the mysterious Englishman known as the Scarlet Pimpernel had created a great deal of popular satisfaction; but it was obvious that not only was the public mind not allowed to associate that capture with the escape of little Capet from the Temple, but it soon became clear to Ffoulkes that the news of that escape was still being kept a profound secret.

On one occasion he had succeeded in spying on the Chief Agent of the Committee of General Security, whom he knew by sight, while the latter was sitting at dinner in the company of a stout, florid man with pock-marked face and podgy hands covered with rings.

Sir Andrew marvelled who this man might be. Héron spoke to him in ambiguous phrases that would have been unintelligible to anyone who did not know the circumstances of the Dauphin's escape and the part that the League of the Scarlet Pimpernel had played in it. But to Sir Andrew Ffoulkes, who – cleverly disguised as a farrier, grimy after his day's work – was straining his ears to listen while apparently consuming huge slabs of boiled beef, it soon became clear that the chief agent and his fat friend were talking of the Dauphin and of Blakeney.

'He won't hold out much longer, citizen,' the chief agent was saying in a confident voice; 'our men are absolutely unremitting in their task. Two of them watch him night and day; they look after him well, and practically never lose sight of him, but the moment he tries to get any sleep one of them rushes into the cell with a loud banging of bayonet and sabre, and noisy tread on the flagstones, and shouts at the top of his voice: "Now then, aristo, where's the brat? Tell us now, and you shall lie down and go to sleep." I have done it myself all through one day just for the pleasure of it. It's a little tiring, for you have to shout a good deal now, and sometimes give the cursed Englishman a good shake up. He has had five days of it, and not one wink of sleep during that time – not one single minute of rest – and he only gets enough food to keep him alive. I tell you he can't last. Citizen Chauvelin had a splendid idea there. It will all come right in a day or two.'

'H'm!' grunted the other sulkily; 'those Englishmen are tough.'

'Yes!' retorted Héron, with a grim laugh and a leer of savagery that made his gaunt face look positively hideous – 'you would have given out after three days, friend de Batz, would you not? And I warned you, didn't I? I told you if you tampered with the brat I would make you cry in mercy to me for death.'

'And I warned you,' said the other imperturbably, 'not to worry so much about me, but to keep your eyes open for those cursed Englishmen.'

'I am keeping my eyes open for you, nevertheless, my friend. If I thought you knew where the vermin's spawn was at this moment I would —'

'You would put me on the same rack that you or your precious friend, Chauvelin, have devised for the Englishman. But I don't know where the lad is. If I did I would not be in Paris.'

'I know that,' assented Héron with a sneer; 'you would soon be after the reward – over in Austria, what? – but I have your movements tracked day and night, my friend. I dare say you are as anxious as we are as to the whereabouts of the child. Had he been taken over the frontier you would have been the first to hear of it, eh? No,' he added confidently, and as if anxious to reassure himself, 'my firm belief is that the original idea of these confounded Englishmen was to try and get the child over to England, and that they alone know where he is. I tell you it won't be many days before that very withered Scarlet Pimpernel will order his followers to give little Capet up to us. Oh! they are hanging about Paris some of them, I know that; citizen Chauvelin is convinced that the wife isn't very far away. Give her a sight of her husband now, say I, and she'll make the others give the child up soon enough.'

Perspiration stood up in beads on Sir Andrew's brow when he thought of his friend, brought down by want of sleep to – what? His physique was exceedingly powerful, but could it stand against such racking torment for long? And the clear, the alert mind, the scheming brain, the reckless daring – how soon would these become enfeebled by the slow, steady torture of an utter want of rest?

CHAPTER XVI

The bitterest foe

THE next evening Sir Andrew Ffoulkes, having announced his intention of gleaning further news of Armand, if possible, went out shortly after seven o'clock, promising to be home again about nine. Marguerite sat at the open window long after he had gone out, watching the few small flickers of light that blinked across from the other side of the river, and which came from the windows of the Châtelet towers. The windows of the Conciergerie she could not see, for these gave on one of the inner courtyards; but there was a melancholy consolation even in gazing on those walls that held in their cruel, grim enbrace all that she loved in the world.

She turned away from the window, for the night was getting bitterly cold. From the tower of St Germain l'Auxerrois the clock slowly struck eight. Even as the last sound of the historic bell died away in the distance she heard a timid knocking at the door.

'Enter!' she called unthinkingly.

She thought it was her landlady, come up with more wood, mayhap, for the fire, so she did not turn to the door when she heard it being slowly opened, then closed again, and presently a soft tread on the threadbare carpet.

'May I crave your kind attention, Lady Blakeney?' said a harsh voice, subdued to tones of ordinary courtesy.

She quickly repressed a cry of terror. How well she knew that voice! She turned and faced the man who was her bitterest foe.

'Chauvelin!' she gasped.

'Himself at your service, dear lady,' he said simply.

He stood in the full light of the lamp, his trim, small figure boldly cut out against the dark wall beyond. He wore the usual sable-coloured clothes, which he affected, with the primly-folded jabot and cuffs edged with narrow lace.

Without waiting for permission from her, he quietly and deliberately placed his hat and cloak on a chair. Then he turned once more towards her, and made a movement as if to advance into the room; but instinctively she put up a hand as if to ward off the calamity of his approach.

He shrugged his shoulders, and the shadow of a smile that had neither mirth nor kindliness in it hovered round the corners of his thin lips.

'Have I your permission to sit?' he asked.

'As you will,' she replied slowly, keeping her wide-open eyes fixed upon him, as does a frightened bird upon the serpent whom it loathes and fears.

'And may I crave a few moments of your undivided attention, Lady Blakeney?' he continued, taking a chair, and so placing it beside the table that the light of the lamp when he sat remained behind him and his face was left in shadow.

'Is it necessary?' asked Marguerite.

'It is,' he replied curtly, 'if you desire to see and speak with your husband – to be of use to him before it is too late.'

'Then, I pray you speak, citizen, and I will listen.'

She sank into a chair, not heeding whether the light of the lamp fell on her face or not, whether the lines in her haggard cheeks or her tear-dimmed eyes showed plainly the sorrow and despair that had traced them. She had nothing to hide from this man, the cause of all the tortures which she endured. She knew that neither courage nor sorrow would move him, and that hatred for Percy – personal deadly hatred for the man who had twice foiled him – had long crushed the last spark of humanity in his heart.

'Perhaps, Lady Blakeney,' he began after a slight pause and in his smooth, even voice, 'it would interest you to hear how I succeeded in procuring for myself this pleasure of an interview with you?'

'Your spies did their usual work, I suppose,' she said coldly.

'Exactly. We have been on your track for three days, and yesterday evening an unguarded movement on the part of Sir Andrew Ffoulkes gave us the final clue to your whereabouts.'

'Of Sir Andrew Ffoulkes?' she asked, greated puzzled.

'He was in an eating-house, cleverly disguised I own, trying to glean information, no doubt, as to the probable fate of Sir Percy Blakeney. As chance would have it, my friend Héron, of the Committee of General Security, chanced to be discussing with reprehensible openness – er – certain – what shall I say? – certain measures which at my advice the Committee of Public Safety have been forced to adopt with a view to —'

'A truce to your smooth-tongued speeches, citizen Chauvelin,' she interposed firmly. 'Sir Andrew Ffoulkes has told me naught of this – so I pray you speak plainly and to the point, if you can.'

He bowed with marked irony.

'As you please,' he said. 'Sir Andrew Ffoulkes, hearing certain matters of which I will tell you anon, made a movement which betrayed him to one of our spies. At a word from citizen Héron this man followed on the heels of the young farrier who had shown such interest in the conversation of the Chief Agent. Sir Andrew, I imagine, burning with indignation at what he had heard, was perhaps not quite so cautious as he usually is. Anyway, the man on his track followed him to this door. It was quite simple, as you see. As for me. I had guessed a week ago that we would see the beautiful Lady Blakeney in Paris before long. When I knew where Sir Andrew Ffoulkes lodged, I had no difficulty in guessing that Lady Blakeney would not be far off.'

'And what was there in citizen Héron's conversation last night,' she asked quietly, 'that so aroused Sir Andrew's indignation?'

'He has not told you?'

'No.'

'Oh! it is very simple. Let me tell you, Lady Blakeney, exactly how matters stand. Sir Percy Blakeney – before lucky chance at last delivered him into our hands – thought fit, as no doubt you know, to meddle with our most important prisoner of State.'

'A child. I know it, sir – the son of a murdered father, whom you and your friends were slowly doing to death.'

'That is as it may be, Lady Blakeney,' rejoined Chauvelin calmly; 'but it was none of Sir Percy Blakeney's business. This, however, he chose to disregard. He succeeded in carrying little Capet from the Temple, and two days later we had him under lock and key.'

'Through some infamous and treacherous trick, sir,' she retorted.

Chauvelin made no immediate reply; his pale, inscrutable eyes were fixed upon her face, and the smile of irony round his mouth appeared more strongly marked than before.

'That, again, as it may be,' he said suavely; 'but anyhow for the moment we have the upper hand. Sir Percy is in the Conciergerie, guarded day and night, more closely than Marie Antoinette even was guarded.'

'And he laughs at your bolts and bars, sir,' she rejoined proudly. 'Remember Calais, remember Boulogne! His laugh at your discomfiture, then, must resound in your ear even today.'

'Yes; but for the moment laughter is on our side. Still we are willing to forgo even that pleasure if Sir Percy will but move a finger towards his own freedom.'

'Again some infamous letter?' she asked with bitter contempt; 'some attempt against his honour?'

'No, no, Lady Blakeney,' he interposed with perfect blandness. 'Matters are so much simpler now, you see. We hold Sir Percy at our mercy. We could send him to the guillotine tomorrow, but we might be willing – remember, I only say we might – to exercise our prerogative of mercy if Sir Percy Blakeney will on his side accede to a request from us.'

'And that request?'

'Is a very natural one. He took Capet away from us, and it is but credible that he knows at the present moment exactly where the child is. Let him instruct his followers – and I mistake not, Lady Blakeney, there are several of them not very far from Paris just now – let him, I say, instruct these followers of his to return the person of young Capet to us, and not only will we undertake to give these same gentlemen a safe conduct back to England, but we even might be inclined to deal somewhat less harshly with the gallant Scarlet Pimpernel himself.'

She laughed a hard, mirthless, contemptuous laugh.

'I don't think that I quite understand,' she said after a moment or two. 'You want my husband – the Scarlet Pimpernel, citizen – to deliver the little King of France to you after he has risked his life to save the child from your clutches? Is that what you are trying to say?'

'It is,' rejoined Chauvelin complacently, 'just what we have been saying to Sir Percy Blakeney for the past six days, madame.'

'Well! then you have had your answer, have you not?'

'Yes,' he replied slowly; 'but the answer has become weaker day by day.'

'Weaker! I don't understand.'

'Let me explain, Lady Blakeney,' said Chauvelin, now with measured emphasis. He put both elbows on the table and leaned well forward, peering into her face, lest one of its varied expressions escaped him. 'Just now you taunted me with my failure in Calais, and again at Boulogne; with a proud toss of the head, which I own is excessively becoming, you threw the name of the Scarlet Pimpernel in my face like a challenge which I no longer dare to accept. "The Scarlet Pimpernel," you would say to me, "stands for loyalty, for honour, and for indomitable courage. Think you he would sacrifice his honour to obtain your mercy? Remember Boulogne and your discomfiture!" All of which, dear lady, is perfectly charming and womanly and enthusiastic, and I, bowing my humble head, must own that I was fooled in Calais and baffled in Boulogne. But in Boulogne I made a grave mistake, and one from which I learned a lesson, which I am putting into practice now. Sir Percy Blakeney has been in the prison of the Conciergerie for exactly one week, Lady Blakeney,' he continued, speaking very slowly, and letting every one of his words sink impressively into her mind. 'Even before he had time to take the bearings of his cell or to plan on his own behalf one of those remarkable escapes for which he is so justly famous, our men began to work on a scheme which I am proud to say originated with myself. A week has gone by since then, Lady Blakeney, and during that time a special company of prison guards, acting under the orders of the Committees of General Security and of Public Safety, have questioned the prisoner unremittingly – unremittingly, remember – day and night. Two by two these men take it in turns to enter the prisoner's cell every quarter of an hour – lately it has had to be more often – and ask him the question, "Where is little Capet?" Up to now we have received no satisfactory reply, although we have explained to Sir Percy that many of his followers are honouring the neighbourhood of Paris with their visit, and that all we ask for from him are instructions to those gallant gentlemen to bring young Capet back to us. It is all very simple; unfortunately the prisoner is somewhat obstinate. At first, even the idea seemed to amuse him; he used to laugh and say that he always had the faculty of sleeping with his eyes open. But our soldiers are untiring in their efforts, and the want of sleep as well as of a sufficiency of food and of fresh air is certainly beginning to tell on Sir Percy Blakeney's magnificent physique. I don't think that it will be very long before he gives way to our gentle persuasions; and in any case now, I assure you, dear lady, that we need not fear any attempt on his part to escape. I doubt if he could walk very steadily across this room —'

Marguerite sat quite silent and apparently impassive.

'So you came tonight to tell me all this?' she asked as soon as she could trust herself to speak. Her impulse was to shriek out her indignation, her horror of him, but her words of loathing would only have added to his delight.

'You have had your wish,' she added coldly, 'now I pray you, go.'

'Your pardon, Lady Blakeney,' he said with all his habitual blandness; 'my object in coming to see you tonight was twofold. Methought that I was acting as your friend in giving you authentic news of Sir Percy, and in suggesting the possibility of your adding your persuasion to ours.'

'My persuasion? You mean that I —'

'You would wish to see your husband, would you not, Lady Blakeney?'

'Yes.'

'Then I pray you command me. I will grant you the permission whenever you wish to go.'

'You are in the hope, citizen,' she said, 'that I will do my best to break my husband's spirit by my tears or my prayers – is that it?'

'Not necessarily,' he replied pleasantly. 'I assure you that we can manage to do that ourselves, in time.'

'You devil!' The cry of pain and of horror was involuntarily wrung from the depths of her soul. 'Are you not afraid that God's hand will strike you where you stand?'

'No,' he said lightly; 'I am not afraid, Lady Blakeney. You see, I do not happen to believe in God. Come!' he added more seriously, 'have I not proved to you that my offer is disinterested? Yet I repeat it even now. If you desire to see Sir Percy in prison, command me, and the doors shall be open to you.'

She waited a moment, looking him straight and quite dispassionately in the face; then she said coldly :

'Very well! I will go.'

'When?' he asked.

'This evening.'

'Just as you wish. I would have to go and see my friend Héron first, and arrange with him for your visit.'

'Then go. I will follow in half an hour.'

'*C'est entendu.* Will you be at the main entrance of the Conciergerie at half past nine? You know it, perhaps – no? It is in the Rue de la Barillerie, immediately on the right at the foot of the great staircase of the house of Justice.'

'Of the house of Justice!' she exclaimed involuntarily, a world of bitter contempt in her cry. Then she added in her former matter-of-fact tones :

'Very good, citizen. At half past nine I will be at the entrance you name.'

'And I will be at the door prepared to escort you.'

He took up his hat and cloak and bowed ceremoniously to her. Then he turned to go. At the door a cry from her – involuntary enough, God knows! – made him pause.

'My interview with the prisoner,' she said, vainly trying, poor soul! to repress that quiver of anxiety in her voice, 'it will be private?'

'Oh yes! Of course,' he replied with a reassuring smile. '*Au revoir*, Lady Blakeney! Half past nine, remember —'

CHAPTER XVII

The caged lion

MARGUERITE, accompanied by Sir Andrew Ffoulkes, walked rapidly along the quay. It lacked ten minutes to the half hour; the night was dark and bitterly cold. Snow was still falling in sparse, thin flakes, and lay like a crisp and glittering mantle over the parapets of the bridges and the grim towers of the Châtelet prison.

They walked on silently now. All that they had wanted to say to one another had been said inside the squalid room of their lodgings when Sir Andrew Ffoulkes had come home and learned that Chauvelin had been.

'They are killing him by inches, Sir Andrew,' had been the heart-rending cry which burst from Marguerite's oppressed heart as soon as her hands rested in the kindly ones of her best friend. 'Is there aught that we can do?'

There was, of course, very little that could be done. One or two fine steel files which Sir Andrew gave to her to conceal beneath the folds of her kerchief; also a tiny dagger with sharp, poisoned blade, which for a moment she held in her hand, hesitating, her eyes filled with tears, her heart throbbing with unspeakable sorrow.

Then slowly – very slowly – she raised the small, death-dealing instrument to her lips, and reverently kissed the narrow blade.

'If it must be!' she murmured, 'God in His mercy will forgive!'

She sheathed the dagger, and this, too, she hid in the folds of her gown.

'Can you think of anything else, Sir Andrew, that he might want?' she asked. 'I have money in plenty, in case those soldiers —'

Sir Andrew sighed, and turned away from her so as to hide the hopelessness which he felt. For three days now he had been exhausting every conceivable means of getting at the prison guard with bribery and corruption. But Chauvelin and his friends had taken excellent precautions. The prison of the Conciergerie, situated as it was in the very heart of the labyrinthine and complicated structure of the Châtelet and the house of Justice, and isolated from every other group of cells in the building, was inaccessible save from one narrow doorway which gave on the guard-room first, and thence on the inner cell beyond. Just as all attempts to rescue the late unfortunate Queen from that prison had failed, so now every attempt to reach the imprisoned Scarlet Pimpernel was equally doomed to bitter disappointment.

'Courage, Lady Blakeney,' he said to Marguerite, when anon they had crossed the Pont au Change, and were wending their way slowly along the Rue de la Barillerie; 'remember our proud dictum: the Scarlet Pimpernel never fails! And also this, that whatever messages Blakeney gives to you for us, whatever he wishes us to do, we are to a man ready to do it, and to give our lives for our chief. Courage! Something tells me that a man like Percy is not going to die at the hands of such vermin as Chauvelin and his friends.'

They had reached the great iron gates of the house of Justice. Marguerite, trying to smile, extended her trembling hand to this faithful, loyal comrade.

'I'll not be far,' he said. 'When you come out do not look to the right or left, but make straight for home; I'll not lose sight of you for a moment, and as soon as possible will overtake you. God bless you both.'

He pressed his lips on her cold little hand, and watched her tall, elegant figure as she passed through the great gates until the veil of falling snow hid her from his gaze. Then with a deep sigh of bitter anguish and sorrow he turned away and was soon lost in the gloom.

Marguerite found the gate at the bottom of the monumental stairs open when she arrived. Chauvelin was standing immediately inside the building waiting for her.

'We are prepared for your visit, Lady Blakeney,' he said, 'and the prisoner knows that you are coming.'

He led the way down one of the numerous and interminable corridors of the building, and she followed briskly, pressing her hand against her bosom, there where the folds of her kerchief hid the steel files and the precious dagger.

Presently Chauvelin paused beside a door. His hand was on the latch, for it did not appear to be locked, and he turned towards Marguerite.

'I am very sorry, Lady Blakeney,' he said in simple, deferential tones, 'that the prison authorities have made a slight condition to your visit.'

'A condition?' she asked. 'What is it?'

'You must forgive me,' he said, as if purposely evading her question, 'for I give you my word that I had nothing to do with a regulation that you might justly feel was derogatory to your dignity. If you will kindly step in here a wardress in charge will explain to you what is required.'

He pushed open the door, and stood aside ceremoniously in order to allow her to pass in.

She walked into the room, past Chauvelin, who whispered as she went by:

'I will wait for you here. And, I pray you, if you have aught to complain of, summon me at once.'

Then he closed the door behind her.

The room in which Marguerite now found herself was a small unventilated quadrangle, dimly lighted by a hanging lamp. A woman in a soiled cotton gown and lank grey hair brushed away from a parchment-like forehead rose from the chair in which she had been sitting when Marguerite entered, and put away some knitting on which she had apparently been engaged.

'I was to tell you, citizeness,' she said the moment the door had been closed and she was alone with Marguerite, 'that the prison authorities have given orders that I should search you before you visit the prisoner.'

'That you should search me!' reiterated Marguerite slowly, trying to understand.

'Yes,' replied the woman. 'I was to tell you to take off your clothes, so that I might look them through and through. I have often had to do this before when visitors have been allowed inside the prison, so it no use your trying to deceive me in any way. I am very sharp at finding out if anyone has papers, or files or ropes concealed in an underpetticoat. Come,' she added more roughly, seeing that Marguerite had remained motionless in the middle of the room; 'the quicker you are about it the sooner you will be taken to see the prisoner.'

These words had their desired effect. The proud Lady Blakeney, inwardly revolting at the outrage, knew that resistance would be worse than useless. Chauvelin was the other side of the door. A call from the woman would being him to her assistance, and Marguerite was only longing to hasten the moment when she could be with her husband.

She took off her kerchief and her gown and calmly submitted to the woman's rough hands as they wandered with sureness and accuracy to the various pockets and folds that might conceal prohibited articles. The woman did her work with peculiar stolidity; she did not utter a word when she found the tiny steel files and placed them on a table beside her. In equal silence she laid the little dagger beside them, and the purse which contained twenty gold pieces. These she counted in front of Marguerite and then replaced them in the purse. Her face expressed neither surprise nor greed nor pity. She was obviously beyond the reach of bribery – just a machine paid by the prison authorities to do this unpleasant work, and no doubt terrorized into doing it conscientiously.

When she had satisfied herself that Marguerite had nothing further concealed about her person, she allowed her to put her dress on once more. She even offered to help her on with it. When Marguerite was fully dressed she opened the door for her. Chauvelin was standing in the passage waiting patiently. At sight of Marguerite, whose pale, set face betrayed nothing of the indignation which she felt, he turned quick, inquiring eyes on the woman.

'Two files, a dagger and a purse with twenty louis,' said the latter curtly.

Chauvelin made no comment. He received the information quite placidly, as if it had no special interest for him. Then he said quietly:

'This way, citizeness!'

Was there some instinct of humanity left in the soldier who allowed Marguerite through the barrier into the prisoner's cell?

Certain it is that as soon as Marguerite passed the barrier he put himself on guard against it, with his back to the interior of the cell and to her.

Marguerite had paused on the threshold.

After the glaring light of the guard-room the cell seemed dark, and at first she could hardly see. The whole length of the long, narrow cubicle lay to her left, with a slight recess at its further end, so that from the threshold of the doorway she could not see into the distant corner. Swift as a lightning flash the remembrance came back to her of proud Marie Antoinette narrowing her life to that dark corner where the insolent eyes of the rabble soldiery would not spy her every movement.

Marguerite stepped farther into the room. Gradually by the dim light of an oil lamp placed upon a table in the recess, she began to distinguish various objects: one or two chairs, another table, and a small but very comfortable-looking camp bedstead.

Just for a few seconds she only saw those inanimate things, then she became conscious of Percy's presence.

He sat on a chair, with his left arm half-stretched out upon the table, his head hidden in the bend of the elbow.

Marguerite did not utter a cry; she did not even tremble. Just for one brief instant she closed her eyes, so as to gather up all her courage before she dared to look again. Then with a steady and noiseless step she came quite close to him. She knelt on the flagstones at his feet, and raised reverently to her lips the hand that hung nerveless and limp by his side.

He gave a start; a shiver seemed to go right through him; he half raised his head and murmured in a hoarse whisper:

'I tell you that I do not know, and if I did —'

She put her arms round him and pillowed her head upon his breast. He turned his head slowly towards her, and now his eyes – hollowed and rimmed with purple – looked straight into hers.

'My beloved,' he said, 'I knew that you would come.'

His arms closed round her. There was nothing of lifelessness or of weariness in the passion of that embrace; and when she looked up again it seemed to her as if that first vision which she had had of him, with weary head bent, and wan, haggard face was not reality, only a dream born of her own anxiety for him; for now the hot, ardent blood coursed just as swiftly as ever through his veins, as if life – strong, tenacious, pulsating life – throbbed with unabated vigour in those massive limbs, and behind that square, clear brow, as though the body, but half subdued, had transferred its vanishing strength to the kind and noble heart that was beating with the fervour of self-sacrifice.

'Percy,' she said gently, 'they will only give us a few moments together. They thought that my tears would break your spirit where their devilry had failed.'

'Dear heart,' he said with a quaint sigh, while he buried his face in the soft masses of her hair, 'until you came I was so d—d fatigued.'

He was laughing, and the old look of boyish love of mischief illumined his haggard face.

'Is it not lucky, dear heart,' he said a moment or two later, 'that those brutes do not leave me unshaved? I could not have faced you with a week's growth of beard round my chin. By dint of promises and bribery I have persuaded one of that rabble to come and shave me every morning. They will not allow me to handle a razor myself. They are afraid I should cut my throat – or one of theirs. But mostly I am too d—d sleepy to think of such a thing.'

'Percy!' she exclaimed, with tender and passionate reproach.

'I know – I know, dear,' he murmured, 'what a brute I am! Ah, God did a cruel thing the day that He threw me in your path. To think that once – not so very long ago – we were drifting apart, you and I. You would have suffered less, dear heart, if we had continued to drift.'

Then as he saw that his bantering tone pained her, he covered her hands with kisses, entreating her forgiveness.

'Dear heart,' he said merrily, 'I deserve that you should leave me to rot in this abominable cage. They haven't got me yet, little woman, you know; I am not yet dead – only d—d sleepy at times. But I'll cheat them even now, never fear.'

'How, Percy – how?' she moaned, for her heart was aching with intolerable pain; she knew better than he did the precautions which were being taken against his escape, and she saw more clearly than he realized it himself the terrible barrier set up against that escape by ever-encroaching physical weakness.

'Well, dear,' he said simply, 'to tell you the truth, I have not yet thought of that all-important "how". I had to wait, you see, until you came. I was so sure that you would come! I have succeeded in putting on paper all my instructions to Ffoulkes, and the others. I will give them to you anon. I knew that you would come, and that I could give them to you; until then I had but to think of one thing, and that was of keeping body and soul together. My chance of seeing you was to let them have their will with me. Those brutes were sure, sooner or later, to bring you to me, that you might see the caged fox worn down to imbecility, eh? That you might add your tears to their persuasion, and succeed where they have failed.'

He laughed lightly with an unstrained note of gaiety, only Marguerite's sensitive ears caught the faint tone of bitterness which rang through the laugh.

'Once I know that the little King of France is safe,' he said, 'I can think of how best to rob those d—d murderers of my skin.'

Then suddenly his manner changed. He still held her with one arm closely to him, but the other now lay across the table, and the slender, emaciated hand was tightly clutched. He did not look at her, but straight ahead; the eyes, unnaturally large now, with their deep purple rims, looked beyond the stone walls of this grim, cruel prison.

'My beautiful one,' he said softly, 'the moments are very precious. God knows I could spend eternity thus with your dear form nestling against my heart. But those d—d murderers will only give us half an hour, and I want your help, my beloved, now that I am a helpless cur caught in their trap. Will you listen attentively, dear heart, to what I am going to say?'

'Yes, Percy, I will listen,' she replied.

'And have you the courage to do just what I tell you, dear?'

'I would not have courage to do aught else,' she said simply.

'It means going from hence today, dear heart, and perhaps not meeting again. Hush-sh-sh, my beloved,' he said, tenderly placing his thin hand over her mouth, from which a sharp cry of pain had well-nigh escaped; 'your exquisite soul will be with me always. Try – try not to give way to despair. Why! your love alone, which I see shining from your dear eyes, is enough to make a man cling to life with all his might. Tell me! will you do as I ask you?'

And she replied firmly and courageously:

'I will do just what you ask, Percy.'

'God bless you for your courage, dear. You will have need of it.'

CHAPTER XVIII

For the sake of that helpless innocent

THE next instant he was kneeling on the floor and his hands were wandering over the small, irregular flagstones immediately underneath the table. Marguerite had risen to her feet; she watched her husband with intent and puzzled eyes; she saw him suddenly pass his slender fingers along a crevice between two flagstones, then raise one of these slightly, and from beneath it extract a small bundle of papers, each carefully folded and sealed. Then he replaced the stone and once more rose to his knees.

He gave a quick glance towards the doorway. Reassured that his movements could not have been and were not watched, he drew Marguerite closer to him.

'Dear heart,' he whispered, 'I want to place these papers in your care. Look upon them as my last will and testament. I succeeded in fooling those brutes one day by pretending to be willing to accede to their will. They gave me pen and ink and paper and wax, and I was to write out an order to my followers to bring the Dauphin hither. They left me in peace for one quarter of an hour, which gave me time to write three letters – one for Armand and the other two for Ffoulkes, and to hide them under the flooring of my cell. You see, dear, I knew that you would come and that I could give them to you then.'

He was pressing one of the papers into her hand, holding her fingers tightly in his, and compelling her gaze with the ardent excitement of his own.

'This first letter is for Ffoulkes,' he said. 'It relates to the final measures for the safety of the Dauphin. They are my instructions to those members of the League who are in or near Paris at the present moment. Ffoulkes, I know, must be with you – he was not likely, God bless his loyalty! to let you come to Paris alone. Then give this letter to him, dear heart, at once, tonight, and tell him that it is my express command that he and the others shall act in minute accordance with my instructions.'

'But the Dauphin surely is safe now,' she urged. 'Ffoulkes and the others are here in order to help you.'

'To help me, dear heart?' he interposed earnestly. 'God alone can do that now, and such of my poor wits as these devils do not succeed in crushing out of me within the next ten days.'

'Ten days!'

'I have waited a week, until this hour when I could place this packet in your hands; another ten days should see the Dauphin out of France – after that, we shall see.'

'Percy,' she exclaimed in an agony of horror, 'you cannot endure this another ten days – and live!'

'Nay!' he said in a tone that was almost insolent in its proud defiance, 'there is but little that a man cannot do an he sets his mind to it. For the rest, 'tis in God's hands!' he added more gently. 'Dear heart! you swore that you would be brave. The Dauphin is still in France, and until he is out of it he will not really be safe. His friends wanted to keep him inside the country! God only knows what they still hope; had I been free I should not have allowed him to remain so long; now those good people at Mantes will yield to my letter and to Ffoulkes' earnest appeal – they will allow one of our League to convey the child safely out of France, and I'll wait here until I know that he is safe. If I tried to get away now, and succeeded – why, Heaven help us! the hue and cry might turn against the child, and he might be captured before I could get to him. Dear heart, dear, dear heart! try to understand! The safety of that child is bound with mine honour, but I swear to you, my sweet love, that the day on which I feel that safety is assured I will save mine own skin – what there is left of it – if I can!'

'Percy!' she cried with a sudden outburst of passionate revolt, 'you speak as if the safety of that child were of more moment than your own. Ten days! – but, God in Heaven! have you thought how I shall live these ten days, while slowly, inch by inch, you give your dear, your precious life for a forlorn cause?'

She had tried to speak calmly, never raising her voice beyond a whisper. Her hands still clutched that paper, which seemed to sear her fingers, the paper which she felt held writ upon its smooth surface the death-sentence of the man she loved.

But his look did not answer her firm appeal; it was fixed far away beyond the prison walls, on a lonely country road outside Paris, with the rain falling in a thin drizzle and leaden clouds overhead chasing one another, driven by the gale.

'Poor mite,' he murmured softly; 'he walked so bravely by my side, until the little feet grew weary; then he nestled in my arms and slept until we met Ffoulkes waiting with the cart. He was no King of France just then, only a helpless innocent whom Heaven aided me to save.'

Marguerite bowed her head in silence. There was nothing more that she could say, no plea that she could urge. Indeed, she had understood, as he had begged her to understand. She understood that long ago he had mapped out the course of his life, and now that that course happened to lead up to a Calvary of humiliation and of suffering, he was not likely to turn back, even though on the summit death already was waiting and beckoning with no uncertain hand; not until he could murmur, in the wake of the great and divine sacrifice itself, the sublime words: 'It is accomplished.'

'But the Dauphin is safe enough now!' was all that she said, after that one moment's silence when her heart, too, had offered up to God the supreme abnegation of self, and calmly faced a sorrow which threatened to break it at last.

'Yes!' he rejoined quietly, 'safe enough for the moment. But he would be safer still if he were out of France. I had hoped to take him one day with me to England. But in this plan damnable Fate has interfered. His adherents wanted to get him to Vienna, and their wish had best be fulfilled now. In my instructions to Ffoulkes I have mapped out a simple way for accomplishing the journey. Tony will be the one best suited to lead the expedition, and I want him to make straight for Holland; the Northern frontiers are not so closely watched as are the Austrian ones. There is a faithful adherent of the Bourbon cause who lives at Delft, and who will give the shelter of his name and home to the fugitive King of France until he can be conveyed to Vienna: he has name Naundorff. Once I feel that the child is safe in his hands I will look after myself, never fear.'

He paused, for his strength, which was only factitious, born of the excitement that Marguerite's presence had called forth, was threatening to give way. His voice, though he had spoken in a whisper all along, was very hoarse, and his temples were throbbing with the sustained effort to speak.

'If those fiends had only thought of denying me food instead of sleep,' he murmured involuntarily, 'I could have held out until —'

Then with characteristic swiftness his mood changed in a moment. His arms closed round Marguerite once more with a passion of self-reproach.

'Heaven forgive me for a selfish brute,' he said, while the ghost of a smile once more lit up the whole of his face. 'Dear soul, I must have forgotten your sweet presence, thus brooding over my own troubles while your loving heart has a graver burden –

God help me! — than it can possibly bear. Listen, my beloved, for I don't know how many minutes longer they intend to give us, and I have not yet spoken to you about Armand —'

'Armand!' she cried.

A twinge of remorse had gripped her. For fully ten minutes now she had relegated all thoughts of her brother to a distant cell of her memory.

'We have no news of Armand,' she said. 'Sir Andrew has searched all the prison registers. Oh! were not my heart atrophied by all that it has endured this past sennight it would feel a final throb of agonizing pain at every thought of Armand.'

A curious look, which even her loving eyes failed to interpret, passed like a shadow over her husband's face. But the shadow lifted in a moment, and it was with a reassuring smile that he said to her:

'Dear heart! Armand is comparatively safe for the moment. Tell Ffoulkes not to search the prison registers for him, rather to seek out Mademoiselle Lange. She will know where to find Armand.'

'Jeanne Lange!' she exclaimed with a world of bitterness in the tone of her voice, 'the girl whom Armand loved, it seems, with a passion greater than his loyalty. Oh! Sir Andrew tried to disguise my brother's folly, but I guessed what he did not choose to tell me. It was his disobedience, his want of trust, that brought this unspeakable misery on us all.'

'Do not blame him overmuch, dear heart. Armand was in love, and love excuses every sin committed in its name.'

He checked himself abruptly, and once more that strange, enigmatical look crept into his eyes.

'I took Jeanne Lange to a place of comparative safety,' he said after a slight pause, 'but since then she has been set entirely free.'

'Free?'

'Yes. Chauvelin himself brought me the news,' he replied with a quick, mirthless laugh, wholly unlike his usual lighthearted gaiety. 'He had to ask me where to find Jeanne, for I alone knew where she was. As for Armand, they'll not worry about him while I am here. Another reason why I must bide a while longer. But in the meanwhile, dear, I pray you find Mademoiselle Lange; she lives at No. 5, Square du Roule. Through her I know that you can get to see Armand. This second letter,' he added, pressing a smaller packet into her hand, 'is for him. Give it to him, dear heart; it will, I hope, tend to cheer him. I fear me the poor lad frets; yet he only sinned because he loved, and to me he will always be your brother – the man who held your affection for all the years before I came into your life. Give him this letter, dear; they are my instructions to him, as the others are for Ffoulkes; but tell him to read them when he is all alone. You will do that, dear heart, will you not?'

'Yes, Percy,' she said simply. 'I promise.'

'Then there is one thing more,' he said. 'There are others in this cruel city, dear heart, who have trusted me, and whom I must not fail – Marie de Marmontel and her brother, faithful servants of the late Queen; they were on the eve of arrest when I succeeded in getting them to a place of comparative safety; and there are others there, too – all of these poor victims have trusted me implicitly. They are waiting for me, trusting in my promise to convey them to England. Sweetheart, you must redeem my promise to them.'

'I promise, Percy,' she said once more.

'Then go, dear, tomorrow, in the late afternoon, to No. 98, Rue de Charonne. Ffoulkes and all the others know these people and know the house; Armand by the same token knows it too. Marie de Marmontel and her brother are there, and several others; the old Comte de Lézardière, the Abbé de Firmont; their names spell suffering, loyalty, and hopelessness. I was lucky enough to convey them safely to that hidden shelter. They trust me implicitly, dear heart. They are waiting for me there, trusting in my promise to them. Ffoulkes has some certificates of safety by him, and the old clothes dealer will supply the necessary disguises; he has a covered cart which he uses for his business, and which you can borrow from him. Ffoulkes will drive the little party to Achard's farm in St Germain, where other members of the League should be in waiting for the final journey to England. Ffoulkes will know how to arrange for everything; he was always my most able lieutenant. Once everything is organized he can appoint Hastings to lead the party. But you, dear heart, must do as you wish, Achard's farm would be a safe retreat for you and for Ffoulkes if ... I know – I know, dear,' he added with infinite tenderness. 'See! I do not even suggest that you should leave me. Ffoulkes will be with you, and I know that neither he nor you would go even if I commanded. Either Achard's farm, or even the house in the Rue de Charonne, would be quite safe for you, dear, under Ffoulkes's protection, until the time when I myself can carry you back – you, my precious burden – to England in mine own arms, or until ... Hush-sh-sh, dear heart,' he entreated, smothering with a passionate kiss the low moan of pain which had escaped her lips; 'it is all in God's hands now; I am in a tight corner – tighter than ever I have been before; but I am not dead yet, and those brutes have not yet paid the full price for my life. Tell me, dear heart, that you have understood.' She reiterated firmly :

'I have understood every word that you said to me, Percy, and I promise to do what you ask.'

He uttered a deep sigh of satisfaction, and even at that moment there came from the guard-room beyond the sound of a harsh voice, saying peremptorily :

'That half-hour is nearly over, sergeant; 'tis time you interfered.'

'Three minutes more, citizen,' was the curt reply.

'Three minutes, you devils,' murmured Blakeney between set teeth, while a sudden light which even Marguerite's keen gaze failed to interpret leapt into his eyes. Then he pressed the third letter into her hand.

Once more his close, intent gaze compelled hers; their faces were close one to the other, so near to him did he draw her, so tightly did he hold her to him. The paper was in her hand and his fingers were pressed firmly on hers.

'For the next ten days the Dauphin will be on the high roads of France, on his way to safety. Every stage of his journey will be known to me. I can from between these four walls follow him and his escort step by step. Well, dear, I am but a man, already brought to shameful weakness by mere physical discomfort – the want of sleep – such a trifle after all; but in case my reason tottered – God knows what I might do – then give this packet to Ffoulkes – it contains my final instructions – and he will know how to act. Promise me, dear heart, that you will not open the packet unless – unless mine own dishonour seems to you imminent – unless I have yielded to these brutes in this prison, and sent Ffoulkes or one of the others orders to exchange the Dauphin's life for mine; then, when mine own handwriting hath proclaimed me a coward, then and then only, give this packet to Ffoulkes. Promise me that, and also that when you and he have mastered its contents you will act exactly as I have commanded.'

Through the sobs that well-nigh choked her she murmured the promise he desired.

His voice had grown hoarser and more spent with the inevitable reaction after the long and sustained effort, but the vigour of the spirit was untouched, the fervour, the enthusiasm.

'Dear heart,' he murmured, 'do not look on me with those dear, scared eyes of yours. If there is aught that puzzles you in what I said, try and trust me a while longer. Remember, I must save the Dauphin at all costs; mine honour is bound with his safety. What happens to me after that matters but little, yet I wish to live for your dear sake.'

He drew a long breath which had naught of weariness in it. The haggard look had completely vanished from his face, the eyes were lighted up from within, the very soul of reckless daring and immortal gaiety illumined his whole personality.

'Do not look so sad, little woman,' he said with a strange and sudden recrudescence of power; 'those d—d murderers have not got me yet – even now.'

Then he went down like a log.

The iron bar was raised and thrown back with a loud crash, the butt-ends of muskets were grounded against the floor, and two soldiers made noisy irruption into the cell.

'Holà, citizen! Wake up,' shouted one of the men; 'you have not told us yet what you have done with Capet!'

Marguerite uttered a cry of horror. Instinctively her arms were interposed between the unconscious man and these inhuman creatures, with a beautiful gesture of protecting motherhood.

'He has fainted,' she said, her voice quivering with indignation. 'My God! are you devils that you have not one spark of manhood in you?'

'Tell him to say what he has done with Capet,' said one of the soldiers, and this rough command was accompanied with a coarse jest that sent the blood flaring up into Marguerite's pale cheeks.

The brutal laugh, the coarse words which accompanied it, the insult flung at Marguerite, had penetrated to Blakeney's slowly returning consciousness. With sudden strength, that appeared almost supernatural, he jumped to his feet, and before any of the others could interfere he had with clenched fist struck the soldier a full blow on the mouth.

The man staggered back with a curse, the other shouted for help; in a moment the narrow place swarmed with soldiers; Marguerite was roughly torn away from the prisoner's side, and thrust into the far corner of the cell, from where she only saw a confused mass of blue coats and white belts, and – towering for one brief moment above what seemed to her fevered fancy like a veritable sea of heads – the pale face of her husband, with widely dilated eyes searching the gloom for hers.

'Remember!' he shouted, and his voice for that brief moment rang out clear and sharp above the din.

CHAPTER XIX

Afterwards

'I AM sorry, Lady Blakeney,' said a harsh, dry voice close to her; 'the incident at the end of your visit was none of our making, remember.'

She turned away, sickened with horror at the thought of contact with this wretch. She had heard the heavy oaken door swing to behind her on its ponderous hinges, and the key once again turn in the lock. She felt as if she had suddenly been thrust into a coffin, and that clods of earth were being thrown upon her breast, oppressing her heart so that she could not breathe.

Had she looked for the last time on the man whom she loved beyond everything else on earth, whom she worshipped more ardently day by day? Was she even now carrying within the folds of her kerchief a message from a dying man to his comrades?

Mechanically she followed Chauvelin down the corridor and along the passages which she had traversed a brief half-hour ago. From some distant church tower a clock tolled the hour of ten. It had then really only been little more than thirty brief minutes since first she had entered this grim building, which seemed less stony than the monsters who held authority within it; to her it seemed that centuries had gone over her head during that time. She felt like an old woman, unable to straighten her back or to steady her limbs; she could only dimly see some few paces ahead the trim figure of Chauvelin walking with measured steps, his hands held behind his back, his head thrown up with what looked like triumphant defiance.

At the door of the cubicle where she had been forced to submit to the indignity of being searched by a wardress, the latter was now standing, waiting with characteristic stolidity. In her hand she held the steel files, the dagger, and the purse which, as Marguerite passed, she held out to her.

'Your property, citizeness,' she said placidly.

She emptied the purse into her own hand, and solemnly

counted out the twenty pieces of gold. She was about to replace them all into the purse, when Marguerite pressed one of them back into her wrinkled hand.

'Nineteen will be enough, citizeness,' she said; 'keep one for yourself, not only for me, but for all the poor women who come here with their heart full of hope, and go hence with it full of despair.'

The woman turned calm, lack-lustre eyes on her, and silently pocketed the gold piece with a grudgingly muttered word of thanks.

Chauvelin during this brief interlude had walked thoughtlessly on ahead. Marguerite, peering down the length of the narrow corridor, spied his sable-clad figure some hundred metres farther on as it crossed the dim circle of light thrown by one of the lamps.

She was about to follow, when it seemed to her as if someone was moving in the darkness close beside her. The wardress was even now in the act of closing the door of her cubicle, and there were a couple of soldiers who were disappearing from view round one end of the passage, while Chauvelin's retreating form was lost in the gloom at the other.

There was no light close to where she herself was standing, and the blackness around her was as impenetrable as a veil; the sound of a human creature moving and breathing close to her in this intense darkness acted weirdly on her overwrought nerves.

'*Qui va là?*' she called.

There was a more distinct movement among the shadows this time, as of a swift tread on the flagstones of the corridor. All else was silent round her, and now she could plainly hear those footsteps running rapidly down the passage away from her. She strained her eyes to see more clearly, and anon in one of the dim circles of light on ahead she spied a man's figure – slender and darkly clad – walking quickly yet furtively like one pursued. As he crossed the light the man turned to look back. It was her brother Armand.

Her first instinct was to call to him; the second checked that call upon her lips.

Percy had said that Armand was in no danger; then why should he be sneaking along the dark corridors of this awful house of Justice if he was free and safe?

Certainly, even at a distance, her brother's movements suggested to Marguerite that he was in danger of being seen. He cowered in the darkness, tried to avoid the circles of light thrown by the lamps in the passage. At all costs Marguerite felt that she must warn him that the way he was going now would lead him straight into Chauvelin's arms, and she longed to let him know that she was close by.

Feeling sure that he would recognize her voice, she made pretence to turn back to the cubicle through the door of which the wardress had already disappeared, and called out as loudly as she dared:

'Good night, citizeness!'

But Armand – who surely must have heard – did not pause at the sound. Rather was he walking on now more rapidly than before. In less than a minute he would be reaching the spot where Chauvelin stood waiting for Marguerite. That end of the corridor, however, received no light from any of the lamps; strive how she might, Marguerite could see nothing now either of Chauvelin or of Armand.

Blindly, instinctively, she ran forward, thinking only to reach Armand, and to warn him to turn back before it was too late; before he found himself face to face with the most bitter enemy he and his nearest and dearest had ever had. But as she at last came to a halt at the end of the corridor, panting with the exertion of running and the fear for Armand, she almost fell up against Chauvelin, who was standing there alone and imperturbable, seemingly having waited patiently for her. She could only dimly distinguish his face, the sharp features and thin cruel mouth, but she felt – more than she actually saw – his cold, steely eyes fixed with a strange expression of mockery upon her.

But of Armand there was no sign, and she – poor soul! – had difficulty in not betraying the anxiety which she felt for her brother. Had the flagstones swallowed him up? A door on the right was the only one that gave on the corridor at this point; it led to the concierge's lodge, and thence out into the courtyard. Had Chauvelin been dreaming, sleeping with his eyes open, while he stood waiting for her, and had Armand succeeded in slipping past him under cover of the darkness and through that door to safety that lay beyond these prison walls?

Marguerite, miserably agitated, not knowing what to think, looked somewhat wild-eyed on Chauvelin; he smiled, that inscrutable, mirthless smile of his, and said blandly:

'Is there aught else that I can do for you, citizeness? This is your nearest way out. No doubt Sir Andrew will be waiting to escort you home.'

Then as she – not daring either to reply or to question – walked straight up to the door, he hurried forward, prepared to open it for her. But before he did so he turned to her once again:

'I trust that your visit has pleased you, Lady Blakeney,' he said suavely. 'At what hour do you desire to repeat it tomorrow?'

'Tomorrow?' she reiterated in a vague, absent manner, for she was still dazed with the strange incident of Armand's appearance and his flight.

'Yes. You would like to see Sir Percy again tomorrow, would you not? I myself would gladly pay him a visit from time to time, but he does not care for my company.'

Madly she longed to accept his suggestion. The very thought of seeing Percy on the morrow was solace to her aching heart; it could feed on hope tonight instead of on its own bitter pain. But even during this brief moment of hesitancy, and while her whole being cried out for this joy that her enemy was holding out to her, even then in the gloom ahead of her she seemed to see a vision of a pale face raised above a crowd of swaying heads, and of the eyes of the dreamer searching for her own, while the last sublime cry of perfect self-devotion once more echoed in her ear:

'Remember!'

The promise which she had given him, that would she fulfil. The burden which he had laid on her shoulders she would try to bear as heroically as he was bearing his own. She wanted, above all, not to arouse Chauvelin's suspicions by markedly refusing to visit the prisoner again – suspicions that might lead to her being searched once more and the precious packet filched from her. Therefore she said to him earnestly now:

'I thank you, citizen, for your solicitude on my behalf, but you will understand, I think, that my visit to the prisoner has been almost more than I could bear. I cannot tell you at this moment whether tomorrow I should be in a fit state to repeat it.'

'As you please,' he replied urbanely. 'But I pray you to remember one thing, and that is —'

He paused a moment while his restless eyes wandered rapidly over her face, trying, as it were, to get at the soul of this woman, at her innermost thoughts, which he felt were hidden from him.

'Yes, citizen,' she said quietly; 'what is it that I am to remember?'

'That it rests with you, Lady Blakeney, to put an end to the present situation.'

'How?'

'Surely you can persuade Sir Percy's friends not to leave their chief in durance vile. They themselves could put an end to his troubles tomorrow.'

'By giving up the Dauphin to you, you mean?' she retorted coldly.

'Precisely.'

'And you hoped – you still hope that by placing before me the picture of your own fiendish cruelty against my husband you will induce me to act the part of a traitor towards him and a coward before his followers?'

'Oh!' he said deprecatingly, 'the cruelty is no longer mine. Sir Percy's release is in your hands, Lady Blakeney – in those of his followers. I should only be too willing to end the present intolerable situation. You and your friends are applying the last turn of the thumb-screw, not I —'

She smothered the cry of horror that had risen to her lips. The man's cold-blooded sophistry was threatening to make a breach in her armour of self-control.

She would no longer trust herself to speak, but made a quick movement towards the door.

He shrugged his shoulders as if the matter were now entirely out of his control. Then he opened the door for her to pass out, and as her skirts brushed against him he bowed with studied deference, murmuring a cordial 'Good night!'

'And remember, Lady Blakeney,' he added politely, 'that should you at any time desire to communicate with me at my rooms, 19, Rue Dupuy, I hold myself entirely at your service.'

CHAPTER XX

Sisters

THE morning found her fagged out, but more calm. Later on she managed to drink some coffee, and having washed and dressed, she prepared to go out.

Sir Andrew appeared in time to ascertain her wishes.

'I promised Percy to go to the Rue de Charonne in the late afternoon,' she said. 'I have some hours to spare, and mean to employ them in trying to find speech with Mademoiselle Lange.'

'Blakeney has told you where she lives?'

'Yes. In the Square du Roule. I know it well. I can be there in half an hour.'

He, of course, begged to be allowed to accompany her, and anon they were walking together quickly up towards the Faubourg St Honoré. The snow had ceased falling, but it was still very cold, but neither Marguerite nor Sir Andrew were conscious of the temperature or of any outward signs around them. They walked on silently until they reached the torn-down gates of the Square du Roule; there Sir Andrew parted from Marguerite after having appointed to meet her an hour later at a small eating-house he knew of where they could have some food together, before starting on their long expedition to the Rue de Charonne.

Five minutes later Marguerite Blakeney was shown by worthy Madame Belhomme, into the quaint and pretty drawing-room with its soft-toned hangings and old-world air of faded grace. Mademoiselle Lange was sitting there, in a capacious armchair, which encircled her delicate figure with its framework of dull old gold.

She rose when Marguerite entered, obviously puzzled at the unexpected visit, and somewhat awed at the appearance of this beautiful woman with the sad look in her eyes.

'I must crave your pardon, mademoiselle,' said Lady Blakeney as soon as the door had once more closed on Madame Belhomme, and she found herself alone with the young girl. 'This visit at such an early hour must seem to you an intrusion. But I am Marguerite St Just, and —'

Her smile and outstretched hand completed the sentence.

'St Just!' exclaimed Jeanne.

'Yes. Armand's sister!'

A swift blush rushed to the girl's pale cheeks; her brown eyes expressed unadulterated joy. Marguerite, who was studying her closely, was conscious that her poor aching heart went out to this exquisite child, the far-off innocent cause of so much misery.

Jeanne, a little shy, a little confused and nervous in her movements, was pulling a chair close to the fire, begging Marguerite to sit. Her words came out all the while in short, jerky sentences, and from time to time she stole swift, shy glances at Armand's sister.

'You will forgive me, mademoiselle,' said Marguerite, whose simple and calm manner quickly tended to soothe Jeanne Lange's confusion; 'but I was so anxious about my brother – I do not know where to find him.'

'And so you came to me, Madame?'

'Was I wrong?'

'Oh, no! But what made you think that – that I would know?'

'I guessed,' said Marguerite, with a smile.

'You had heard about me then?'

'Oh, yes!'

'Through whom? Did Armand tell you about me?'

'No, alas! I have not seen him this past fortnight, since you, mademoiselle, came into his life; but many of Armand's friends are in Paris just now; one of them knew, and he told me.'

The soft blush had now overspread the whole of the girl's face, even down to her graceful neck. She waited to see Marguerite comfortably installed in an armchair, then she resumed shyly:

'And it was Armand who told me all about you. He loves you so dearly.'

'Armand and I were very young children when we lost our parents,' said Marguerite softly, 'and we were all in all to each other then. And until I married he was the man I loved best in all the world!'

'He told me you were married – to an Englishman.'

'Yes?'

'He loves England too. At first he always talked of my going there with him as his wife, and of the happiness we should find there together.'

'Why do you say "at first"?'

'He talks less about England now.'

'Perhaps he feels that now you know all about it, and that you understand each other with regard to the future.'

'Perhaps.'

'Mademoiselle Lange,' said Marguerite gently, 'do you not feel that you can trust me?'

She held out her two hands to the girl, and Jeanne slowly turned to her. The next moment she was kneeling at Marguerite's feet and kissing the beautiful kind hands that had been stretched out to her with such sisterly love.

'Indeed, indeed, I do trust you,' she said, and looked with tear-dimmed eyes in the pale face above her. 'I have longed for someone in whom I could confide. I have been so lonely lately, and Armand —'

With an impatient little gesture she brushed away the tears which had gathered in her eyes.

'What has Armand been doing?' asked Marguerite, with an encouraging smile.

'Oh, nothing to grieve me!' replied the young girl eagerly, 'for he is kind, and good, and chivalrous and noble. Oh, I love him with all my heart! I loved him from the moment that I set eyes on him, and then he came to see me – perhaps you know! And he talked so beautifully about England, and so nobly about his leader the Scarlet Pimpernel. Have you heard of him?'

'Yes,' said Marguerite, smiling. 'I have heard of him.'

'It was that day that citizen Héron came with his soldiers! Oh! you do not know citizen Héron. He is the most cruel man in France. In Paris he is hated by everyone, and no one is safe from his spies. He came to arrest Armand, but I was able to fool him and to save Armand. And after that,' she added with charming naïveté, 'I felt as if, having saved Armand's life, he belonged to me – and his love for me had made me his.'

'Then I was arrested,' she continued, after a slight pause, and at the recollection of what she had endured then her fresh voice still trembled with horror.

'They dragged me to prison, and I spent two days in a dark cell, where —'

She hid her face in her hands, while a few sobs shook her whole frame; then she resumed more calmly :

'I had seen nothing of Armand. I wondered where he was, and I knew that he would be eating out his heart with anxiety for me. But God was watching over me. At first I was transferred to the Temple prison, and there a kind creature – a sort of man-of-all-work in the prison – took compassion on me. I did not know how he contrived it, but one morning very early he brought me some filthy old rags which he told me to put on quickly, and when I had done that he bade me follow him. Oh! he was a very dirty, wretched man himself, but he must have had a kind heart. He took me by the hand and made me carry his broom and brushes. Nobody took much notice of us, the dawn was only just breaking, and the passages were very dark and deserted; only once some soldiers began to chaff him about me : 'C'est ma fille – quoi?' he said roughly. I very nearly laughed then, only I had the good sense to restrain myself, for I knew that my freedom, and perhaps my life, depended on my not betraying myself. My grimy, tattered guide took me with him right through the interminable corridors of that awful building, while I prayed fervently to God for him and for myself. We got out by one of the service stairs and exit, and then he dragged me through some narrow streets until we came to a corner where a covered cart stood waiting. My kind friend told me to get into the cart, and then he bade the driver on the box take me straight to a house in the Rue St Germain l'Auxerrois. Oh! I was infinitely grateful to the poor creature who had helped me to get out of that awful prison, and I would gladly have given him some money, for I am sure he was very poor; but I had none by me. He told me that I should be quite safe in the house in the Rue St Germain l'Auxerrois, and begged me to wait there patiently for a few days, until I heard from one who had my welfare at heart, and who would further arrange for my safety.'

Marguerite had listened silently to this narrative so naïvely told by this child, who obviously had no idea to whom she owed her freedom and her life. While the girl talked, her mind could follow with unspeakable pride and happiness every phase of that scene in the early dawn when that mysterious, ragged man-of-all-work, unbeknown even to the woman whom he was saving, risked his own noble life for the sake of her whom his friend and comrade loved.

'And did you never see again the kind man to whom you owe your life?' she asked.

'No!' replied Jeanne. 'I never saw him since; but when I arrived at the Rue St Germain l'Auxerrois I was told by the good people who took charge of me that the ragged man-of-all-work had been none other than the mysterious Englishman whom Armand reveres, he whom they call the Scarlet Pimpernel.'

'But you did not stay very long in the Rue St Germain l'Auxerrois, did you?'

'No. Only three days. The third day I received a *communiqué* from the Committee of General Security, together with an unconditional certificate of safety. It meant that I was free – quite free. Oh! I could scarcely believe it. I laughed and I cried until the people in the house thought that I had gone mad. The past few days had been such a horrible nightmare.'

'And then you saw Armand again?'

'Yes. They told him that I was free. And he came here to see me. He often comes; he will be here anon.'

'But are you not afraid on his account and your own? He is – he must be still – "suspect"; a well-known adherent of the Scarlet Pimpernel, he would be safer out of Paris.'

'No! oh no! Armand is in no danger. He, too, has an unconditional certificate of safety.'

'An unconditional certificate of safety?' asked Marguerite, while a deep frown of grave puzzlement appeared between her brows. 'What does that mean?'

'It means that he is free to come and go as he likes; that neither he nor I have anything to fear from Héron and his awful spies. Oh! but for that sad and careworn look on Armand's face we could be so happy; but he is so unlike himself. He is Armand and yet another; his look at times quite frightens me.'

'Yet you know why he is so sad,' said Marguerite in a strange, toneless voice which she seemed quite able to control, for that tonelessness came from a terrible sense of suffocation, of a feeling as if her heart-strings were being gripped by huge, hard hands.

'Yes, I know,' said Jeanne half hesitatingly, as if knowing, she was still unconvinced.

'His chief, his comrade, the friend of whom you speak, the Scarlet Pimpernel, who risked his life in order to save yours, Mademoiselle, is a prisoner in the hands of those that hate him.'

'Oh yes!' she said with a deep, sad sigh, while the ever-ready tears once more gathered in her eyes, 'Armand is very unhappy because of him. The Scarlet Pimpernel was his friend; Armand loved and revered him.'

'I have news for Armand,' whispered Marguerite, 'that will comfort him, a message – a letter from his friend. You will see, dear, that when Armand reads it he will become a changed man; you see, Armand acted a little foolishly a few days ago. His chief had given him orders which he disregarded – he was so anxious about you – he should have obeyed, and now, mayhap, he feels that his disobedience may have been the – the innocent cause of much misery to others; that is, no doubt, the reason why he is so sad. The letter from his friend will cheer him, you will see.'

'Do you really think so, madame?' murmured Jeanne, in whose tear-stained eyes the indomitable hopefulness of youth was already striving to shine.

'I am sure of it,' assented Marguerite.

CHAPTER XXI

The letter

THE two women, both so young still, but each of them with a mark of sorrow already indelibly graven in her heart, were clinging to one another, bound together by the strong bond of sympathy. And but for the sadness of it all it were difficult to conjure up a more beautiful picture than that which they presented as they stood side by side; Marguerite, tall and stately as an exquisite lily, with the crown of her ardent hair and the glory of her deep blue eyes, and Jeanne Lange, dainty and delicate, with the brown curls and the childlike droop of the soft, moist lips.

Thus Armand saw them when, a moment of two later, he entered unannounced. He had pushed open the door, and looked on the two women silently for a second or two; on the girl whom he loved so dearly, for whose sake he had committed the great, the unpardonable sin which would send him for ever henceforth, Cain-like, a wanderer on the face of the earth; and the other, his sister, her whom a Judas act would condemn to lonely sorrow and widowhood.

He could have cried out in an agony of remorse, and it was the groan of acute soul anguish which escaped his lips that drew Marguerite's attention to his presence.

Even though many things that Jeanne Lange had said had prepared her for a change in her brother, she was immeasurably shocked by his appearance. He had always been slim and rather below the average in height, but now his usually upright and trim figure seemed to have shrunken within itself; his clothes hung baggy on his shoulders, his hands appeared waxen and emaciated, but the greatest change was in his face, in the wide circles round the eyes that spoke of wakeful nights, in the hollow cheeks, and the mouth that had wholly forgotten how to smile.

Percy after a week's misery immured in a dark and miserable prison, deprived of food and rest, did not look such a physical wreck as did Armand St Just, who was free.

Marguerite's heart reproached her for what she felt had been neglect, callousness on her part.

'Armand!' she cried.

And the loving arms that had guided his baby footsteps long ago, the tender hands that had wiped his boyish tears, were stretched out with unalterable love towards him.

'I have a message for you, dear,' she said gently – 'a letter from him. Mademoiselle Jeanne allowed me to wait here for you until you came.'

Silently, like a little shy mouse, Jeanne had slipped out of the room. Her pure love for Armand had ennobled every one of her thoughts, and her innate kindliness and refinement had already suggested that brother and sister would wish to be alone. At the door she had turned and met Armand's look. That look had satisfied her; she felt that in it she had read the expression of his love, and to it she had responded with a glance that spoke of hope for a future meeting.

As soon as the door had closed on Jeanne Lange, Armand, with an impulse that refused to be checked, threw himself into his sister's arms. The present, with all its sorrows, its remorse and its shame, had sunk away; only the past remained – the unforgettable past, when Marguerite was 'little mother' – the soother, the comforter, the healer, the ever-willing receptacle wherein he had been wont to pour the burden of his childish griefs, of his boyish escapades.

'And I have brought you a message from Percy,' she repeated, 'a letter which he begged me to give you as soon as maybe.'

'You have seen him?' he asked.

She nodded silently, unable to speak. Not now, not when her nerves were strung to breaking pitch, would she trust herself to speak of that awful yesterday. She groped in the folds of her gown and took the packet which Percy had given her for Armand. It felt quite bulky in her hand.

'There is quite a good deal there for you to read, dear,' she said. 'Percy beggged me to give you this, and then to let you read it when you were alone.'

She pressed the packet into his hand. Armand's face was ashen pale. He clung to her with strange, nervous tenacity; the paper which he held in one hand seemed to sear his fingers.

'I will slip away now,' she said. 'You will make my excuses to Mademoiselle Lange,' she said, trying to smile. 'When you have read, you will wish to see her alone.'

Gently she disengaged herself from Armand's grasp and made for the door. He appeared dazed, staring down at that paper which was scorching his fingers. Only when her hand was on the latch did he seem to realize that she was going.

'When shall I see you again?' he asked.

'Read your letter, dear,' she replied, 'and when you have read it, if you care to impart its contents to me, come tonight to my lodgings. Quai de la Ferraille, above the saddler's shop. But if there is aught in it that you do not wish me to know, then do not come; I shall understand. Goodbye, dear.'

She took his head between her two cold hands, and as it was still bowed she placed a tender kiss, as of a long farewell, upon his hair.

Then she went out of the room.

* * *

Armand sat in the arm-chair in front of the fire. His head rested against one hand; in the other he held the letter written by the friend whom he had betrayed.

Twice he had read it now, and already was every word of that minute, clear writing graven upon the innermost fibres of his body, upon the most secret cells of his brain.

'Armand, I know. I knew even before Chauvelin came to tell me, and stood there hoping to gloat over the soul-agony of a man who finds that he has been betrayed by his dearest friend. But that d—d reprobate did not get that satisfaction, for I was prepared. Not only do I know, Armand, but I *understand*. I, who do not know what love is, have realized how small a thing is honour, loyalty, or friendship when weighed in the balance of a loved one's need.

'To save Jeanne you sold me to Héron and his crowd. We are men, Armand, and the word "Forgiveness" has only been spoken once these past two thousand years, and then it was spoken by Divine lips. But Marguerite loves you, and mayhap soon you will be all that is left her to love on this earth. Because of this she must never know.... As for you, Armand – well, God help you! But mesems that the hell which you are enduring now is ten thousand times worse than mine. I have heard your furtive footsteps in the corridor outside the grated window of this cell, and would not then have exchanged my hell for yours. Therefore, Armand, and because Marguerite loves you, I would wish to turn to you in the hour that I need help. I am in a tight corner, but the hour may come when a comrade's hand might mean life to me. I have thought of you, Armand: partly because having taken more than my life, your own belongs to me, and partly because the plan which I have in my mind will carry with it grave risks for the man who stands by me.

'I swore once that never would I risk a comrade's life to save mine own; but matters are so different now ... we are both in hell, Armand, and I in striving to get out of mine will be showing you a way out of yours.

'Will you retake possession of your lodgings in the Rue de la Croix Blanche? I should always know then where to find you in an emergency. But if at any time you receive another letter from me, be its contents what they may, act in accordance with the letter, and send a copy of it at once to Ffoulkes or to Marguerite. Keep in close touch with them both. Tell her I so far forgave your disobedience (there was nothing more) that I may yet trust my life and mine honour in your hands.

'I shall have no means of ascertaining definitely whether you will do all that I ask; but somehow, Armand, I know that you will.'

For the third time Armand read the letter through.

'But, Armand,' he repeated, murmuring the words softly under his breath, 'I know that you will.'

Prompted by some indefinable instinct, moved by a force that compelled, he allowed himself to glide from the chair on to the floor, on to his knees.

All the pent-up bitterness, the humiliation, the shame of the past few days, surged up from his heart to his lips in one great cry of pain.

'My God!' he whispered, 'give me the chance of giving my life for him.'

Alone and unwatched, he gave himself over for a few brief moments to the almost voluptuous delight of giving free rein to his grief. The hot Latin blood in him, tempestuous in all its passions, was firing his heart and brain now with the glow of devotion and of self-sacrifice.

Soon his mood calmed down, his look grew less wan and haggard. Hearing Jeanne's discreet and mouse-like steps in the next room, he rose quickly and hid the letter in the pocket of his coat.

She came in and inquired anxiously about Marguerite; a hurriedly expressed excuse from him, however, satisfied her easily enough. She wanted to be alone with Armand, happy to see that he held his head more erect today, and that the look as of a hunted creature had entirely gone from his eyes.

She ascribed this happy change to Marguerite, finding it in her heart to be grateful to the sister for having accomplished what the *fiancée* had failed to do.

For a while they remained together, sitting side by side, speaking at times, but mostly silent, seeming to savour the return of truant happiness, Armand felt like a sick man who had obtained a sudden surcease from pain. He looked round him with a kind of melancholy delight on this room which he had entered for the first time less than a fortnight ago, and which already was so full of memories.

Those first hours spent at the feet of Jeanne Lange, how exquisite they had been, how fleeting in the perfection of their happiness! Now they seemed to belong to a far distant past, evanescent like the perfume of violets, swift in their flight like the winged steps of youth. Blakeney's letter had effectually taken the bitter sting from out of his remorse, but it had increased his already over-heavy load of inconsolable sorrow.

Later in the day he turned his footsteps in the direction of the river, to the house in the Quai de la Ferraille above the saddler's shop. Marguerite had returned alone from the expedition to the Rue de Charonne. While Sir Andrew took charge of the little party of fugitives and escorted them out of Paris, she came back to her lodgings in order to collect her belongings, preparatory to taking up her quarters in the house of Lucas, the old-clothes dealer. She returned also because she hoped to see Armand.

'If you care to impart the contents of the letter to me, come to my lodgings tonight,' she had said.

All day a phantom had haunted her, the phantom of an agonizing suspicion.

But now the phantom had vanished never to return. Armand was sitting close beside her, and he told her that the chief had selected him among all the others to stand by him inside the walls of Paris until the last.

'I shall mayhap,' thus closed that precious document, 'have no means of ascertaining definitely whether you will act in accordance with this letter. But somehow, Armand, I know that you will.'

'I know that you will, Armand,' reiterated Marguerite fervently. She had only been too eager to be convinced.

Armand, trying to read his sister's thoughts in the depths of her blue eyes, found the look in them limpid and clear. Percy's message had reassured her just as he had intended that it should do. Fate had dealt over harshly with her as it was, and Blakeney's remorse for the sorrow which he had already caused her was scarcely less keen than Armand's. He did not wish her to bear the intolerable burden of hatred against her brother; and by binding St Just close to him at the supreme hour of danger he hoped to prove to the woman whom he loved so passionately that Armand was worthy of trust.

PART III

CHAPTER XXII

The last phase

'WELL? How is it now?'

'The last phase, I think.'

'He will yield?'

'He must.'

'Bah! you have said it yourself often enough; those English are tough.'

'It takes time to hack them to pieces, perhaps. In this case even you, citizen Chauvelin, said that it would take time. Well, it has taken just seventeen days, and now the end is in sight.'

It was close on midnight in the guard-room, which gave on the innermost cell of the Conciergerie. Héron had just visited the prisoner as was his wont at this hour of the night. He had watched the changing of the guard, inspected the night-watch, questioned the sergeant in charge, and finally he had been on the point of retiring to his own new quarters in the house of Justice, in the near vicinity of the Conciergerie, when citizen Chauvelin entered the guard-room unexpectedly and detained his colleague with the peremptory question:

'How is it now?'

'If you are so near the end, citizen Héron,' he now said, sinking his voice to a whisper, 'why not make a final effort and end it tonight?'

'I wish I could; the anxiety is wearing me out more than him,' he added with a jerky movement of the head in the direction of the inner cell.

'Shall I try?' rejoined Chauvelin grimly.

'Yes, as you wish.'

Chauvelin looked on his friend and associate with no small measure of contempt. He would no doubt have vastly preferred to conclude the present difficult transaction entirely in his own way and alone; but equally there was no doubt that the Committee of Public Safety did not trust him quite so fully as it used to do before the *fiasco* at Calais and the blunders at Boulogne.

Héron, on the other hand, enjoyed to its uttermost the confidence of his colleagues.

As far as the bringing of prisoners to trial was concerned the chief agent of the Committee of General Security had been given a perfectly free hand by the decree of the 27th Nivôse. At first, therefore, he had experienced no difficulty when he desired to keep the Englishman in close confinement for a time without hurrying on that summary trial and condemnation which the populace had loudly demanded, and to which they felt that they were entitled as a public holiday. The death of the Scarlet Pimpernel on the guillotine had been a spectacle promised by every demagogue who desired to purchase a few votes by holding out visions of pleasant doings to come; and during the first few days the mob of Paris was content to enjoy the delights of expectation.

But now seventeen days had gone by and still the Englishman was not being brought to trial. The pleasure-loving public was waxing impatient, and earlier this evening, when citizen Héron had shown himself in the stalls of the National Theatre, he was greeted by a crowded audience with decided expressions of disapproval and open mutterings of :

'What of the Scarlet Pimpernel?'

It almost looked as if he would have to bring that accursed Englishman to the guillotine without having wrested from him the secret which he would have given a fortune to possess. Chauvelin, who had also been present at the theatre, had heard the expressions of discontent; hence his visit to his colleague at this late hour of the night.

'Shall I try?' he had queried with some impatiece, and a deep sigh of satisfaction escaped his thin lips when the chief agent, wearied and discouraged, had reluctantly agreed.

'Let the men make as much noise as they like,' he added with an enigmatical smile. 'The Englishman and I will want an accompaniment to our pleasant conversation.'

Héron growled a surly assent, and without another word Chauvelin turned towards the inner cell. As he stepped in he allowed the iron bar to fall into its socket behind him. Then he went farther into the room until the distant recess was fully revealed to him. His tread had been furtive and almost noiseless. Now he paused, for he had caught sight of the prisoner. For a moment he stood quite still, with his hands clasped behind his back in his wonted animal attitude – quite still save for a strange, involuntary twitching of his mouth, and the nervous clasping and interlocking of his fingers behind his back. He was savouring to its utmost fulsomeness the supremest joy which animal man can ever know – the joy of looking on a fallen enemy.

Blakeney sat at the table with one arm resting on it, the emaciated hand tightly clutched, the body leaning forward, the eyes looking into nothingness.

For the moment he was unconscious of Chauvelin's presence, and the latter could gaze on him to the full content of his heart.

Indeed, to all outward appearances there sat a man whom privations of every sort and kind, the want of fresh air, of proper food, above all, of rest, had worn him down physically to a shadow. There was not a particle of colour in cheeks or lips, the skin was grey in hue, the eyes looked like deep caverns, wherein the glow of fever was all that was left of life.

Chauvelin now made a slight movement, and suddenly Blakeney became conscious of his presence, and swift as a flash a smile lit up his wan face.

'Why! if it is not my engaging friend Monsieur Chambertin,' he said gaily.

He rose and stepped forward in the most approved fashion prescribed by the elaborate etiquette of the time. But Chauvelin smiled grimly and a look of almost animal lust gleamed in his pale eyes, for he had noted that as he rose Sir Percy had to seek support of the table, even while a dull film appeared to gather over his eyes.

The gesture had been quick and cleverly disguised, but it had been there nevertheless – that and the livid hue that overspread the face as if consciousness was threatening to go. All of which was sufficient still further to assure the looker-on that that mighty physical strength was giving way at last, that strength which he had hated in his enemy almost as much as he had hated the thinly veiled insolence of his manner.

'And what procures me, sir, the honour of your visit?' continued Blakeney, who had – at any rate, outwardly – soon recovered himself, and whose voice, though distinctly hoarse and spent, rang quite cheerfully across the dank narrow cell.

'My desire for your welfare, Sir Percy,' replied Chauvelin with equal pleasantry.

'La, sir; but have you not gratified that desire already, to an extent which leaves no room for further solicitude? But I pray you, will you not sit down?' he continued, turning back towards the table. 'I was about to partake of the lavish supper which your friends have provided for me. Will you not share it, sir?

You are most royally welcome, and it will mayhap remind you of that supper we shared together in Calais, eh? when you, Monsieur Chambertin, were temporarily in holy orders.'

He laughed, offering his enemy a chair, and pointed with inviting gesture to the hunk of brown bread and the mug of water which stood on the table.

'Such as it is, sir,' he said with a pleasant smile, 'it is yours to command.'

Chauvelin sat down. He held his lower lip tightly between his teeth, so tightly that a few drops of blood appeared upon its narrow surface. He was making vigorous efforts to keep his temper under control, for he would not give his enemy the satisfaction of seeing him resent his insolence. He could afford to keep calm now that victory was at last in sight, now that he knew that he had but to raise a finger, and those smiling, impudent lips would be closed for ever at last.

'Sir Percy,' he resumed quietly, 'no doubt it affords you a certain amount of pleasure to aim your sarcastic shafts at me. I will not begrudge you that pleasure; in your present position, sir, your shafts have little or no sting.'

'And I shall have but few chances left to aim them at your charming self,' interposed Blakeney, who had drawn another chair close to the table and was now sitting opposite his enemy, with the light of the lamp falling on his own face, as if he wished his enemy to know that he had nothing to hide, no thought, no hope, no fear.

'Exactly,' said Chauvelin dryly. 'That being the case, Sir Percy, what say you to no longer wasting the few chances which are left to you for safety? The time is getting on. You are not, I imagine, quite as hopeful as you were even a week ago ... you have never been over-comfortable in this cell, why not end this unpleasant state of affairs now – once and for all? You'll not have cause to regret it. My word on it.'

Sir Percy leaned back in his chair. He yawned loudly and ostentatiously.

'I pray you, sir, forgive me,' he said. 'Never have I been so d—d fatigued. I have not slept for more than a fortnight.'

'Exactly, Sir Percy. A night's rest would do you a world of good.'

'A night, sir?' exclaimed Blakeney with what seemed like an echo of his former inimitable laugh. 'La! I should want a week.'

'I am afraid we could not arrange for that, but one night would greatly refresh you.'

'You are right, sir, you are right; but those d—d fellows in the next room make so much noise.'

'I would give strict orders that perfect quietude reigned in the guard-room this night,' said Chauvelin, murmuring softly, and there was a gentle purr in his voice, 'and that you were left undisturbed for several hours. I would give orders that a comforting supper be served to you at once, and that everything be done to minister to your wants.'

'That sounds d—d alluring, sir. Why did you not suggest this before?'

'You were so – what shall I say – so obstinate, Sir Percy?'

'Call it pig-headed, my dear Monsieur Chambertin,' retorted Blakeney gaily, 'truly you would oblige me.'

'In any case you, sir, were acting in direct opposition to your own interests.'

'Therefore you came,' concluded Blakeney airily, 'like the good Samaritan to take compassion on me and my troubles, and to lead me straight away to comfort, a good supper and a downy bed.'

'Admirably put, Sir Percy,' said Chauvelin blandly; 'that is exactly my mission.'

'How will you set to work, Monsieur Chambertin?'

'Quite easily, if you, Sir Percy, will yield to the persuasion of my friend citizen Héron.'

'Ah!'

'Why, yes! He is anxious to know where little Capet is. A reasonable whim, you will own, considering that the disappearance of the child is causing him grave anxiety.'

'And you, Monsieur Chambertin?' queried Sir Percy with that suspicion of insolence in his manner which had the power to irritate his enemy even now. 'And yourself, sir; what are your wishes in the matter?'

'Mine, Sir Percy?' retorted Chauvelin. 'Mine? Why, to tell you the truth, the fate of little Capet interests me but little. Let him rot in Austria or in our prisons, I care not which. He'll never trouble France overmuch, I imagine. The teachings of old Simon will not tend to make a leader or a king out of the puny brat whom you chose to drag out of our keeping. My wishes, sir, are the annihilation of your accursed League, and the lasting disgrace, if not the death, of its chief.'

While he spoke Blakeney had once more leaned forward, resting his elbows upon the table. Now he drew nearer to him the wooden platter on which reposed that very uninviting piece of dry bread. With solemn intentness he proceeded to break the bread into pieces; then he offered the platter to Chauvelin.

'I am sorry,' he said pleasantly, 'that I cannot spare you more dainty fare, sir.'

He crumbled some of the dry bread into his slender fingers, then started munching the crumbs with apparent relish. He poured out some water into the mug and drank it. Then he said with a light laugh :

'Even the vinegar which that ruffian Brogard served us at Calais was preferable to this, do you not imagine so, my good Monsieur Chambertin?'

Chauvelin made no reply. Like a feline creature on the prowl, he was watching the prey that had so nearly succumbed to his talons. Blakeney's face now was positively ghastly. The effort to speak, to laugh, to appear unconcerned, was apparently beyond his strength. His cheeks and lips were livid in hue, the skin clung like a thin layer of wax to the bones of cheek and jaw, and the heavy lids that fell over the eyes had purple patches on them like lead.

To a system in such an advanced state of exhaustion the stale water and dusty bread must have been terribly nauseating, and Chauvelin himself, callous and thirsting for vengeance though he was, could hardly bear to look calmly on the martyrdom of this man whom he and his colleagues were torturing in order to gain their own ends.

An ashen hue, which seemed like the shadow of the hand of death passed over the prisoner's face. Chauvelin felt compelled to avert his gaze.

When he looked round a second or two later that ephemeral fit of remorse did its final vanishing; he had once more encountered the pleasant smile, the laughing if ashen-pale face of his unconquered foe.

'Only a passing giddiness, my dear sir,' said Sir Percy lightly. 'As you were saying —'

At the airily spoken words, at the smile that accompanied them, Chauvelin had jumped to his feet. There was something almost supernatural, weird, and impish about the present situation, about this dying man who, like an impudent schoolboy, seemed to be mocking Death with his tongue in his cheek, about his laugh that appeared to find its echo in a widely yawning grave.

'In the name of God, Sir Percy,' he said roughly, as he brought his clenched fist crashing down upon the table, 'this situation is intolerable. Bring it to an end tonight!'

'Why, sir?' retorted Blakeney, 'methought you and your kind did not believe in God.'

'No. But you English do.'

'We do. But we do not care to hear His name on your lips.'

'Then in the name of the wife whom you love —'

But even before the words had died upon his lips, Sir Percy, too, had risen to his feet.

'Have done, man – have done,' he broke in hoarsely, and despite weakness, despite exhaustion and weariness, there was such a dangerous look in his hollow eyes as he leaned across the table that Chauvelin drew back a step or two, and – vaguely fearful – looked furtively towards the opening into the guard-room. 'Have done,' he reiterated for the third time; 'do not name her, or by the living God whom you dared invoke I'll find strength yet to smite you in the face.'

But Chauvelin, after that first moment of almost superstitious fear, had quickly recovered his *sang-froid*.

'Little Capet, Sir Percy,' he said, meeting the other's threatening glance with an imperturbable smile, 'tell me where to find him, and you may yet live to savour the caresses of the most beautiful woman in England.'

He had meant it as a taunt, the final turn of the thumb-screw applied to a dying man, and he had in that watchful, keen mind of his well-weighed the full consequences of the taunt.

The next moment he had paid to the full the anticipated price. Sir Percy had picked up the pewter mug from the table – it was half filled with brackish water – and with a hand that trembled but slightly he hurled it straight at his opponent's face.

The heavy mug did not hit citizen Chauvelin; it went crashing against the stone wall opposite. But the water was trickling from the top of his head, all down his eyes and cheeks. He shrugged his shoulders with a look of benign indulgence directed at his enemy, who had fallen back in his chair, exhausted with the effort.

Then he took out his handkerchief and calmly wiped the water from his face.

'Not quite so straight a shot as you used to be, Sir Percy,' he said mockingly.

'No, sir – apparently – not.'

The words came out in gasps. He was like a man only partly conscious. The lips were parted, the eyes closed, the head leaning against the high back of the chair. For the space of one second

Chauvelin feared that his zeal had outrun his prudence, that he had dealt a death-blow to a man in the last stage of exhaustion, where he had only wished to fan the flickering flame of life. Hastily – for the seconds seemed precious – he ran to the opening that led into the guard-room.

'Brandy – quick!' he cried.

Héron looked up, roused from the state of semi-somnolence in which he had lain for the past half-hour. He disentangled his long limbs from out of the guard-room chair.

'Eh?' he queried. 'What is it?'

'Brandy,' reiterated Chauvelin impatiently; 'the prisoner has fainted.'

'Bah!' retorted the other with a callous shrug of the shoulders, 'you are not going to revive him with brandy, I imagine.'

'No. But you will, citizen Héron,' rejoined the other dryly, 'for if you do not he'll be dead in an hour!'

'Devils in hell!' exclaimed Héron, 'you have not killed him? You – you d—d fool!'

He was wide awake enough now; wide awake and shaking with fury. Almost foaming at the mouth and uttering volleys of the choicest oaths, he elbowed his way roughly through the groups of soldiers who were crowding round the centre table of the guard-room, smoking and throwing dice or playing cards. They made way for him as hurriedly as they could, for it was not safe to thwart the citizen agent when he was in a rage.

Héron walked across to the opening and lifted the iron bar. With scant ceremony he pushed his colleague aside and strode into the cell, while Chauvelin, seemingly not resenting the other's ruffianly manners and violent language, followed closely upon his heel.

In the centre of the room both men paused, and Héron turned with a surly growl to his friend.

'You vowed he would be dead in an hour,' he said reproachfully.

The other shrugged his shoulders.

'It does not look like it now certainly,' he said dryly.

Blakeney was sitting – as was his wont – close to the table, with one arm leaning on it, the other, tightly clenched, resting upon his knee. A ghost of a smile hovered round his lips.

'Not in an hour, citizen Héron,' he said, and his voice now was scarce above a whisper, 'nor yet in two.'

'You are a fool, man,' said Héron roughly. 'You have had seventeen days of this. Are you not sick of it?'

'Heartily, my dear friend,' replied Blakeney a little more firmly.

'Seventeen days,' reiterated the other, nodding his shaggy head; 'you came here on the 2nd of Pluviôse, today is the 19th.'

'The 19th Pluviôse?' interposed Sir Percy, and a strange gleam suddenly flashed in his eyes. 'Demn it, sir, and in Christian parlance what may that day be?'

'The 7th of February at your service, Sir Percy,' replied Chauvelin quietly.

'I thank you, sir. In this d—d hole I had lost count of time.'

Chauvelin had been watching the prisoner very closely for the last moment or two, and even as he gazed, Blakeney slowly turned his eyes full upon him. Chauvelin's heart gave a triumphant bound. He knew that what he was watching now was no longer the last phase of a long and noble martyrdom; it was the end – the inevitable end – that for which he had schemed and striven.

Silence reigned in the narrow cell for a few moments, while two human jackals stood motionless over their captured prey. A savage triumph gleamed in Chauvelin's eyes, and even Héron, dull and brutal though he was, had become vaguely conscious of the great change that had come over the prisoner.

Blakeney, with a gesture and a sigh of hopeless exhaustion, had once more rested both his elbows on the table; his head fell heavy and almost lifeless downward in his arms.

'Curse you, man!' cried Héron almost involuntarily. 'Why in the name of hell did you wait so long?'

Then, as the prisoner made no reply, but only raised his head slightly, and looked on the other two men with dulled, wearied eyes, Chauvelin interposed calmly:

'More than a fortnight has been wasted in useless obstinacy, Sir Percy. Fortunately it is not too late.'

'Capet?' said Héron hoarsely, 'tell us, where is Capet?'

He leaned across the table, his eyes were bloodshot with the keenness of his excitement, his voice shook with the passionate desire for the crowning triumph.

'If you'll only not worry me,' murmured the prisoner; and the whisper came so laboriously and so low that both men were forced to bend their ears close to the scarcely moving lips; 'if you will let me sleep and rest, and leave me in peace —'

'The peace of the grave, man,' retorted Chauvelin roughly; 'if you will only speak. Where is Capet?'

'I cannot tell you; the way is long, the road – intricate.'

'Bah!'

'I'll lead you to him, if you will give me rest.'

'We don't want you to lead us anywhere,' growled Héron with a smothered curse; 'tell us where Capet is; we'll find him right enough.'

'I cannot explain; the way is intricate; the place off the beaten track, unknown except to me and my friends.'

Once more that shadow, which was so like the passing of the hand of Death, overspread the prisoner's face; his head rolled back against the chair.

'He'll die before he can speak,' muttered Chauvelin under his breath. 'You usually are well provided with brandy, citizen Héron.'

The latter no longer demurred. He saw the danger as clearly as did his colleague. It had been hell's own luck if the prisoner were to die now when he seemed ready to give in. He produced a flask from the pocket of his coat, and this he held to Blakeney's lips.

'Beastly stuff,' murmured the latter feebly. 'I think I'd sooner faint – than drink.'

'Capet? where is Capet?' reiterated Héron impatiently.

'One – two – three hundred leagues from here. I must let one of my friends know; he'll communicate with the others; they must be prepared,' replied the prisoner slowly.

Héron uttered a blasphemous oath.

'Where is Capet? Tell us where Capet is, or —'

He was like a raging tiger that had thought to hold its prey and suddenly realized that it was being snatched from him. He raised his fist, and without doubt the next moment he would have silenced for ever the lips that held the precious secret, but Chauvelin fortunately was quick enough to seize his wrist.

'Have a care, citizen,' he said peremptorily; 'have a care! You called me a fool just now when you thought I had killed the prisoner. It is his secret we want first; his death can follow afterwards.'

'I'll die in the open,' he whispered, 'not in this d—d hole.'

'Then tell us where Capet is.'

'I cannot; I wish to God I could. But I'll take you to him, I swear I will. I'll make my friends give him up to you. Do you think that I would not tell you now, if I could.'

Héron, whose every instinct of tyranny revolted against this thwarting of his will, would have continued to heckle the prisoner even now, had not Chauvelin suddenly interposed with an authoritative gesture.

'You'll gain nothing this way, citizen,' he said quietly; 'the man's mind is wandering; he is probably quite unable to give you clear directions at this moment.'

'I'll make that cursed Englishman speak yet,' he said with a fierce oath.

'You cannot,' retorted Chauvelin decisively. 'In his present state he is incapable of doing it, even if he would, which also is doubtful.'

'Ah! then you do think that he still means to cheat us?'

'Yes, I do. But I also know that he is no longer in a physical state to do it. No doubt he thinks that he is. A man of that type is sure to overvalue his own strength; but look at him, citizen Héron. Surely you must see that we have nothing to fear from him now.'

'I wish I were quite sure,' Héron said sullenly, 'that you were body and soul in accord with me.'

'I am in accord with you, citizen Héron,' rejoined the other earnestly – 'body and soul in accord with you. Do you not believe that I hate this man – aye! hate him with a hatred ten thousand times more strong than yours? I want his death – Heaven or hell alone knows how I long for that – but what I long for most is his lasting disgrace. For that I have worked, citizen Héron – for that I advised and helped you. When first you captured this man you wanted summarily to try him, to send him to the guillotine amidst the joy of the populace of Paris, and crowned with a splendid halo of martyrdom. That man, citizen Héron, would have baffled you, mocked you, and fooled you even on the steps of the scaffold. In the zenith of his strength and of his insurmountable good luck you and all your myrmidons and all the assembled guard of Paris would have had no power over him. The day that you led him out of this cell in order to take him to trial or to the guillotine would have been that of your helpless discomfiture. Having once walked out of this cell hale, hearty and alert, be the escort round him ever so strong, he never would have re-entered it again.'

'Yet you talk now of letting him walk out of this cell tomorrow?'

'He is a different man now, citizen Héron. On my advice you placed him on a régime that has counteracted the supernatural power by simple physical exhaustion, and driven to the four winds the host of demons who no doubt fled in the face of starvation.'

'If only I thought that the recapture of Capet was as vital to you as it is to me,' said Héron, still unconvinced.

'The capture of Capet is just as vital to me as it is to you,' rejoined Chauvelin earnestly, 'if it is brought about through the instrumentality of the Englishman.'

He paused, looking intently on his colleague, whose shifty eyes encountered his own. Thus eye to eye the two men at last understood one another.

'Ah!' said Héron with a snort, 'I think I understand.'

'I am sure that you do,' responded Chauvelin dryly. 'The disgrace of this cursed Scarlet Pimpernel and his League is as vital to me, and more, as the capture of Capet is to you. That is why I showed you the way to bring that meddlesome adventurer to his knees; that is why I will help you now both to find Capet with his aid and to wreak what reprisals you like on him in the end.'

Héron before he spoke again cast one more look on the prisoner. The latter had not stirred; his face was hidden, but the hands, emaciated, nerveless, and waxen, like those of the dead, told a more eloquent tale, mayhap, than the eyes could do. The chief agent of the Committee of General Security walked deliberately round the table until he stood once more close beside the man from whom he longed with passionate ardour to wrest an all-important secret. With brutal, grimy hand he raised the head that lay, sunken and inert, against the table; with callous eyes he gazed attentively on the face that was then revealed to him: he looked on the waxen flesh, the hollow eyes, the bloodless lips; then he shrugged his wide shoulders, and with a laugh that surely must have caused joy in hell, he allowed the wearied head to fall back against the outstretched arms, and turned once again to his colleague.

'I think you are right, citizen Chauvelin,' he said; 'there is not much supernatural power here. Let me hear your advice.'

CHAPTER XXIII

Capitulation

WHAT occurred within the inner cell of the Conciergerie prison within the next half-hour of that 19th day of Pluviôse in the year II. of the Republic is, perhaps, too well known to history to need or bear overfull repetition.

Chroniclers, intimate with the inner history of those infamous days, have told us how the chief agent of the Committee of General Security gave orders one hour after midnight that hot soup, white bread and wine be served to the prisoner, who for close on fourteen days previously had been kept on short rations of black bread and water; the sergeant in charge of the guard-room watch for the night also received strict orders that that same prisoner was on no account to be disturbed until the hour of six in the morning, when he was to be served with anything in the way of breakfast that he might fancy.

All this we know, and also that citizen Héron, having given all necessary orders for the morning's expedition, returned to the Conciergerie, and found his colleague Chauvelin waiting for him in the guard-room.

'Well?' he asked with febrile impatience – 'the prisoner?'

'He seems better and stronger,' replied Chauvelin.

'Not so well, I hope.'

'No, no, only just well enough.'

'You have seen him – since his supper?'

'Only from the doorway. It seems he ate and drank hardly at all, and the sergeant had some difficulty in keeping him awake until you came.'

'Well, now for the letter,' concluded Héron with the same marked feverishness of manner which sat so curiously on his uncouth personality. 'Pen, ink and paper, sergeant!' he commanded.

'On the table, in the prisoner's cell, citizen,' replied the sergeant.

He preceded the two citizens across the guard-room to the doorway, and raised for them the iron bar, lowering it back after them.

The next moment Héron and Chauvelin were once more face to face with their prisoner.

Whether by accident of design the lamp had been so placed that as the two men approached its light fell full upon their faces, while that of the prisoner remained in shadow. He was leaning forward with both elbows on the table, his thin, tapering fingers toying with the pen and ink-horn which had been placed close to his hand.

'I trust that everything has been arranged for your comfort, Sir Percy?' Chauvelin asked with a sarcastic little smile.

'I thank you, sir,' replied Blakeney politely.

'You feel refreshed, I hope?'

'Greatly so, I assure you. But I am still demmed sleepy; and if you would kindly be brief —'

'You have not changed your mind, sir?' queried Chauvelin, and a note of anxiety, which he vainly tried to conceal, quivered in his voice.

'No, my good M. Chambertin,' replied Blakeney with the same urbane courtesy, 'I have not changed my mind.'

A sigh of relief escaped the lips of both the men. The prisoner certainly had spoken in a clearer and firmer voice; but whatever renewed strength wine and food had imparted to him he apparently did not mean to employ in renewed obstinacy. Chauvelin, after a moment's pause, resumed more calmly:

'You are prepared to direct us to the place where little Capet lies hidden?'

'I am prepared to do anything, sir, to get out of this d—d hole.'

'Very well. My colleague, citizen Héron, has arranged for an escort of twenty men picked from the best regiment of the Garde de Paris to accompany us – yourself, him, and me – to wherever you will direct us. Is that clear?'

'Perfectly, sir.'

'You must not imagine for a moment that we, on the other hand, guarantee to give you your life and freedom even if this expedition prove unsuccessful.'

'I would not venture on suggesting such a wild proposition, sir,' said Blakeney placidly.

Chauvelin looked keenly on him. There was something in the tone of that voice that he did not altogether like – something that reminded him of an evening at Calais, and yet again of a day at Boulogne. He could not read the expression in the eyes, so with a quick gesture he pulled the lamp forward so that its light now fell full on the face of the prisoner.

'Ah! that is certainly better, is it not, my dear M. Chambertin?' said Sir Percy, beaming on his adversary with a pleasant smile.

His face, though still of the same hue, looked serene if hopelessly wearied; the eyes seemed to mock, but this Chauvelin decided in himself must have been a trick of his overwrought fancy. After a brief moment's pause he resumed dryly:

'If, however, the expedition turns out successful in every way – if little Capet, without much trouble to our escort, falls safe and sound into our hands – if certain contingencies which I am about to tell you all fall out as we wish – then, Sir Percy, I see no reason why the Government of this country should not exercise its prerogative of mercy towards you after all.'

'An exercise, my dear M. Chambertin, which must have wearied through frequent repetition,' retorted Blakeney with the same imperturbable smile.

'The contingency at present is somewhat remote; when the time comes we'll talk this matter over....I will make no promise ... and, anyhow, we can discuss it later.'

'At present we are but wasting our valuable time over so trifling a matter....If you'll excuse me, sir ... I am so demmed fatigued —'

'Then you will be glad to have everything settled quickly, I am sure.'

'Exactly, sir.'

'I see with pleasure, Sir Percy,' he said, 'that we thoroughly understand one another. Having had a few hours' rest you will, I know, feel quite ready for the expedition. Will you kindly indicate to me the direction in which we will have to travel?'

'Northwards all the way.'

'Towards the coast?'

'The place to which we must go is about seven leagues from the sea.'

'Our first objective then will be Beauvais, Amiens, Abbeville, Crécy, and so on?'

'Precisely.'

'As far as the forest of Boulogne, shall we say?'

'Where we shall come off the beaten track, and you will have to trust to my guidance.'

'We might go there now, Sir Percy, and leave you here.'

'You might. But you would not then find the child. Seven leagues is not far from the coast. He might slip through your fingers.'

'And my colleague Héron, being disappointed, would inevitably send you to the guillotine.'

'Quite so,' rejoined the prisoner placidly. 'Methought, sir, that we had decided that I should lead this little expedition? Surely,' he added, 'it is not so much the Dauphin whom you want as my share in this betrayal.'

'You are right as usual, Sir Percy. Therefore let us take that as settled. We go as far as Crécy, and thence place ourselves entirely in your hands.'

'The journey should not take more than three days, sir.'

'During which you will travel in a coach in the company of my friend Héron.'

'I could have chosen pleasanter company, sir; still, it will serve.'

'This being settled, Sir Percy, I understand that you desire to communicate with one of your followers.'

'Someone must let the others know ... those who have the Dauphin in their charge.'

'Quite so. Therefore I pray you write to one of your friends that you have decided to deliver the Dauphin into our hands in exchange for your own safety.'

'You said just now that this you would not guarantee?' interposed Blakeney quietly.

'If all turns out well,' retorted Chauvelin with a show of contempt, 'and if you will write the exact letter which I shall dictate, we might even give you that guarantee.'

'The quality of your mercy, sir, passes belief.'

'Then I pray you write. Which of your followers will have the honour of the communication?'

'My brother-in-law, Armand St Just; he is still in Paris, I believe. He can let the others know.'

Chauvelin paused awhile, hesitating. Would Sir Percy Blakeney be ready – if his own safety demanded it – to sacrifice the man who had betrayed him?

But the friend as hostage was only destined to be a minor leverage for the final breaking-up of the League of the Scarlet Pimpernel through the disgrace of its chief.

Blakeney quietly drew pen and paper towards him, and made ready to write.

'What do you wish me to say?' he asked simply.

'Will that young blackguard answer your purpose, citizen Chauvelin?' queried Héron roughly.

Obviously the same doubt had crossed his mind. Chauvelin quickly reassured him.

'Better than anyone else,' he said firmly. 'Will you write in French and at my dictation, Sir Percy?'

'I am waiting to do so, my dear sir.'

'Begin your letter as you wish, then; now continue.'

And he began to dictate slowly – in French – and watching every word as it left Blakeney's pen.

' "I cannot stand my present position any longer. Citizen Héron and also M. Chauvelin—" Yes, Sir Percy, Chauvelin, not Chambertin ... C, H, A, U, V, E, L, I, N ... . That is quite right – "have made this prison a perfect hell for me." '

Sir Percy looked up from his writing, smiling.

'You wrong yourself my dear M. Chambertin!' he said; 'I have really been most comfortable.'

'I wish to place the matter before your friends in as indulgent a manner as I can,' retorted Chauvelin dryly.

'I thank you, sir. Pray proceed.'

'... "a perfect hell for me,"' resumed the other. 'Have you that? ... "and I have been forced to give way. Tomorrow we start from here at dawn; and I will guide citizen Héron to the place where he can find the Dauphin. But the authorities demand that one of my followers, one who has once been a member of the League of the Scarlet Pimpernel, shall accompany me on this expedition. I therefore ask you? – or "desire you" or "beg you" – whichever you prefer, Sir Percy ...'

' "Ask you" will do quite nicely. This is really very interesting, you know.'

'... "to be prepared to join the expedition. We start at dawn, and you would be required to be at the main gate of the house of Justice at six o'clock precisely. I have an assurance from the authorities that your life shall be inviolate, but if you refuse to accompany me the guillotine will await me on the morrow.'

' "The guillotine will await me on the morrow." That sounds quite cheerful, does it not, M. Chambertin,' said the prisoner, who had not evinced the slightest surprise at the wording of the letter while he wrote at the other's dictation. 'Do you know, I quite enjoyed writing this letter; it so reminded me of happy days in Boulogne.'

'The conditions are somewhat different now,' he said placidly, 'from those that reigned in Boulogne. But will you not sign your letter, Sir Percy?'

'With pleasure, sir,' responded Blakeney, as with an elaborate flourish of the pen he appended his name to the missive.

Chauvelin was watching him with eyes that would have shamed a lynx by their keenness. He took up the completed letter, read it through very carefully, as if to find some hidden meaning behind the very words which he himself had dictated; he studied the signature, and looked vainly for a mark or sign that might convey a different sense to that which he had intended. Finally, finding none, he folded the letter up with his own hand, and at once slipped it in the pocket of his coat.

'Take care, M. Chambertin,' said Blakeney lightly; 'it will burn a hole in that elegant vest of yours.'

'It will have no time to do that, Sir Percy,' retorted Chauvelin blandly; 'and if you will furnish me with citizen St Just's present address I will myself convey the letter to him at once.'

'At this hour of the night? Poor old Armand, he'll be abed. But his address, sir, is No. 32, Rue de la Croix Blanche, on the first floor, the door on your right as you mount the stairs; you know the room well, citizen Chauvelin; you have been in it before. And now,' he added with a loud and ostentatious yawn, 'shall we all go to bed? We start at dawn, you said, and I am so d—d fatigued.'

Frankly, he did not look it now. Chauvelin himself, despite his matured plans, despite all the precautions that he meant to take for the success of this gigantic scheme, felt a sudden strange sense of fear creeping into his bones. Half an hour ago he had seen a man in what looked like the last stage of utter physical exhaustion, a hunched-up figure, listless and limp, hands that twitched nervously, the face as of a dying man. Now those outward symptoms were still there certainly; the face by the light of the lamp still looked livid, the lips bloodless, the hands emaciated and waxen; but the eyes! – they were still hollow with heavy lids still purple, but in their depths there was a curious, mysterious light, a look that seemed to see something that was hidden to natural sight.

Citizen Chauvelin thought that Héron, too, must be conscious of this, but the Committee's agent was sprawling on a chair, sucking a short-stemmed pipe, and gazing with entire animal satisfaction on the prisoner.

'The most perfect piece of work we have ever accomplished, you and I, citizen Chauvelin,' he said complacently.

'You think that everything is quite satisfactory?' asked the other, with anxious stress on his words.

'Everything, of course. Now, you see to the letter. I will give final orders for tomorrow, but I shall sleep in the guard-room.'

'And I on that inviting bed,' interposed the prisoner lightly, as he rose to his feet. 'Your servant, citizens!'

He bowed his head slightly, and stood by the table while the two men prepared to go. Chauvelin took a final long look at the man whom he firmly believed he had at last brought down to abject disgrace.

Blakeney was standing erect, watching the two retreating figures – one slender hand was on the table. Chauvelin saw that it was leaning rather heavily, as if for support and that even while a final mocking laugh sped him and his colleague on their way, the tall figure of the conquered lion swayed like a stalwart oak that is forced to bend to the mighty fury of an all-compelling wind.

With a sigh of content Chauvelin took his colleague by the arm, and together the two men walked out of the cell.

*   *   *

Two hours after midnight Armand St Just was wakened from sleep by a peremptory pull at his bell. In these days in Paris but one meaning could, as a rule, be attached to such a summons at this hour of the night, and Armand, though possessed of an unconditional certificate of safety, sat up in bed, quite convinced that for some reason which would presently be explained to him he had once more been placed on the list of the 'suspect', and that his trial and condemnation on a trumped-up charge would follow in due course.

'In the name of the people!'

He had expected to hear not only those words, but also the grounding of arms and the brief command to halt. He had expected to see before him the white facings of the uniform of the Guarde de Paris, and to feel himself roughly pushed back into his room preparatory to the search being made of all his effects and the placing of irons on his wrists.

Instead of this, it was a quiet, dry voice that said without undue harshness:

'In the name of the people!'

And instead of the uniforms, the bayonets and the scarlet caps with tricolour cockades, he was confronted by a slight, sable-clad figure, whose face, lit by the flickering light of the tallow candle, looked strangely pale and earnest.

'Citizen Chauvelin!' gasped Armand, more surprised than frightened at this unexpected apparition.

'Himself, citizen, at your service,' replied Chauvelin, with his quiet, ironical manner. 'I am the bearer of a letter for you from Sir Percy Blakeney. Have I your permission to enter?'

Mechanically Armand stood aside, allowing the other man to pass in. He closed the door behind his nocturnal visitor, then, candle in hand, he preceded him into the inner room.

'Shall I light the lamp?' he asked.

'Quite unnecessary,' replied Chauvelin curtly. 'I have only a letter to deliver, and after that to ask you one brief question.'

From the pocket of his coat he drew the letter which Blakeney had written an hour ago.

'The prisoner wrote this in my presence,' he said as he handed the letter over to Armand. 'Will you read it?'

Armand took it from him, and sat down close to the table; leaning forward, he held the paper near the light, and began to read. He read the letter through very slowly to the end, then once again from the beginning. He was trying to do that which Chauvelin had wished to do an hour ago; he was trying to find the inner meaning which he felt must inevitably lie behind these words, which Percy had written with his own hand.

Swiftly his thoughts flew back to that other letter, the one which Marguerite had given him – the letter full of pity and of friendship, which had brought him hope and a joy and peace which he had thought at one time that he would never know again. And suddenly one sentence in that letter stood out so clearly before his eyes that it blurred the actual, tangible ones on the paper which even now rustled in his hand.

'But if at any time you receive another letter from me – be its contents what they may – act in accordance with the letter, and send a copy of it at once to Ffoulkes or to Marguerite.'

Now everything seemed at once quite clear; his duty, his next actions, every word that he would speak to Chauvelin. Those that Percy had written to him were already indelibly graven on his memory.

Chauvelin had waited with his usual patience, silent and imperturbable, while the young man read. Now, when he saw that Armand had finished, he said quietly:

'Just one question, citizen, and I need not detain you longer. But, first, will you kindly give me back that letter? It is a precious document which will for ever remain in the archives of the nation.'

But even while he spoke Armand, with one of those quick intuitions that come in moments of acute crisis, had done just that which he felt Blakeney would wish him to do. He had held the letter close to the candle. A corner of the thin crisp paper immediately caught fire, and before Chauvelin could utter a word of anger or make a movement to prevent the conflagration the flames had licked up fully one half of the letter, and Armand had only just time to throw the remainder on the floor and to stamp out the blaze with his foot.

'I am sorry, citizen,' he said calmly; 'an accident.'

'A useless act of devotion,' interposed Chauvelin, who already had smothered the oath that had risen to his lips. 'The Scarlet Pimpernel's actions in the present matter will not lose their merited publicity through the foolish destruction of this document.'

'I had no thought, citizen,' retorted the young man, 'of commenting on the actions of my chief, or of trying to deny them that publicity which you seem to desire for them almost as much as I do.'

'More, citizen, a great deal more! The impeccable Scarlet Pimpernel, the noble and gallant English gentleman, has agreed to deliver into our hands the uncrowned King of France – in exchange for his own life and freedom. Methinks that even his worst enemy would not wish for a better ending to a career of adventure and a reputation for bravery unequalled in Europe. But no more of this, time is pressing, I must help citizen Héron with his final preparations for his journey. You, of course, citizen St Just, will act in accordance with Sir Percy Blakeney's wishes?'

'Of course,' replied Armand.

'You will present yourself at the main entrance of the house of Justice at six o'clock this morning.'

'I will not fail you.'

'You will be a hostage in our hands, citizen; your life a guarantee that your chief has no thought of playing us false.'

'I have spent the last fortnight in praying to God that my life might yet be given for his,' retorted Armand, proud and defiant.

'Even were Sir Percy Blakeney prepared to wreak personal revenge on you, he would scarcely be so foolish as to risk the other life which we shall also hold as hostage for his good faith.'

'The other life?'

'Yes. Your sister, Lady Blakeney, will also join the expedition tomorrow. This Sir Percy does not yet know; but it will come as a pleasant surprise for him. At the slightest suspicion of false play on Sir Percy's part, at his slightest attempt at escape, your life and that of your sister are forfeit; you will both be summarily shot before his eyes. I think that I need not detain you any longer, citizen St Just. I wish you good night, citizen.'

'Good night,' murmured Armand mechanically.

He took the candle and escorted his visitor back to the door.

He waited on the landing, candle in hand, while Chauvelin descended the narrow winding stairs. Then, satisfied that Chauvelin had finally gone, he turned back to his own rooms and carefully locked the outer door. Then he lit the lamp, for the candle gave but a flickering light, and he had some important work to do.

Firstly, he picked up the charred fragment of the letter and smoothed it out carefully and reverently as he would a relic. Tears had gathered in his eyes, but he was not ashamed of them, for no one saw them; but they eased his heart, and helped to strengthen his resolve. It was a mere fragment that had been spared by the flame, but Armand knew every word of the letter by heart.

He had pen, ink and paper ready to his hand, and from memory wrote out a copy of it. To this he added a covering letter from himself to Marguerite:

'This – which I had from Percy through the hands of Chauvelin – I neither question nor understand.... He wrote the letter, and I have no thought but to obey. In his previous letter to me he enjoined me, if ever he wrote to me again, to obey him implicitly, and to communicate with you. To both these commands do I submit with a glad heart. But of this must I give you warning – Chauvelin desires you also to accompany us tomorrow.... Percy does not know this yet, else he would never start. But those fiends fear that his readiness is a blind ... and that he has some plan in his head for his own escape and the continued safety of the Dauphin. ... This plan they hope to frustrate through holding you and me as hostages for his good faith. God only knows how gladly I would give my life for my chief ... but your life is sacred above all.... I think that I do right in warning you. God help us all.'

Having written the letter, he sealed it, together with the copy of Percy's letter which he had made. Then he took up the candle and went downstairs.

There was no longer any light in the concierge's lodge, and Armand had some difficulty in making himself heard. At last the woman came to the door. She was tired and cross after two interruptions of her night's rest, but she had a partiality for her young lodger, whose pleasant ways and easy liberality had been like a pale ray of sunshine through the squalor of everyday misery.

'It is a letter, *citoyenne*,' said Armand, with earnest entreaty, 'for my sister. She lives in the Rue de Charonne, near the fortifications, and must have it within an hour; it is a matter of life and death to her, to me, and to another who is very dear to us both.'

The concierge threw up her hands in horror.

'Rue de Charonne, near the fortifications,' she exclaimed, 'and within an hour! By the Holy Virgin, citizen, that is impossible. Who will take it? There is no way.'

'A way must be found, *citoyenne*,' said Armand firmly, 'and at once; it is not far, and there are five golden louis waiting for the messenger!'

Five golden louis! The poor, hard-working woman's eyes gleamed at the thought. Five louis meant food for at least two months if one was careful, and—

'Give me the letter, citizen,' she said, 'time to slip on a warm petticoat and a shawl, and I'll go myself. It's not fit for the boy to go at this hour.'

'You will bring me back a line from my sister in reply to this,' said Armand, whom circumstances had at last rendered cautious. 'Bring it up to my room that I may give you the five louis in exchange.'

CHAPTER XXIV

God help us all

In a small upstairs room in the Rue de Charonne, above the shop of Lucas the old-clothes dealer, Marguerite sat with Sir Andrew Ffoulkes. Armand's letter, with its message and its warning, lay open on the table between them, and she had in her hand the sealed packet which Percy had given her just ten days ago, and which she was only to open if all hope seemed to be dead, if nothing appeared to stand any longer between that one dear life and irretrievable shame.

A small lamp placed on the table threw a feeble yellow light on the squalid, ill-furnished room, for it lacked still an hour or so before dawn. Armand's concierge had brought her lodger's letter, and Marguerite had quickly dispatched a brief reply to him, a reply that held love and also encouragement.

Then she had summoned Sir Andrew. He never had a thought of leaving her during these days of dire trouble, and he had lodged all this while in a tiny room on the topmost floor of this house in the Rue de Charonne.

At her call he had come down very quickly, and now they sat together at the table, with the oil-lamp illuminating their pale, anxious faces; she the wife and he the friend holding a consultation together in this most miserable hour that preceded the cold wintry dawn.

'I can see now,' said Marguerite in that calm voice which comes so naturally in moments of infinite despair – 'I can see now exactly what Percy meant when he made me promise not to open this packet until it seemed to me – to me and to you, Sir Andrew – that he was about to play the part of a coward. A coward! Great God!' She checked the sob that had risen to her throat, and continued in the same calm manner and quiet, even voice:

'You do think with me, do you not, that the time has come, and that we must open this packet?'

'Without a doubt, Lady Blakeney,' replied Ffoulkes with equal earnestness. 'I would stake my life that already a fortnight ago Blakeney had that same plan in his mind which he has now matured. Escape from that awful Conciergerie prison with all the precautions so carefully taken against it was impossible. I knew that alas! from the first. But in the open all might yet be different. I'll not believe it that a man like Blakeney is destined to perish at the hands of those curs.'

'God bless you, Sir Andrew, for your enthusiasm and for your trust,' she said with a sad little smile; 'but for you I should long ago have lost all courage, and these last ten days – what a cycle of misery they represent – would have been maddening but for your help and your loyalty. God knows I would have courage for everything in life, for everything save one. But just that – his death – that would be beyond my strength – neither reason nor body could stand it. Therefore, I am so afraid, Sir Andrew....' she added piteously.

'Of what, Lady Blakeney?'

'That when he knows that I too am to go as hostage, as Armand says in his letter, that my life is to be guarantee for his, I am afraid that he will draw back ... that he will....Oh, my God!' she cried with sudden fervour, 'tell me what to do!'

'Shall we open the packet?' asked Ffoulkes gently, 'and then just make up our minds to act exactly as Blakeney has enjoined us to do, neither more nor less, but just word for word, deed for deed, and I believe that that will be right – whatever may betide – in the end.'

Once more his quiet strength, his earnestness, and his faith comforted her. She dried her eyes and broke open the seal. There were two separate letters in the packet, one unaddressed; obviously intended for her and Ffoulkes, the other was addressed to

M. le Baron Jean de Batz, 15 Rue St Jean de Latran à Paris.

'A letter addressed to that awful Baron de Batz,' said Marguerite, looking with puzzled eyes on the paper as she turned it over and over in her hand, 'to that bombastic windbag! I know him and his ways well! What can Percy have to say to him?'

Sir Andrew too looked puzzled. But neither of then had the mind to waste time in useless speculations. Marguerite unfolded the letter which was intended for her, and after a final look on her friend, whose kind face was quivering with excitement, she began slowly to read aloud:

'I need not ask either of you two to trust me, knowing that you will. But I could not die inside this hole like a rat in a trap – I had to try and free myself, at the worst to die in the open beneath God's sky. You two will understand, and understanding you will trust me to the end. Send the enclosed letter at once to its address. And you, Ffoulkes my most sincere and most loyal friend, I beg with all my soul to see to the safety of Marguerite. Armand will stay by me – but you, Ffoulkes, do not leave her, stand by her. As soon as you read this letter – and you will not read it until both she and you have felt that hope has fled and I myself am about to throw up the sponge – try and persuade her to make for the coast as quickly as may be.... At Calais you can open up communications with the *Daydream* in the usual way, and embark on her at once. Let no member of the League remain on French soil an hour longer after that. Then tell the skipper to make for Le Portel – the place which he knows – and there to keep a sharp outlook for another three nights. After that make straight for home, for it will be no use waiting any longer. I shall not come. These measures are for Marguerite's safety, and for you all who are in France at this moment. Comrade, I entreat you to look on these measures as on my dying wish. To de Batz I have given *rendezvous* at the Chapelle of the Holy Sepulchre, just outside the park of the Château d'Ourde. He will help me to save the Dauphin, and if by good luck he also helps me to save myself I shall be within seven leagues of Le Portel, and with the Liane frozen as she is I could reach the coast.

'But Marguerite's safety I leave in your hands, Ffoulkes. Would that I could look more clearly into the future, and know that those devils will not drag her into danger. Beg her to start at once for Calais immediately you have both read this. I only beg, I do not command. I know that you, Ffoulkes, will stand by her whatever she may wish to do. God's blessing be for ever on you both.'

'We can but hope, Lady Blakeney,' said Sir Andrew Ffoulkes after a while, 'that you will be allowed out of Paris; but from what Armand says —'

'And Percy does not actually send me away,' she rejoined with a pathetic little smile.

'No. He cannot compel you, Lady Blakeney. You are not a member of the League.'

'Oh, yes I am!' she retorted firmly: 'and I have sworn obedience, just as all of you have done. I will go, just as he bids me, and you, Sir Andrew, you will obey him too?'

'My orders are to stand by you. That is an easy task.'

'You know where this place is?' she asked – 'the Château d'Ourde?'

'Oh, yes, we all know it! It is empty, and the park is a wreck; the owner fled from it at the very outbreak of the revolution; he left some kind of steward nominally in charge, a curious creature, half imbecile; the château and the chapel in the forest just outside the grounds have oft served Blakeney and all of us as a place of refuge on our way to the coast.'

'But the Dauphin is not there?' she said.

'No. According to the first letter which you brought me from Blakeney ten days ago, and on which I acted, Tony, who has charge of the Dauphin, must have crossed into Holland with his little Majesty today.'

'I understand,' she said simply. 'But then – this letter to de Batz?'

'Ah, there I am completely at sea! But I'll deliver it, and at once too, only I don't like to leave you. Will you let me get you out of Paris first? I think just before dawn it could be done. We can get the cart from Lucas, and if we could reach St Germain before noon, I could come straight back then and deliver the letter to de Batz. This, I feel I ought to do myself; but at Achard's farm I would know that you were safe for a few hours.'

'I will do whatever you think right, Sir Andrew,' she said simply; 'my will is bound up with Percy's dying wish. God knows I would rather follow him now, step by step – as hostage, as prisoner – any way so long as I can see him, but —'

She rose and turned to go, almost impassive now in that great calm born of despair.

'Ten minutes and I'll be ready, Sir Andrew,' she said. 'I have but few belongings. Will you the while see Lucas about the cart?'

He did as she desired. Her calm in no way deceiving him; he knew that she must be suffering keenly, and would suffer more keenly still while she would be trying to efface her own personal feelings all through the coming dreary journey to Calais.

He went to see the landlord about the horse and cart and a quarter of an hour later Marguerite came downstairs ready to start. She found Sir Andrew in close converse with an officer of the Garde de Paris, while two soldiers of the same regiment were standing at the horse's head.

When she appeared in the doorway Sir Andrew came at once up to her.

'It is just as I feared, Lady Blakeney,' he said; 'this man has been sent here to take charge of you. Of course, he knows nothing beyond the fact that his orders are to convey you at once to the guard-house of the Rue St Anne, where he is to hand you over to citizen Chauvelin of the Committee of Public Safety.'

Sir Andrew could not fail to see the look of intense relief, which in the midst of all her sorrow, seemed suddenly to have lighted up the whole of Marguerite's wan face. The thought of wending her own way to safety while Percy, mayhap, was fighting an uneven fight with death had been well-nigh intolerable; but she had been ready to obey without a murmur. Now Fate and the enemy himself had decided otherwise. She felt as if a load had been lifted from her heart.

'I will at once go and find de Batz,' Sir Andrew contrived to whisper hurriedly. 'As soon as Percy's letter is safely in his hands I will make my way northwards and communicate with all the members of the League. I myself will go by land to Le Portel, and thence, if I have no news of you or of the expedition, I will slowly work southwards in the direction of the Château d'Ourde. That is all that I can do. If you can contrive to let Percy or even Armand know my movements, do so by all means. I know that I shall be doing right, for, in a way, I shall be watching over you and arranging for your safety, as Blakeney begged me to do. God bless you, Lady Blakeney, and God save the Scarlet Pimpernel!'

He stooped and kissed her hand, and she intimated to the officer that she was ready. He had a hackney coach waiting for her lower down the street. To it she walked with a firm step, and as she entered it she waved a last farewell to Sir Andrew Ffoulkes.

*　　*　　*

The little *cortège* was turning out of the great gates of the house of Justice. It was intensely cold; a bitter north-easterly gale was blowing from across the heights of Montmartre, driving sleet and snow and half frozen rain into the faces of the men, and finding its way up their sleeves, down their collars, and round the knees of their threadbare breeches.

Armand, whose fingers were numb with the cold, could scarcely feel the reins in his hands. Chauvelin was riding close beside him, but the two men had not exchanged one word since the moment when the small troop of some twenty mounted soldiers had filed up inside the courtyard, and Chauvelin, with a curt word of command, had ordered one of the troopers to take Armand's horse on the lead.

A hackney coach brought up the rear of the *cortège*, with a man riding at either door and two more following at a distance of twenty paces. Héron's gaunt, ugly face, crowned with a battered sugar-loaf hat, appeared from time to time at the window of the coach. He was no horseman, and, moreover, preferred to keep the prisoner closely under his own eye. The corporal had told Armand that the prisoner was with citizen Héron inside the coach – in irons. Beyond that, the soldiers could tell him nothing.

At last the more closely populated quarters of the city were left behind and a halt was called.

It was quite light now. As light as it would ever be beneath this leaden sky. Rain and snow still fell in gusts, driven by the blast.

Someone ordered Armand to dismount. He did as he was told, and a trooper led him to the door of an irregular brick building that stood isolated on the right, extended on either side by a low wall, and surrounded by a patch of uncultivated land, which now looked like a sea of mud. Mechanically Armand had followed the soldier to the door of the building. Here Chauvelin was standing, and bade him follow. Chauvelin led the way to a room on the left.

There was a table in the middle of the room, and on it stood cups of hot coffee. Chauvelin bade him drink, suggesting, not unkindly, that the warm beverage would do him good. Armand advanced farther into the room, and saw that there were wooden benches all round against the wall. On one of these sat his sister Marguerite.

When she saw him she made a sudden, instinctive movement to go to him, but Chauvelin interposed in his usual bland, quiet manner.

'Not just now, citizeness,' he said.

She sat down again, and Armand noted how cold and stony seemed her eyes, as if life within her was at a standstill and a shadow that was almost like death had atrophied every emotion in her.

'I trust you have not suffered too much from the cold, Lady Blakeney,' resumed Chauvelin politely; 'we ought not to have kept you waiting here for so long, but delay at departure is sometimes inevitable.'

She made no reply, only acknowledging his reiterated inquiry as to her comfort with an inclination of the head.

Armand had forced himself to swallow some coffee, and for the moment he felt less chilled. He held the cup between his two hands, and gradually some warmth crept into his bones.

'Try and drink some of this, it will do you good,' he said.

'Thank you, dear,' she replied. 'I have had some. I am not cold.'

Then a door at the end of the room was pushed open, and Héron stalked in.

'Are we going to be all day in this confounded hole?' he queried roughly.

Armand, who was watching his sister very closely, saw that she started at sight of the wretch, and seemed immediately to shrink still further within herself, while her eyes, suddenly luminous and dilated, rested on him like those of a captive bird upon an approaching cobra.

But Chauvelin was not to be shaken out of his suave manner.

'One moment, citizen Héron,' he said; 'this coffee is very comforting. Is the prisoner with you?' he added lightly. 'Perhaps, you will be so good, citizen, to invite him hither.'

A second or two later Sir Percy Blakeney stood in the doorway; his hands were behind his back, obviously handcuffed, but he held himself very erect, though it was clear that this caused him a mighty effort. As soon as he had crossed the threshold his quick glance swept round the room.

He saw Armand, and his eyes lit up almost imperceptibly.

Then he caught sight of Marguerite, and his pale face took on suddenly a more ashen hue.

With a slight, imperceptible movement – imperceptible to everyone save to him, she had seemed to handle a piece of paper in her kerchief, then she had nodded slowly, with her eyes – steadfast, reassuring – fixed upon him: and his glance gave answer that he had understood.

But Chauvelin and Héron had seen nothing of this. They were satisfied that there had been no communication between the prisoner and his wife and friend.

'You are no doubt surprised, Sir Percy,' said Chauvelin after a while, 'to see Lady Blakeney here. She, as well as citizen St Just, will accompany our expedition to the place where you will lead us. We none of us know where that place is – citizen Héron and myself are entirely in your hands – you might be leading us to certain death, or again to a spot where your own escape would be an easy matter to yourself. You will not be surprised, therefore, that we have thought fit to take certain precautions both against any little ambuscade which you have prepared for us, or against your making one of those daring attempts to escape for which the noted Scarlet Pimpernel is so justly famous. At the slightest suspicion that you have played us false, your friend and your wife will be summarily shot before your eyes.'

'You leave me no option in that case. As you have remarked before, citizen Héron, why should we wait any longer? Surely we can now go.'

CHAPTER XXV

The halt at Crécy

'Now, then, citizen, don't go to sleep: this is Crécy, our last halt!'

Armand woke up from his last dream. They had been moving steadily on since they left Abbeville soon after dawn; the rumble of the wheels, the swaying of the carriage, the interminable patter of the rain, had lulled him into a kind of wakeful sleep. There had been three days of this awful monotony.

Chauvelin had already alighted from the coach. He was helping Marguerite to descend. Armand shook the stiffness from his limbs and followed in the wake of his sister. Always those miserable soldiers round them, with their dank coats of rough blue cloth and the red caps on their heads! Armand pulled

Marguerite's hand through his arm, and dragged her with him into the house.

The small city lay damp and grey before them; the rough pavement of the narrow street glistened with the wet, reflecting the dull, leaden sky overhead; the rain beat into the puddles; the slate-roofs shone in the cold wintry light.

This was Crécy! The last halt of the journey, so Chauvelin had said. The party had drawn rein in front of a small one-storied building that had a wooden verandah running the whole length of its front.

Marguerite seemed dazed and giddy; she had been five hours in that stuffy coach with nothing to distract her thoughts except the rain-sodden landscape, on which she had ceaselessly gazed since the early dawn.

Armand led her to the bench, and she sank down on it, numb and inert, resting her elbows on the table and her head in her hands.

'If it were only all over!' she sighed involuntarily. 'Armand, at times now I feel as if I were not really sane, as if my reason had already given way! Tell me, do I seem mad to you at times?'

He sat down beside her and tried to chafe her cold little hands.

There was a knock at the door, and without waiting for permission Chauvelin entered the room.

'My humble apologies to you, Lady Blakeney,' he said in his usual suave manner, 'but our worthy host informs me that this is the only room in which he can serve a meal. Therefore I am forced to intrude my presence upon you.'

Though he spoke with outward politeness, his tone had become more peremptory, less bland, and he did not await Marguerite's reply before he sat down opposite to her and continued to talk airily.

'An ill-conditioned fellow, our host,' he said – 'quite reminds me of our friend Brogard, at the Chat Gris, in Calais? You remember him, Lady Blakeney?'

'My sister is giddy, and over-tired,' interposed Armand firmly. 'I pray you, citizen, to have some regard for her.'

'All the regard in the world, citizen St Just,' protested Chauvelin jovially. 'Methought that those pleasant reminiscences would cheer her. Ah! here comes the soup,' he added, as a man in blue blouse and breeches; with sabots on his feet, slouched into the room, carrying a tureen which he incontinently placed upon the table. 'I feel sure that in England Lady Blakeney misses

167

our excellent *croûtes-au-pot*, the glory of our *bourgeois* cookery. Lady Blakeney, a little soup?'

'I thank you, sir,' she murmured.

'Do try and eat something,' Armand whispered in her ear; 'try and keep up your strength, for his sake, if not for mine.'

She turned a wan, pale face to him, and tried to smile.

'I'll try, dear,' she said.

'You have taken bread and meat to the citizens in the coach?' Chauvelin called out to the retreating figure of mine host.

'H'm!' grunted the latter in assent.

'And see that the citizen soldiers are well fed, or there will be trouble.'

'H'm!' grunted the man again. After which he banged the door to behind him.

'Citizen Héron is loath to let the prisoner out of his sight,' explained Chauvelin lightly, 'now that we have reached the last, most important stage of our journey, so he is sharing Sir Percy's midday meal in the interior of the coach.'

He ate his soup with a relish, ostentatiously paying many small attentions to Marguerite all the time. He ordered meat for her – bread, butter – asked if any dainties could be got. He was apparently in the best of tempers.

After he had eaten and drunk he rose and bowed ceremoniously to her.

'Your pardon, Lady Blakeney,' he said, 'but I must confer with the prisoner now, and take from him full directions for the continuance of our journey.' He hurried out of the room, and Armand and Marguerite could hear him ordering the soldiers to take them forthwith back to the coach.

As they came out of the inn they saw the other coach some fifty metres farther up the street. Héron's hideous face, appeared at the carriage window. He cursed violently and at the top of his voice.

'What are those d——d aristos doing out there?' he shouted.

'Just getting into the coach, citizen,' replied the sergeant promptly.

And Armand and Marguerite were immediately ordered back into the coach.

Héron remained at the window for a few moments longer; he had a toothpick in his hand which he was using very freely.

'How much longer are we going to wait in this cursed hole?' he called out to the sergeant.

'Only a few moments longer, citizen. Citizen Chauvelin will be back soon with the guard.'

A quarter of an hour later the clatter of cavalry horses on the rough, uneven pavement drew Marguerite's attention. She lowered the carriage window and looked out. Chauvelin had just returned with the new escort. He was on horseback; his horse's bridle, since he was but an indifferent horseman, was held by one of the troopers.

Outside the inn he dismounted; evidently he had taken full command of the expedition, and scarcely referred to Héron.

He spoke for some moments with the sergeant, also with the driver of his own coach. He went to the window of the other carriage, probably in order to consult with citizen Héron, or to take final directions from the prisoner, for Marguerite, who was watching him, saw him standing on the step and leaning well forward into the interior, while apparently he was taking notes on a small tablet which he had in his hand.

At last everything was in order and the small party ready to start.

'Does anyone know here the Chapel of the Holy Sepulchre, close by the park of the Château d'Ourde?' asked Chauvelin, vaguely addressing the knot of gaffers that stood closest to him.

The men shook their heads.

One of the scouts on ahead turned in his saddle and spoke to citizen Chauvelin :

'I think I know the way pretty well, citizen Chauvelin,' he said; 'at any rate, I know it as far as the forest of Boulogne.'

'Do you know the Château d'Ourde, citizen St Just?' Chauvelin asked abruptly as soon as the carriage began to move.

Armand woke – as was habitual with him these days – from some gloomy reverie.

'Yes, citizen,' he replied. 'I know it.'

'And the Chapel of the Holy Sepulchre?'

'Yes. I know it too.'

Indeed, he knew the château well, and the little chapel in the forest. But Marguerite's aching nerves had thrilled at the name.

The Château d'Ourde! The Chapel of the Holy Sepulchre! That was the place which Percy had mentioned in his letter, the place where he had given rendezvous to de Batz. Sir Andrew had said that the Dauphin could not possibly be there, yet Percy was leading his enemies thither. And this despite that whatever plans, whatever hopes, had been born in his mind when he was still immured in the Conciergerie prison must have been set at naught by the clever counterplot of Chauvelin and Héron, who had effectually not only tied the schemer's hands, but forced him either to deliver the child to them or to sacrifice his wife and his friend.

The *impasse* was so horrible that she could not face it even in her thoughts.

CHAPTER XXVI

The Forest of Boulogne

PROGRESS was not easy, and very slow along the muddy road; the two coaches moved along laboriously, with wheels creaking and sinking deeply from time to time in the quagmire.

When the small party finally reached the edge of the wood the greyish light of this dismal day had changed in the west to a dull reddish glow – a glow that had neither brilliance nor incandescence in it; only a weird tint that hung over the horizon and turned the distance into lines of purple.

Suddenly there was a halt, much shouting, a volley of oaths from the drivers and citizen Chauvelin thrust his head out of the carriage window.

'What is it?' he asked.

'The scouts, citizen,' replied the sergeant, who had been riding close to the coach door all this while; 'they have returned.'

'Tell one man to come straight to me and report.'

Marguerite sat quite still. Indeed, she had almost ceased to live momentarily, for her spirit was absent from her body, which felt neither fatigue, nor cold, nor pain. But she heard the snorting of the horse close by as his rider pulled him up sharply beside the carriage door.

'Well?' said Chauvelin curtly.

'About two leagues from here there is a clearing with a small stone chapel, more like a large shrine, nestling among the trees. Opposite to it the angle of a high wall with large wrought-iron gates at the corner, and from these a wide drive leads through a park.'

'Did you turn into the drive?'

'Only a little way, citizen. We thought we had best report first that all is safe.'

'You saw no one?'

'No one.'

'The château, then, lies some distance from the gates?'

'A league or more, citizen. Close to the gates there are out-houses and stabling, the disused buildings of the home farm, I should say.'

'Good! We are on the right road, that is clear. Keep ahead with your men now, but only some two hundred mètres or so. Stay!' he added, as if on second thoughts. 'Ride down to the other coach and ask the prisoner if we are on the right track.'

The rider turned his horse sharply round. Marguerite heard the clang of metal and the sound of retreating hoofs.

A few moments later the man returned.

'Yes, citizen,' he reported, 'the prisoner says it is quite right. The Château d'Ourde lies a full league from its gates. This is the nearest road to the chapel and the château. He says we should reach the former in half an hour. It will be very dark in there,' he added with a significant nod in the direction of the wood.

Chauvelin made no reply, but quietly stepped out of the coach. Marguerite watched him, leaning out of the window, following his small trim figure as he pushed his way past the groups of mounted men, catching at a horse's bit now and then, or at a bridle, making a way for himself among the restless, champing animals, without the slightest hesitation or fear.

Soon his retreating figure lost its sharp outline silhouetted against the evening sky. It was enfolded in the veil of vapour which was blown out of the horses' nostrils or rising from their damp cruppers; it became more vague, almost ghostlike, through the mist and the fast-gathering gloom.

Presently a group of troopers hid him entirely from her view, but she could hear his thin, smooth voice quite clearly as he called to citizen Héron.

'We are close to the end of our journey now, citizen,' she heard him say. 'If the prisoner has not played us false little Capet should be in our charge within the hour.'

'If he is not,' and Marguerite recognized the harsh tones of citizen Héron – 'if he is not, then two corpses will be rotting in this wood tomorrow.'

Then Chauvelin's voice once more came clearly to her ear:

'My suggestion, citizen,' he was saying, 'is that the prisoner shall now give me an order – couched in whatever terms he may think necessary – but a distinct order to his friends to give up Capet to me without any resistance.'

'You must do as you think right – you planned the whole of this affair – see to it that it works out well in the end.'

'How many men shall I take with me? Our advance guard is here, of course.'

'I couldn't spare you more than four more men – I shall want the others to guard the prisoners.'

'Four men will be quite sufficient, with the four of the advance guard. That will leave you twelve men for guarding your prisoners, and you really only need to guard the woman – her life will answer for the others. Sir Percy, will you be so kind as to scribble the necessary words on these tablets?'

There was a long pause. Then Chauvelin's voice was raised again.

'I thank you,' he said, 'this certainly should be quite effectual. And now, citizen Héron, I do not think that under the circumstances we need fear an ambuscade or any kind of trickery – you hold the hostages. And if by any chance I and my men are attacked, or if we encounter armed resistance at the château, I will dispatch a rider back straightway to you, and – well, you will know what to do.'

Chauvelin and his picked escort detached themselves from the main body of the squad. Soon the dull thud of their horses' hoofs treading the soft ground came more softly – then more softly still as they turned into the woodland and the purple shadows seemed to enfold every sound and finally to swallow them completely.

Armand and Marguerite from the depth of the carriage heard Héron's voice ordering his own driver now to take the lead.

Héron's head, with its battered sugar-loaf hat, and a soiled bandage round the brow, was as usual out of the carriage window. He had fallen during the journey and cut his head.

He gave sharp orders to the men to close up round the carriages, and then gave the curt word of command:

'En avant!'

The diminished party was moving at foot-pace in the darkness that seemed to grow denser at every step, and through that silence which was so full of mysterious sounds.

There was another halt, the coach-wheels groaned and creaked on their axles, one or two horses reared with the sudden drawing up of the curb.

'What is it now?' came Héron's hoarse voice through the darkness.

'It is pitch-dark, citizen,' was the response from ahead. 'The drivers cannot see their horses' ears. They want to know if they may light their lanthorns and then lead their horses.'

'They can lead their horses,' replied Héron roughly, 'but I'll have no lanthorns lighted. We don't know what fools may be lurking behind trees, hoping to put a bullet through my head – or yours, sergeant – we don't want to make a lighted target of ourselves – what? But let the drivers lead their horses, and one or two of you who are riding greys might dismount too and lead the way – the greys would show up perhaps in this cursed blackness.'

While his orders were being carried out he called out once more :

'Are we far now from that confounded chapel?'

'We can't be far, citizen; the whole forest is not more than six leagues wide at any point, and we have gone two since we turned into it.'

'Hush!' Héron's voice suddenly broke in hoarsely. 'What was that? Silence, I say. Damn you – can't you hear?'

There was a hush – every ear straining to listen; but the horses were not still – they continued to champ their bits, to paw the ground, and to toss their heads, impatient to get on. Only now and again there would come a lull, even through these sounds – a second or two, mayhap, of perfect, unbroken silence – and then it seemed as if right through the darkness a mysterious echo sent back those same sounds – the champing of bits, the pawing of soft ground, the tossing and snorting of animals, human life that breathed far out there among the trees.

'It is citizen Chauvelin and his men,' said the sergeant after a while, and speaking in a whisper.

'Yes, it must be citizen Chauvelin,' said Héron at last; but the tone of his voice sounded as if he were anxious and only half convinced; 'but I thought he would be at the château by now.'

'He may have had to go at foot pace; it is very dark, citizen Héron,' remarked the sergeant.

'*En avant*, then,' quoth the other; 'the sooner we come up with him the better.'

And the squad of mounted men, the two coaches, the drivers and the advance section, who were leading their horses, slowly restarted on the way. The horses snorted, the bits and stirrups clanged, and the springs and wheels of the coaches creaked and groaned dismally as the ramshackle vehicles began once more to plough the carpet of pine-needles that lay thick upon the road.

But inside the carriage Armand and Marguerite held one another tightly by the hand.

'It is de Batz – with his friends,' she whispered scarce above her breath.

'De Batz?' he asked vaguely and fearfully, for in the dark he could not see her face, and as he did not understand why she should suddenly be talking of de Batz, he thought with horror that mayhap her prophecy anent herself had come true, and that her mind – wearied and overwrought – had become suddenly unhinged.

'Yes, de Batz,' she replied. 'Percy sent him a message, through me, to meet him – here. I am not mad, Armand,' she added more calmly. 'Sir Andrew took Percy's letter to de Batz the day that we started from Paris.'

'Great God!' exclaimed Armand, and instinctively, with a sense of protection, he put his arms round his sister. 'Then, if Chauvelin or the squad is attacked – if —'

'Yes,' she said calmly; 'if de Batz makes an attack on Chauvelin, or if he reaches the château first and tries to defend it, they will shoot us, Armand . . . and Percy.'

'But is the Dauphin at the Château d'Ourde?'

'No, no! I think not.'

'Then why should Percy have invoked the aid of de Batz? Now, when —'

'I don't know,' she murmured helplessly. 'Of course, when he wrote the letter he could not guess that they would hold us as hostages. He may have thought that under cover of darkness and of an unexpected attack he might have saved himself had he been alone; but now that you and I are here — Oh! it is all so horrible, and I cannot understand it all.'

'Hark!' broke in Armand, suddenly gripping her arm more tightly.

'Halt!' rang the sergeant's voice through the night.

This time there was no mistaking the sound; already it came from no far distance. It was the sound of a man running and panting, and now and again calling out as he ran.

For a moment there was stillness in the very air, the wind itself was hushed between two gusts, even the rain had ceased its incessant pattering. Héron's harsh voice was raised in the stillness.

'What is it now?' he demanded.

'A runner, citizen,' replied the sergeant, 'coming through the wood from the right.'

'From the right?' and the exclamation was accompanied by a volley of oaths; 'the direction of the château? Chauvelin has

been attacked; he is sending a messenger back to me. Sergeant —
sergeant, close up round that coach; guard your prisoners as you
value your life, and —'

The rest of his words were drowned in a yell of such violent
fury that the horses, already over-nervous and fidgety, reared in
mad terror, and the men had the greatest difficulty in holding
them in. For a few minutes noisy confusion prevailed, until the
men could quieten their quivering animals with soft words and
gentle pattings.

Then the troopers obeyed, closing up round the coach wherein
brother and sister sat huddled against one another.

One of the men said under his breath :

'Ah! but the citizen agent knows how to curse! One day he
will break his gullet with the fury of his oaths.'

In the meanwhile the runner had come nearer, always at the
same breathless speed.

The next moment he was challenged :

'*Qui va là?*'

'A friend!' he replied, panting and exhausted. 'Where is
citizen Héron?'

'Here!' came the reply in a voice hoarse with passionate
excitement. 'Come up, damn you. Be quick!'

'A lanthorn, citizen,' suggested one of the drivers.

'No — no — not now. Here! Where the devil are we?'

'We are close to the chapel on our left, citizen,' said the
sergeant.

The runner, whose eyes were no doubt accustomed to the
gloom, had drawn nearer to the carriage.

'The gates of the château,' he said, still somewhat breath-
lessly, 'are just opposite here on the right, citizen. I have just
come through them.'

'Speak up, man!' and Héron's voice now sounded as if choked
with passion. 'Citizen Chauvelin sent you?'

'Yes. He bade me tell you that he has gained access to the
château, and that Capet is not there.'

A series of citizen Héron's choicest oaths interrupted the
man's speech. Then he was curtly ordered to proceed, and he
resumed his report.

'Citizen Chauvelin rang at the door of the château; after a
while he was admitted by an old servant, who appeared to be in
charge, but the place seemed otherwise absolutely deserted —
only —'

'Only what? Go on; what is it?'

'As we rode through the park it seemed to us as if we were being watched and followed. We heard distinctly the sound of horses behind and around us, but we could see nothing; and now, when I ran back, again I heard ... There are others in the park tonight besides us, citizen.'

There was silence after that. It seemed as if the flood of Héron's blasphemous eloquence had spent itself at last.

'Others in the park!' And now his voice was scarcely above a whisper, hoarse and trembling. 'How many? Could you see?'

'No, citizen, we could not see; but there are horsemen lurking round the château now. Citizen Chauvelin took four men into the house with him and left the others on guard outside. He bade me tell you it might be safer to send him a few more men if you could spare them. There are a number of disused farm buildings quite close to the gates, and he suggested that all the horses be put up there for the night, and that the men come up to the château on foot; it would be quicker and safer, for the darkness is intense.'

Even while the man spoke the forest in the distance seemed to wake from its solemn silence, the wind on its wings brought sounds of life and movement different from the prowling of beasts or the screeching of night-birds. It was the furtive advance of men, the quick whispers of command, of encouragement, of the human animal preparing to attack his kind. But all in the distance still, all muffled, all furtive as yet.

'Sergeant!' It was Héron's voice, but it was subdued, and almost calm now; 'can you see the chapel?'

'More clearly, citizen,' replied the sergeant. 'It is on our left; quite a small building, I think.'

'Then dismount, and walk all round it. See that there are no windows or door in the rear.'

There was a prolonged silence, during which those distant sounds of men moving, of furtive preparations for attack, struck distinctly through the night.

Marguerite and Armand, clinging to one another, not knowing what to think, nor yet what to fear, heard the sounds mingling with those immediately around them, and Marguerite murmured under her breath:

'It is de Batz and some of his friends; but what can they do? What can Percy hope for now?'

CHAPTER XXVII

The Chapel of the Holy Sepulchre

THE sergeant's voice broke in upon her misery.

The man had apparently done as the citizen agent had ordered, and had closely examined the little building that stood on the left – a vague, black mass more dense than the surrounding gloom.

'It is all solid stone, citizen,' he said; 'iron gates in front, closed but not locked, rusty key in the lock, which turns quite easily; no windows or door in the rear.'

'You are quite sure?'

'Quite certain, citizen : it is plain, solid stone at the back, and the only possible access to the interior is through the iron gate in front.'

'Good.'

Marguerite could only just hear Héron speaking to the sergeant. Darkness enveloped every form and deadened every sound. Even the harsh voice which she had learned to loathe and to dread sounded curiously subdued and unfamiliar. Héron no longer seemed inclined to storm, to rage, or to curse. The momentary danger, the thought of failure, the hope of revenge, had apparently cooled his temper, strengthened his determination, and forced his voice down to little above a whisper. He gave his orders clearly and firmly, and the words came to Marguerite on the wings of the wind with strange distinctness, borne to her ears by the darkness itself, and the hush that lay over the wood.

'Take half a dozen men with you, sergeant,' she heard him say, 'and join citizen Chauvelin at the château. You can stable your horses in the farm buildings close by, as he suggests, and run to him on foot. You and your men should quickly get the best of a handful of midnight prowlers; you are well armed and they only civilians. Tell citizen Chauvelin that I in the meanwhile will take care of our prisoners. The Englishman I shall put in irons and lock up inside the chapel, with five men under the command of your corporal to guard him, the other two I will drive myself straight to Crécy with what is left of the escort. You understand?'

'Yes, citizen.'

'We may not reach Crécy until two hours after midnight, but

directly I arrive I will send citizen Chauvelin further reinforcements, which, however, I hope may not prove necessary, but which will reach him in the early morning. Even if he is seriously attacked, he can, with the fourteen men he will have with him, hold out inside the castle through the night. Tell him also that at dawn the two prisoners who will be with me will be shot in the courtyard of the guard-house at Crécy, but that whether he has got hold of Capet or not he had best pick up the Englishman in the chapel in the morning and bring him straight to Crécy, where I shall be awaiting him ready to return to Paris. You understand?'

'Yes, citizen.'

'Then repeat what I said.'

'I am to take six men with me to reinforce citizen Chauvelin now.'

'Yes.'

'And you, citizen, will drive straight back to Crécy, and will send us further reinforcements from there, which will reach us in the early morning.'

'Yes.'

'We are to hold the château against those unknown marauders if necessary until the reinforcements come from Crécy. Having routed them, we return here, pick up the Englishman whom you will have locked up in the chapel under a strong guard commanded by Corporal Cassard, and join you forthwith at Crécy.'

'This, whether citizen Chauvelin has got hold of Capet or not.'

'Yes, citizen, I understand,' concluded the sergeant imperturbably; 'and I am also to tell citizen Chauvelin that the two prisoners will be shot at dawn in the courtyard of the guard-house at Crécy.'

'Yes. That is all. Try to find the leader of the attacking party, and bring him along to Crécy with the Englishman; but unless they are in very small numbers do not trouble about the others. Now *en avant*; citizen Chauvelin might be glad of your help. And – stay – order all the men to dismount, and take the horses out of one of the coaches, then let the men you are taking with you each lead a horse, or even two, and stable them all in the farm buildings. I shall not need them, and could not spare any of my men for the work later on. Remember that, above all, silence is the order. When you are ready to start, come back to me here.'

The sergeant moved away, and Marguerite heard him transmitting the citizen agent's orders to the soldiers. The dismounting was carried on in wonderful silence – for silence had been one of the principal commands – only one or two words reached her ears.

'First section and first half of second section fall in! Right wheel! First section each take two horses on the lead. Quietly now there; don't tug at his bridle – let him go.'

And after that a simple report:

'All ready, citizen!'

'Good!' was the response. 'Now detail your corporal and two men to come here to me, so that we may put the Englishman in irons, and take him at once to the chapel, and four men to stand guard at the doors of the other coach.'

The necessary orders were given, and after that there came the curt command:

'*En avant!*'

The sergeant, with his squad and all the horses, was slowly moving away in the night. The horses' hoofs hardly made a noise on the soft carpet of pine-needles and of dead fallen leaves, but the champing of the bits was of course audible, and now and then the snorting of some poor, tired horse longing for his stable.

Marguerite tried to open the carriage door, but it was held from without, and a harsh voice cursed her, ordering her to sit still. But she could lean out of the window and strain her eyes to see. They were by now accustomed to the gloom, the dilated pupils taking in pictures of vague forms moving like ghouls in the shadows. The other coach was not far, and she could hear Héron's voice, still subdued and calm, and the curses of the men. But not a sound from Percy.

'I think the prisoner is unconscious,' she heard one of the men say.

'Lift him out of the carriage, then,' was Héron's curt command; 'and you go and throw open the chapel gates.'

Marguerite saw it all. The movement, the crowd of men, two vague, black forms lifting another one, which appeared heavy and inert, out of the coach, and carrying it staggering up towards the chapel.

Then the forms disappeared, swallowed up by the more dense mass of the little building, merged in with it, immovable as the stone itself.

Only a few words reached her now.

'He is unconscious.'

'Leave him there, then; he'll not move.'

'Now close the gates!'

There was a loud clang, and Marguerite gave a piercing scream. She tore at the handle of the carriage door.

'Armand, Armand, go to him!' she cried; and all her self-control, all her enforced calm, vanished in an outburst of wild, agonizing passion. 'Let me get to him, Armand! This is the end; get me to him, in the name of God!'

'Stop that woman screaming,' came Héron's voice clearly through the night. 'Put her and the other prisoner in irons – quick!'

But while Marguerite expended her feeble strength in a mad, pathetic effort to reach her husband, even now at this last hour, when all hope was dead and Death was so nigh, Armand had already wrenched the carriage door from the grasp of the soldier who was guarding it. He was of the South, and knew the trick of charging an unsuspecting adversary with head thrust forward like a bull inside a ring. Thus he knocked one of the soldiers down and made a quick rush for the chapel gates.

The men, attacked so suddenly and in such complete darkness, did not wait for orders. They closed in round Armand; one man drew his sabre and hacked away with it in aimless rage.

But for the moment he evaded them all, pushing his way through them, not heeding the blows that came on him out of the darkness. At last he reached the chapel.

With one bound he was at the gate, his numb fingers fumbling for the lock, which he could not see.

It was a vigorous blow from Héron's fist that brought him at last to his knees. Then it was that the heavy blow on his head caused him a sensation of sickness, and he fell on his knees, still gripping the ironwork.

Stronger hands than his were forcing him to loosen his hold; blows that hurt terribly rained on his numbed fingers; he felt himself dragged away, carried like an inert mass farther and farther from that gate which he would have given his life-blood to force open.

And Marguerite heard all this from the inside of the coach, where she was imprisoned as effectually as was Percy's unconscious body inside that dark chapel. She could hear the noise and scramble, and Héron's hoarse commands, the swift sabre strokes as they cut through the air.

Already a trooper had clapped irons on her wrists, two others held the carriage doors. Now Armand was lifted back into the coach, and she could not even help to make him comfortable, though as he was lifted in she heard him feebly moaning. Then the carriage doors were banged again.

'Do not allow either of the prisoners out again, on peril of your lives!' came with a vigorous curse from Héron.

After which there was a moment's silence; whispered commands came spasmodically in deadened sounds to her ear.

'Will the key turn?'

'Yes, citizen.'

'All secure?'

'Yes, citizen. The prisoner is groaning.'

'Let him groan.'

'The empty coach, citizen? The horses have been taken out.'

'Leave it standing where it is, then; citizen Chauvelin will need it in the morning.'

'Armand,' whispered Marguerite inside the coach, 'did you see Percy?'

'It was so dark,' murmured Armand feebly; 'but I saw him, just inside the gates, where they had laid him down. I heard him groaning. Oh, my God!'

'Hush, dear!' she said. 'We can do nothing more, only die as he lived, bravely and with a smile on our lips, in memory of him.'

'Number 35 is wounded, citizen,' said one of the men.

'Curse the fool who did the mischief,' was the placid response. 'Leave him here with the guard.'

'How many of you are there left then?' asked the same voice a moment later.

'Only two, citizen; if one whole section remains with me at the chapel door, and also the wounded man.'

'Two are enough for me, and five are not too many at the chapel door.' And Héron's coarse cruel laugh echoed against the stone walls of the little chapel. 'Now then, one of you get into the coach, and the other go to the horses' heads; and remember, Corporal Cassard, that you and your men who stay here to guard that chapel door are answerable to the whole nation with your lives for the safety of the Englishman.'

The carriage door was thrown open, and a soldier stepped in and sat down opposite Marguerite and Armand. Héron in the meanwhile was apparently scrambling up the box. Marguerite could hear him muttering curses as he groped for the reins and finally gathered them into his hand.

The springs of the coach creaked and groaned as the vehicle slowly swung round; the wheels ploughed deeply through the soft carpet of dead leaves.

Marguerite felt Armand's inert body leaning heavily against her shoulder.

'Are you in pain, dear?' she asked softly.

He made no reply, and she thought that he had fainted. It was better so; at least the next dreary hours would flit by for him in the blissful state of unconsciousness. Now at last the heavy carriage began to move more evenly. The soldier at the horses' heads was stepping along at a rapid pace.

Marguerite would have given much even now to look back once more at the dense black mass – blacker and denser than any shadow that had ever descended before on God's earth – which held between its cold, cruel walls all that she loved in the world.

But her wrists were fettered by the irons which cut into her flesh when she moved. She could no longer lean out of the window, and she could not even hear. The whole forest was hushed, the wind was lulled to rest; wild beasts and night birds were silent and still. And the wheels of the coach creaked in the ruts, bearing Marguerite with every turn farther and farther away from the man who lay helpless in the chapel of the Holy Sepulchre.

CHAPTER XXVIII

The waning moon

ARMAND had wakened from his attack of faintness, and brother and sister sat close to one another, shoulder touching shoulder. That sense of nearness was the one tiny spark of comfort to both of them on this dreary, dreary way.

The coach had lumbered on unceasingly since all eternity – so it seemed to them both. Once there had been a brief halt, when Héron's rough voice had ordered the soldier at the horses' heads to climb on the box beside him, and once – it had been a very little while ago – a terrible cry of pain and terror had rung through the stillness of the night. Immediately after that the horses had been put at a more rapid pace, but it had seemed to Marguerite as if that one cry of pain had been repeated by several others, which sounded more feeble, and soon appeared to be dying away in the distance behind.

The soldier who sat opposite to them must have heard the cry too, for he jumped up, as if awakened from sleep, and put his head out of the window.

'Did you hear that cry, citizen?' he asked.

But only a curse answered him, and a peremptory command not to lose sight of the prisoners by poking his head out of the window.

'Did you hear the cry?' asked the soldier of Marguerite, as he made haste to obey.

'Yes! What could it be?' she murmured.

'It seems dangerous to drive so fast in this darkness,' muttered the soldier.

After which remark he, with the stolidity peculiar to his kind, figuratively shrugged his shoulders, detaching himself, as it were, from the whole affair.

'We should be out of the forest by now,' he remarked in an undertone a little while later; 'the way seemed shorter before.'

Just then the coach gave an unexpected lurch to one side, and after much groaning and creaking of axles and springs it came to a standstill, and the citizen agent was heard cursing loudly and then scrambling down from the box.

The next moment the carriage door was pulled open from without, and the harsh voice called out peremptorily:

'Citizen soldier, here – quick! – quick! – curse you! – we'll have one of the horses down if you don't hurry!'

The soldier struggled to his feet; it was never good to be slow in obeying the citizen agent's commands. He was half-asleep, and no doubt numb with cold and long sitting still; to accelerate his movements he was suddenly gripped by the arm and dragged incontinently out of the coach.

Then the door was slammed to again, either by a rough hand or a sudden gust of wind, Marguerite could not tell; she heard a cry of rage and one of terror, and Héron's raucous curses. She cowered in the corner of the carriage with Armand's head against her shoulder, and tried to close her ears to all those hideous sounds.

Then suddenly all the sounds were hushed and all around everything became perfectly calm and still – so still that at first the silence oppressed her with a vague, nameless dread. It was as if Nature herself had paused, that she might listen; and the silence became more and more absolute, until Marguerite could hear Armand's soft, regular breathing close to her ear.

The window nearest to her was open, and as she leaned forward with that paralysing sense of oppression a breath of pure air struck full upon her nostrils and brought with it a briny taste as if from the sea.

It was not quite so dark; and there was a sense as of open

country stretching out to the limits of the horizon. Overhead a vague greyish light suffused the sky, and the wind swept the clouds in great rolling banks right across that light.

Marguerite gazed upward with a more calm feeling that was akin to gratitude. That pale light, though so wan and feeble, was thrice welcome after that inky blackness wherein shadows were less dark than the lights. She watched eagerly the bank of clouds driven by the dying gale.

The light grew brighter and faintly golden, now the banks of clouds – storm-tossed and fleecy – raced past one another, parted and reunited like veils of unseen giant dancers waved by hands that controlled infinite space – advanced and rushed and slackened speed again – united and finally tore asunder to reveal the waning moon, honey-coloured and mysterious, rising as if from an invisible ocean far away.

The wan pale light spread over the whole stretch of country, throwing over it as it spread dull tones of indigo and of blue. Here and there sparse, stunted trees with fringed gaunt arms bending to prevailing winds proclaimed the neighbourhood of the sea.

Marguerite gazed on the picture which the waning moon had so suddenly revealed; but she gazed with eyes that knew not what they saw. The moon had risen on her right – there lay the east – and the coach must have been travelling due north, whereas Crécy . . .

In the absolute silence that reigned she could perceive from far, very far away, the sound of a church clock striking the midnight hour; and now it seemed to her super-sensitive senses that a firm footstep was treading the soft earth, a footstep that drew nearer – and then nearer still.

Nature did pause to listen. The wind was hushed, the night-birds in the forest had gone to rest. Marguerite's heart beat so fast that its throbbings choked her, and a dizziness clouded her consciousness.

But through this state of torpor she heard the opening of the carriage door, she felt the onrush of that pure, briny air, and she felt a long, burning kiss upon her hands.

She thought then that she was really dead, and that God in His infinite love had opened to her the outer gates of Paradise.

'My love!' she murmured.

She was leaning back in the carriage and her eyes were closed, but she felt that firm fingers removed the irons from her wrists, and that a pair of warm lips were pressed there in their stead.

'There, little woman, that's better so – is it not? Now let me get hold of poor old Armand!'

It was Heaven, of course, else how could earth hold such heavenly joy?

'Percy!' exclaimed Armand in an awed voice.

'Hush, dear!' murmured Marguerite feebly; 'we are in Heaven, you and I —'

Whereupon a ringing laugh woke the echoes of the silent night.

'In Heaven, dear heart!' And the voice had a delicious earthly ring in its whole-hearted merriment. 'Please God, you'll both be at Portel with me before dawn.'

Then she was indeed forced to believe. She put out her hands and groped for him, for it was dark inside the carriage; she groped, and felt his massive shoulders leaning across the body of the coach, while his fingers busied themselves with the irons on Armand's wrist.

'Don't touch that brute's filthy coat with your dainty fingers, dear heart,' he said gaily. 'Great Lord! I have worn that wretch's clothes for over two hours; I feel as if the dirt had penetrated to my bones.'

Then, with that gesture so habitual to him, he took her head between his two hands, and drawing her to him until the wan light from without lit up the face that he worshipped, he gazed his fill into her eyes.

She could only see the outline of his head silhouetted against the wind-tossed sky; she could not see his eyes, nor his lips, but she felt his nearness, and the happiness of that almost caused her to swoon.

'Come out into the open, my lady fair,' he murmured, and though she could not see, she could feel that he smiled; 'let God's pure air blow through your hair and round your dear head. Then, if you can walk so far, there's a small half-way house close by here. I have knocked up the none too amiable host. You and Armand could have half an hour's rest there before we go farther on our way.'

'But you, Percy? – are you safe?'

'Yes, m'dear, we are all of us safe until morning – time enough to reach Le Portel, and to be aboard the *Daydream* before mine amiable friend M. Chambertin has discovered his worthy colleague lying gagged and bound inside the chapel of the Holy Sepulchre. By Gad! how old Héron will curse – the moment he can open his mouth!'

He half helped, half lifted her out of the carriage. The strong pure air suddenly rushing right through to her lungs made her feel faint, and she almost fell. But it was good to feel herself falling, when one pair of arms among the millions on the earth were there to receive her.

'Can you walk, dear heart?' he asked. 'Lean well on me – it is not far, and the rest will do you good.'

'But you, Percy —'

He laughed, and the most complete joy of living seemed to resound through that laugh. Her arm was in his, and for one moment he stood still while his eyes swept the far reaches of the country, the mellow distance still wrapped in its mantle of indigo, still untouched by the mysterious light of the waning moon.

He pressed her arm against his heart, but his right hand was stretched out towards the black wall of the forest behind him, towards the dark crests of the pines in which the dying wind sent its last mournful sighs.

'Dear heart,' he said, and his voice quivered with the intensity of his excitement, 'beyond the stretch of that wood, far from away over there, there are cries and moans of anguish that come to my ear even now. But for you, dear, I would cross that wood tonight and re-enter Paris tomorrow. But for you, dear – but for you,' he reiterated earnestly as he pressed her closer to him, for a bitter cry had risen to her lips.

She went on in silence. Her happiness was great – as great as was her pain. She had found him again, the man whom she worshipped, the husband whom she thought never to see again on earth. She had found him, and not even now – not after those terrible weeks of misery and suffering unspeakable – could she feel that love had triumphed over the wild, adventurous spirit, the reckless enthusiasm, the ardour of self-sacrifice.

CHAPTER XXIX

The land of Eldorado

IT seems that in the pocket of Héron's coat there was a letter-case with some few hundred francs. It was amusing to think that the brute's money helped to bribe the ill-tempered keeper of the half-way house to receive guests at midnight, and to ply them well with food, drink, and the shelter of a stuffy coffee-room.

Marguerite sat silently beside her husband, her hand in his. Armand, opposite to them, had both elbows on the table. He looked pale and wan, with a bandage across his forehead, and his glowing eyes were resting on his chief.

'Yes! you demned young idiot,' said Blakeney merrily, 'you nearly upset my plan in the end, with your yelling and screaming outside the chapel gates.'

'I wanted to get to you, Percy. I thought those brutes had got you there inside that building.'

'Not they!' he exclaimed. 'It was my friend Héron whom they had trussed and gagged, and whom my amiable friend M. Chambertin will find in there tomorrow morning. By Gad! I would go back if only for the pleasure of hearing Héron curse when first the gag is taken from his mouth.'

'But how was it all done, Percy? And there was de Batz —'

'De Batz was part of the scheme I had planned for mine own escape before I knew that those brutes meant to take Marguerite and you as hostages for my good behaviour. What I hoped then was that under cover of a tussle or a fight I could somehow or other contrive to slip through their fingers. It was a chance, and you know my belief in bald-headed Fortune, with the one solitary hair. Well, I meant to grab that hair; and at the worst I could but die in the open and not caged in that awful hole like some noxious vermin. I knew that de Batz would rise to the bait. I told him in my letter that the Dauphin would be at the Château d'Ourde this night, but that I feared the Revolutionary Government had got wind of this fact, and were sending an armed escort to bring the lad away. This letter Ffoulkes took to him; I knew that he would make a vigorous effort to get the Dauphin into his hands, and that during the scuffle that one hair on Fortune's head would for one second only, mayhap, come within my reach. I had so planned the expedition that we were bound to arrive at the forest of Bologne by nightfall, and night is always a useful ally. But at the guard-house of the Rue St Anne I realized for the first time that those brutes had pressed me into a tighter corner than I had preconceived.'

He paused, and once again that look of recklessness swept over his face, and his eyes, still hollow and circled, shone with the excitement of past memories.

'I was such a weak, miserable wretch then,' he said, in answer to Marguerite's appeal. 'I had to try and build up some strength, when – Heaven forgive me for the sacrilege – I had unwittingly risked your precious life, dear heart, in that blind endeavour to save mine own. By Gad! it was no easy task in that jolting vehicle with that noisome wretch beside me for sole company : yet I ate and drank and I slept for three days and two nights, until the hour when in the darkness I struck Héron from behind, half-strangled him first, then gagged him, and finally slipped into his filthy coat and put that loathsome bandage across my head, and his battered hat above it all. The yell he gave when I first attacked him made every horse rear – you must remember it – the noise effectually drowned our last scuffle in the coach. Chauvelin was the only man who might have suspected what had occurred, but he had gone on ahead, and bald-headed Fortune had passed by me, and I had managed to grab its one hair. After that it was all quite easy. The sergeant and the soldiers had seen very little of Héron and nothing of me; it did not take a great effort to deceive them, and the darkness of the night was my most faithful friend. His raucous voice was not difficult to imitate, and darkness always muffles and changes every tone. Anyway, it was not likely that those loutish soldiers would even remotely suspect the trick that was being played on them. The citizen agent's orders were promptly and implicitly obeyed. The men never even thought to wonder that after insisting on an escort of twenty he should drive off with two prisoners and only two men to guard them. If they did wonder, it was not theirs to question. Those two troopers are spending an uncomfortable night somewhere in the forest of Boulogne, each tied to a tree, and some two leagues apart one from the other. And now,' he added gaily, 'en voiture, my fair lady; and you, too, Armand. 'Tis seven leagues to Le Portel, and we must be there before dawn.'

'Sir Andrew's intention was to make for Calais first, there to open communication with the *Daydream* and then for Le Portel,' said Marguerite; 'after that he meant to strike back for the Château d'Ourde in search of me.'

'Then we'll still find him at Le Portel – I shall know how to lay hands on him; but you two must get aboard the *Daydream* at once, for Ffoulkes and I can always look after ourselves.'

It was one hour after midnight when – refreshed with food and rest – Marguerite, Armand, and Sir Percy left the half-way house. Marguerite was standing in the doorway ready to go. Percy and Armand had gone ahead to bring the coach along.

'Percy,' whispered Armand, 'Marguerite does not know?'

'Of course she does not, you young fool,' retorted Percy lightly. 'If you try and tell her I think I would smash your head.'

'But you —' said the young man with sudden vehemence; 'can you bear the sight of me? My God! when I think —'

'Don't think, my good Armand – not of that anyway. Only think of the woman for whose sake you committed a crime – if she is pure and good woo her and win her – not just now, for it were foolish to go back to Paris after her, but anon, when she comes to England and all these past days are forgotten – then love her as much as you can, Armand. Learn your lesson of love better than I have learnt mine; do not cause Jeanne Lange those tears of anguish which my mad spirit brings to your sister's eyes. You were right, Armand, when you said that I do not know how to love!'

But on board the *Daydream*, when all danger was past, Marguerite felt that he did.

These are other Knight Books

John Buchan

GREENMANTLE

This is the second adventure of Richard Hannay, hero of *The thirty-nine steps*, and is set at the time of the First World War. He visits many remote and dangerous places reaching as far as the Black Sea and Anatolia, and his adventures are rich with suspense and excitement.

Elizabeth Goudge

THE LITTLE WHITE HORSE

The setting of this enchanting story is a West Country village, a hundred years ago. Maria, the heroine, her governess and her dog go to live in the old and rather mysterious Manorhouse of Moonacre. There Maria encounters many queer but delightful people, as well as the little white horse and the wicked black men of the woods.

Awarded the Library Association Carnegie Medal for being 'an outstanding children's book of 1946'.

'Long, wonderful edge-of-magic read'. *The Observer*

Illustrated by C. Walter Hodges.

William Mayne and Dick Caesar

THE GOBBLING BILLY

A little-known book by the famous writer
Entertaining and amusing and set in Ireland, this story
tells about the refurbishing of a dilapidated vintage
car, the Gobbling Billy, in time to enter for the
Bemberger Trophy race.
Bob, its owner, has to work in secrecy, and his task
is further complicated by the efforts of a rival to
ensure he doesn't win the race.

Henry Treece

HOUNDS OF THE KING

1066 – the field of what is now called Hastings. The
Hounds of the King, Harold's personal warriors, gather
for the last time to protect their king against the
Normans.
One of these warriors is Beonorth, and this book is
about his life in Harold's service. It is a story of
heroism and adventure, and a magnificent picture of
Saxon England.

These are other Knight Books

Two books about life and riding on the Hungarian Plains, by Kate Seredy.

THE GOOD MASTER

The famous story about Uncle Marton and his family, and his niece Kate, who comes to live with them.

THE SINGING TREE

It is wartime, and Uncle Marton goes away to fight, leaving his son Jancsi in charge of the ranch.

Both books are newly illustrated by the notable artist Imre Hofbauer who, like the author, was born in Hungary and knows well the life so finely presented here.

Ask your local bookseller, or at your public library, for details of other Knight Books, or write to the Editor-in-Chief, Knight Books, Arlen House, Salisbury Road, Leicester LEI 7QS.